the other sister

By the Same Author

Fiction

Broken News

The Sibius Knot

Non-fiction

(Co-author)

Real Stories of Dealing with Depression

Young Mental Health

The Age of Anxiety

Life Interrupted: Understanding India's Suicide Crisis

the other sister

Amrita Tripathi

TRANQUEBAR

Published by Tranquebar, an imprint of Westland Books, a division of Nasadiya Technologies Private Limited, in 2024

No. 269/2B, First Floor, 'Irai Arul', Vimalraj Street, Nethaji Nagar, Alapakkam Main Road, Maduravoyal, Chennai 600095

ISBN: 9789360456887

10 9 8 7 6 5 4 3 2 1

This is a work of fiction. Names, characters, organisations, places, events and incidents are either products of the author's imagination or used fictitiously.

Typeset by Mukul

Printed at Thomson Press (India) Ltd

For Pops. There aren't enough words.
*And for Rubes, who punched a hole in my heart to make room for *all the good things.*

Contents

PART THREE

PART ONE

1

It's Not You, It's Me

[December 2023]

'Life is short, before you know it, time's up ...' Maya posts on her page, unable to resist the urge to perform the way social media loves (and insists on).

Twenty-two 'likes' and four days later, she disappears, ghosting her friends and a new potential significant other. None of them knows that she is already on a timeout, not till she announced it, but that just goes to show how much attention they were paying in real life.

Maya's previous cryptic status update, 'My best friend has left the building', by now has fifty-five likes (most from people assuming this was some cool reference they weren't aware of, hence a 'like' to keep up, but not enough interest to probe further); she did get some individualised attention, the update having prompted ten inquiries, seven of which were on the site itself.

A couple of people WhatsApp Maya and only one person thinks the post refers to her (and is faintly annoyed at the implication), but Akira is that kind of girl. As people used to say when status updates were the norm, 'It's complicated'.

The thing is, Maya is going offline in no small part to avoid her self-professed BFFs and the BS that passes for everyday social life in this great Capital. *None of them get it,* she thinks. *None of them ever will,* she has known, ever since the trauma hit in high school. She herself, though, lost in a world of her own making, doesn't even realise that she's been looking for an exit, an escape … until she suddenly does.

One person does the old-fashioned thing and calls her on the phone, possibly because he is related to her, and probably because he knows that family ties need to be reinforced periodically, away from the virtual world we all prefer.

In an unusual, dysfunctional family, there are no winners, but we aren't all losers either, and Maya's brother knows (has always known?) that showing up is half the battle won.

2

Notes from a Therapist's Office

Showing up is half the battle when it comes to clients too. But we don't give up on them, even—or especially—when they drop off the face of the planet. It's been a few weeks since Maya decided she's done with therapy, and as a result, I may have filled up her appointment slot with the next person who'd been waitlisted, but I have a feeling she's going to be back.

This is one of those cases that's hard to categorise. It's unresolvable, at least as long as she's gone, mid-word, what feels like mid-paragraph. But it's not as dire as it initially appeared.

The client—who presented with dissociative identity disorder, trauma, depression, and a persona with some sort of messiah complex (TBC)—came into my life on the heels of a broken relationship to tell me a pretty extraordinary story. About heartbreak, abandonment, severe trauma, yes, we'd started to discuss these issues, but we'd also just about got to the stuff we don't often get to … love, the universe, and how it sometimes takes a village well into adulthood.

I have no doubt and, more importantly, I'm convinced *she* is aware that she and her family will be in severe need of therapy and some medication on and off, but there's something that may finally work for her, some puzzle pieces that should fit together. I hope she comes to see it, and maybe there are other things that will stand out for her—how they all found each other, even 'the other sister', and the role she's played in protecting Maya.

Anyway, this is what we work for—hope.

3

The Big D, the Little D and a Timeout

[Present Day with Flashbacks]

It doesn't take Maya long to figure out where to go—it's a flat that she pretty much grew up in, after all. *Chini Auntie is the best,* she thinks, even though she'd never admit to any of her friends that she still enjoys coming to this pokey neighbourhood every so often. Far from the heart of the city when they used to live here back in the day, it's come into its own now, especially with the Metro emerging as a game changer. Maya wonders if her younger self would be surprised to know that flats here are selling for more than a couple of crores.

Do her fancy friends even register money and the need to earn it? She has stopped wondering on that front. Funny, that. She's never really thought about money since that period when she didn't have enough, but just leaving the high-rolling life—not to mention some of her Chhatarpur farmhouse-owning, 'Are you in London this summer, darling?' friends—a few years ago has proven to be a very cash-friendly decision. She also knows that none of them will bother to come find her here, trans-Yamuna (or Yamuna Park, as a friend used to routinely mispronounce it years ago), so it's as good a hideout as any.

Luckily, she has always had a standing invitation from her aunt.

This place, her refuge, reminds her of the one good thing from a childhood riven by abandonment (which she doesn't remember too clearly), bullying, trauma and death (which she can't forget), but more on that later. The One Good Thing was strong and powerful—it was unconditional love. And specifically, it came from one beacon of light, as far as Maya was concerned.

For Maya, Chini Auntie was a harbour and by far the only one who would let her talk endlessly without interrupting. Chini Auntie would let Maya hold her hand and not once attempt to stop her from sitting in her lap, unlike her supposed mother Usha (but more on her later).

Maya may have had an unconventional childhood, shunted between three families all told, but the one constant was Chini Auntie, who would make it a point to visit, even taking her away for a few holidays, before finally transplanting her to the trans-Yamuna flat for good. Chini Auntie effortlessly became the favourite, not just for Maya but also her best friend and brother Gautam Bhaiyya. He was always welcome at Chini Auntie's house, even after the Big D (that is, Death of a parent), and that clinched it. It established Chini Auntie's position as the best of the best.

But there was also the fact that till she moved in with Chini Auntie, no one had ever bothered to give Maya the secret codes that other girls in her school seemed to have been born knowing, like how to know who's actually your friend versus just trying to use you or make you the butt of the joke, or when to speak up and show what you know and when to play dumb. Or how to smile and shrug things off even when your heart is crumbling, and how to deal with boys and the girls who change around them.

But perhaps none were as important as knowing when to blend in and how to fade into the background. Maya treasured this one as the Key. An important tip that would let her crack life, knowing by then as she did that you need to be prepared—life could pull the rug out from under your feet at any moment. No use pretending otherwise.

~

Here in the present, some two and a half decades later, as Maya sees cobwebs between the potted plants on the landing and makes a mental note to water the shrubs, she harks back to one of those lessons.

'You have to give the spirits a few seconds to get out of the way when you first walk in after a long time,' Maya remembers Chini Auntie telling her as she walks through the only-slightly-more-weather-beaten door as an adult and is thrust straight into the heart of her childhood.

'Baby, also remember you must avoid the old banyan trees, especially at night, even if your friends try to take you there.'

'Ghosts?' a young Maya had asked.

'Oh yes, ghosts or spirits, yes. Don't even think about stopping.'

'Okay, Auntie, what else?'

'You shouldn't ever call someone back when they're leaving, or try to stop them, that's bad luck too.'

'Ohhh…' Maya immediately started thinking of all the times she'd tried to call her mother—sorry, Usha—back. *Maybe that explained the bad luck.* She didn't want to ask her aunt, who sometimes got very emotional about Usha, so she saved the thought to mull over later. Maya often had to save things to think about without any company. (Though, sometimes, as it turned out, Akira would take her place in private, with none the wiser.)

'And whatever you do, don't cut down the lemon-chilli strings.'

'Why not, Auntie—'

'Hey. What is this?' An interruption by an only-slightly-exasperated Uncle Pi, who always said it paid to stay Rational, though he put up with Chini's rituals because it was the only way to have Peace of Mind, he said.

Maya quite loved to see them together, talking like this, even though he *had* interrupted.

He laughed as he said, 'This is all just mumbo jumbo, mind you, Maya!'

As he walked into the kitchen, he patted Maya on the head, gave Auntie eyes, and started talking in that grown-up voice.

Maya remembers this scene quite clearly because of what happened next. She was 'revising' when it happened …

So if my left hand itches, someone's going to give me a treat and if my eye twitches, there's going to be trouble.

If the dogs are howling, it's a bad sign.

She had looked up to remember the next tip … but wait, who was that? The woman looked an awful lot like her, but different somehow. Older, yes, but beautiful. The lady had popped out of nowhere, smiled, waved, poked at her specs, and then walked out *through* the wall.

Nan didn't blink—she was just sitting at the window, her usual place those days, nodding to herself. Uncle would say she was lost in her own head, but Maya knew she wasn't actually lost, just probably trying to find Mum, sorry, Usha.

Sometimes Nan would ask Maya about school, about Usha, about Lakshman the cop. Maya never knew quite what to say. Nan never asked about the horrid Neeti, which wasn't surprising, but also never about Gautam Bhaiyya, which was. It was as if that whole time she had gone to live with Lakshman and Neeti had never happened. But it had, hadn't it? She had to check her journal to see how many years it was—close to ten. Could it really have been that long? Of course, she had had extended breaks with Chini Auntie even while she lived with Lakshman, before she finally moved for good, but if it wasn't for her journal, she'd never have remembered.

(Maya will talk to her therapist at some point about what she calls 'trauma brain', which she blames for losing track of time and some of the attendant confusion around her unconventional childhood.)

Maya is surprised that this scene with the glamorous visitor has come back so vividly. She half expects to see her again today.

The woman hadn't said anything to Maya directly but had turned back once. By then young Maya had yelped, startled, getting some adult attention.

'Uhhh ... Did you see that, Uncle, you were there, did you see her, Auntie, did you see her? It looked like someone we know ... Who was that?' Maya spoke in a baby voice, higher pitched than usual.

'Wait, hang on, take a breath ... what did we miss?' Auntie asked, laughing. Her face changed when she saw Uncle looking at Maya a bit strangely.

'What did you see?' he asked. He had looked like this the other day when he came into the sitting room to ask Maya who she was talking to in that harsh tone, and was that bad language she was using? 'Not,' Maya had said, more aggressively than normal, and when he looked a bit queasy, she didn't tell him that Auntie spoke to herself too.

'She looked like me! But older and beautiful,' Maya told them excitedly. 'Was it Mum, do you think?' She was so excited that she forgot to add her usual caveat, 'Sorry, she said to only call her Usha.'

'Oh, mm.' That was Auntie, swallowing.

'No, noooh ... It must be an illusion because of the sun,' Uncle said, sitting down abruptly. Maya remembers being surprised that he looked like he was going to cry. But she hadn't dwelled on that. Was it possible they hadn't seen the woman? Or were they trying to spare her feelings? They did that a lot.

'Ahh … you never know,' Auntie said. She added that she had rustled up something for Maya and brought it over (it was her favourite, banana bread!) and gave her a long hug.

In an aside, she asked her husband, 'Do you think Usha somehow …?'

Uncle just made a strange noise in his throat and tried to change the topic. 'Whoever, whatever it was, don't worry about it.'

Don't worry about it! Possibly a ghost? Or Usha? Coming to see Maya? Too exciting!

But shortly thereafter, Auntie and Uncle made her see the 'nice' doctor to tell him everything, except he wasn't nice at all, was he? (More on that later.)

~

The noise from the market nearby brings Maya back to the present. Just as well she's not superstitious in real life or she wouldn't be able to live alone at all. (Except for Mishraji, she smiles, though her aunt's Man Friday is under strict instructions to take a couple of weeks off with Chini Auntie away.)

Maya knows she'll have company soon enough, after that unusually lengthy phone conversation with her brother. He's more than welcome but she hopes he doesn't try to bring anyone else along. Maybe she can explain. She needs a timeout, to work through her tangle of feelings, and she's not ready to give that up. Though, if she's totally honest, the thought of a timeout has been making her recede into the past a little more than usual. Partly, she blames the therapy sessions that have taken months, leaving her more vulnerable, more porous, not to mention a lot poorer at two thousand bucks a pop (though her savings have held up, tided along by her smart investments from back when she had a regular job, and yes, if she's being honest, the semi-annual deposits from Mark do help).

She's feeling a lot more these days, it's true. But she has also realised she's a little muddy about things she thought she knew … she's noticing lapses in her memory, like she's 'lost' time.

Again.

And yet, she's also somewhat clearer about other things, like recent life choices.

Is it worth it? she wonders. She'd rather not feel so much if that's possible, thank you very much. Like, take the last few sessions.

OCTOBER 2023

'Take me back to your childhood,' Reena Gupta prompted.

Gupta is a therapist who came highly recommended on a crowd-sourced list of therapists, and proved to be a delightful change from the creepy shrink of Maya's youth. But still, the Bad started rearing its head with that question.

Childhood should seriously be a no-go area, Maya thought. *Proceed with caution.*

Silence.

'Mia was his name for you, right?'

Maya was very careful not to breathe differently, or move, or show any sort of reaction.

When had she shared that with Gupta? Clearly, her guard had been down.

Gupta stayed quiet for a while, knowing that Maya would talk sooner than later. There was clearly a lot she wanted (needed) to share.

Maya never let anyone call her Mia anymore. That was mainly her father's name for her and he was long gone, taking with him her (only slightly) more happy-go-lucky self, leaving a brooding, easily enraged husk of a girl behind.

From her diary entry: 'It really is the most dreadful, unfair thing, this life. It's all very well for the people who die, but what about the rest of us? Navigating through life acutely aware that there are huge gaps, massive rents and rips in the fabric of our very lives, while the majority of folks are entirely, blissfully oblivious.'

Ever since the accident that claimed her father's life, Maya hasn't cared for much.

Grief lives in the body, someone told her as an adult, but the younger Maya had no clue how to cope—what could anyone have even said back then? Everyone had expected her to just move on.

But how? There was no guidebook. There was no guide, even.

The daily nausea might have passed after a few months, but for the rest of her childhood, she had broken into tears at the most tangential of memories, fleeting wisps from a happier past. Things her father had showed her (the constellations, the parks, the trees), things he had taught her (to challenge herself, how to listen), things he had told her ('Nothing to beat love and laughter', 'Nobody owes you anything'), but most of all, what he had symbolised—a kinder, safer place than the world had proved to be.

The knowledge that he had been completely wrong and then, having lulled her into a complacent state, completely gone, had made Maya feel first angst-ridden and then superior, armed with a cold, efficient rage. She blanked out what she didn't want to focus on. It was easy enough. Just your garden-variety escapism. Except it wasn't, was it?

No one had really acknowledged or even seemed to have noticed that she would sporadically change, speaking and behaving very differently. No one had clocked it as unusual, in the beginning at least. She had actually had very few friends in her life, and one adult caregiver had deeply disliked her, while the good ones who soon followed ascribed her strange behaviour to the trauma of abandonment and losing a parent so young.

No one could have got a handle on things at that stage. Not even her beloved Gautam Bhaiyya. (Beloved and more real than step-, more real than real, he had promised her when the adoption-related yelling wouldn't stop that awful year before she went, once and for all, to the refuge that was Chini Auntie.)

So Maya had started skipping out on reality and someone else came to take the reins, to take control, to 'protect her', though she didn't learn about this till much, much later.

After the Big D that came out of the blue—just like that, no goodbye, no last words (except the vestiges of an argument, the harshness leaving an afterburn)—Maya had started to view the world with a terrible clarity. Like that woman. *God, she's the worst,* an older Maya still thinks, eviscerating Neeti, her stepmother-for-a-few-years, in her diary.

'Horrid, she was. So nasty to me. And she really let herself go. No friends. Not like Papa,' Maya shared this out loud despite herself, forgetting that she didn't want to get into this phase at all in therapy.

A senior police officer, Lakshman had always had hangers-on, both men and women, to keep him company, keep him happy, fuss over the kids. That was some childhood! She and Gautam Bhaiyya had become quite inseparable after their parents had told them they were born just a few minutes apart, imagine that! At the same nursing home too! This had reassured Maya-then-Mia and Gautam too—it was a bond that was meant to be.

And things could have gone so well, without *some people.*

'I often wonder if the wrong parent died,' an older Maya had written in the diary Lakshman had given her. She still allows herself to use one or two of its pages every year.

'I sometimes feel like ...' she started to say in her second-last therapy session.

What could she tell Gupta, though? Could she say anything without coming off as a terrible person? How to put her thoughts into words that could make a smidge of a difference?

Who cares at this point? she thought.

'Anyway, I miss him a lot is all.'

Maya didn't see the point of going deeper. And she definitely didn't need another person to not get her.

'That's not why I'm here,' she all but growled.

Her therapist had the patience of a saint.

'That's fine,' she reassured Maya. 'That's fine. We can come back and unpack that later. But I want you to hold on to what you're feeling ...'

She needn't have added the last part. Maya-then-Mia was already there, lost in her head.

4

Memories, Therapy and the Lost Time in Between

[Flashbacks to Childhood]

In her mind, it was a year of Epic Proportions, an incredible year that could have been any other year for any other child, except Maya-then-Mia was no ordinary child. She knew this thanks in no small part to Lakshman the cop. He had made it very clear to her and to the rest of the family right from the start that Maya-then-Mia was special, very special.

And his favourite.

That was the one thing she and Gautam Bhaiyya couldn't discuss. They discussed everything else under the sun, their stock of *Phantom* and *Tintin* comics and sweets, the large desert cooler rumbling in the background, creating a picture-perfect postcard of a memory that she would have no trouble accessing, unlike some of the later memory pebbles. A few years spent like this, and then all of a sudden it was time for matching school uniforms and getting dropped off in a Gypsy, though Gautam Bhaiyya often had to just make his own way.

'I don't mind,' he used to tell her. 'School is so close to our house.'

There was nothing missing.

Nothing.

Papa would take her out every night to point out the stars and to teach her something about something. Never about people (they're the most boring, he would laugh) but something about astronomy or geology, something about the plants in their garden. Sometimes he would bring out the old Bajaj scooter and they would take a quick round (no need to tell anyone, he would chuckle as he got her an orange bar just for herself, neither of them acknowledging that her colourful tongue and messy face would be instant giveaways when they returned).

Neeti was hardly around, judging from Maya-then-Mia's scrapbook of memories, but that might just be self-preservation kicking in. The good bits were kept and the rest blanked out.

And things *were* good.

But then again, even in that monumental year before he died (the Big D, in contrast to her own periodic depression), she can remember in flashes the gradations of change, the tone and tenor in the house growing tense towards the summer and then, all of a sudden, Gautam Bhaiyya was quieter, often absent, even on the weekend afternoons that had till then been pledged to her. And then he was sent off to his 'special school' that their father had taken him to one fine day, to meet someone called the Rishi.

No summer holidays lazing about together anymore, *achanak se*.

Maya-then-Mia used to get Gautam Bhaiyya to tell her everything back then, ha! Before, in a more innocent time. There was even a conversation between Lakshman and Neeti about the Pahaari (a witch, the children were told; never meet her alone, Neeti had growled), that Maya-then-Mia couldn't make head or tail of, though the first time she did meet her, the Pahaari (who she knew as Usha) smiled at her sweetly and gave her some chocolates, those fancy imported ones. And then she'd spoken to Gautam Bhaiyya as well.

But it had all been a blur, like maybe she'd dreamed it up. *Maybe she had?* Her diary isn't clear on this point.

She definitely hadn't dreamt up what Gautam Bhaiyya had to go through, her diary is quite clear. How strange it had all been for him, meeting the Rishi for the first time with Papa. Their father had taken him the summer before he died to meet Rishi Uncle (who said not to call him Uncle). 'That's fine, that's how grown-ups are,' she had told Gautam Bhaiyya, while asking him to recount exactly what had happened.

'He's one of yours,' Papa had said to the Rishi in that room in the hills.

Gautam had tried not to flinch.

('One of yours means what? A new family?' Maya had asked Gautam later. Sensitive issue, given what they'd been hearing of Neeti and Lakshman's fights. Although those had always sounded like they were about Maya and that 'good-for-nothing witch'.)

The old man had looked at him from behind horn-rimmed glasses and stroked his long beard, Gautam told her. He gave nothing away.

But a few moments later, his tone was gentle. 'Come. Meet the other boys,' he said, pretending he didn't see any signs of distress. 'Nothing to worry about,' he had added, 'You'll fit right in.' Gautam had noticed that he radiated kindness, somehow.

The other boys had been playing some complicated game that looked like cricket but was not.

Papa had come back after a long smoke, nodded at Gautam and said, 'We'll go back now, come.'

In the Gypsy driving back, he had asked, 'Did you learn anything interesting?'

'No,' Gautam said.

'No?' Lakshman asked again, but for once not sounding disappointed. 'You will.'

Gautam had tried to tell him he wasn't sure where the day had gone. His father had always told him to be honest, but sometimes honesty just made him angry. Not today, though. Today, he was humming quietly.

The children fell into their own strange routines, a bit more independent of each other. In fact, Gautam hardly got the time to check on Maya or even his parents, what with his rigorous spiritual and physical training. He had no time to absorb any of the tension brewing in the house, growing worse by the month.

~

But then came the line his father started using when he was in high school. 'You know, baba, you have to be the man of the house.' Inevitably followed after a five-minute pause with, 'I won't always be around.'

He would laugh at his son's look of shock. 'Don't be a baby like Mia. You know how life is.'

Actually, Gautam didn't know, he confided to his sister. By now he was fourteen going on fifteen, the same age as Mia, not even sure why he was different from everyone else, why he was treated different from her. (*Maybe because she was always being picked on in school*, she'd thought, but that didn't convince him. *More likely because he seemed to be psychic? Though selectively so*, she had noted in her diary as an adult, trying to make sense of their dysfunctional childhood.)

Gautam, sadly, by this point wasn't even sure whether his parents accepted him for who he was. He had overheard one conversation from right outside their bedroom. His father saying, '... a bit slow. But the Rishi's going on about some untapped spiritual potential. Either way, it would be worth it if it helps tone down the strange side.'

Mamma didn't say anything, Gautam noted. *Why did they think he was slow and strange? Maybe he was adopted, like Mia, and they just hadn't told him?* (This thought would come back to him later as an adult.)

Anyway, things were so strange around then that Gautam wasn't entirely surprised to see Papa's friend Usha Auntie a few days before he left for the hills that last time. She was talking to Mia on the stairs near the house.

When Gautam came closer, she patted him on the head and said, 'Hello Gautam, my dear. Thanks for taking care of everything.'

What did surprise him was that she somehow said it without saying anything out loud. He didn't know how, but she was speaking into his head. Must be why Mamma used to say she was 'Bad News … Never talk to her alone'.

'She is so beautiful, though.' He brought that up with Mia in a tone of wonder. Mia, meanwhile, worried obsessively that Usha was preparing to take her away. She told Gautam the story she had overheard about the lady being a Pahaari and a witch and the reason dogs were dying in the neighbourhood.

'Must be scary having a mother who's a witch,' Gautam told her.

Papa used to laugh when Gautam asked him any of these questions. 'You'll understand when you're older,' he would say. Or, 'We'll talk about it when you're older.' And, of course, now they never can. Or rather, they can, but Gautam is tired of the one-way conversations.

Even before the accident though, he had started feeling like an outsider at home. There was the fact that Lakshman favoured Mia. *Not that it was her fault,* Gautam thought loyally. But there was no denying that he and his father couldn't have a conversation without a severe critique on many fronts, like he somehow disappointed his father just by being alive.

The shame of it.

And they couldn't talk about any of it. Not without what felt like a fight unto death between the parents themselves. Neeti and Lakshman never stopped going at it those days and eventually just started avoiding each other whenever possible.

'For God's sake, Lakshman,' Neeti had snapped once within earshot of her son. 'This isn't a home for the abandoned we're running. Take your shit elsewhere.'

What did that mean? Gautam wondered. *Who else was abandoned? It was just Mia, surely?*

Neeti hadn't taken kindly to the news about Mia moving in ten years earlier and she wasn't about to let time get in the way of that attitude. She had been suspicious about Lakshman's behaviour in the whole episode. *Wasn't he supposed to be a police officer, for God's sake? Why couldn't he stand up to that maniac of a girlfriend of his?*

Why couldn't Mamma ever stand up to Papa? Gautam had thought. But he had enough of a survival instinct to keep this to himself. He was the chirpy, chubby child who had opened the door when Papa's friend Usha Auntie had flounced up to their house one fine day and given him a pat on the head, ignoring Neeti completely. He remembered her launching into a long conversation with Papa, who had looked pensive on her departure.

Maybe it was that day that Neeti decided she hated Mia with a vengeance. Even now Gautam remembers fragments of the conversation and how his mother had tried to enlist him in her war against Mia. People would start to talk, Neeti knew. They'd already started looking at her and Lakshman differently when they went out, she told her husband. That inevitable hush in a group of women and an extra-polite 'Namaste Bhabhiji' that didn't quite hide the sting of deliberate humiliation. She had stopped wanting to go out in public, preferring to wallow in her hurt and sadness, trying to imagine how she could control the rapidly spiralling mess around them.

'They know about your affairs,' she had hissed at her husband once when Gautam was with them at dinner. Lakshman was trying to tell her that she was reading too much into everything, that things were just in her head, that she should join him for the weekly outing to the club. She had sworn at him for the first time in her life. 'Fuck you.'

Gautam had been shocked. But he noticed that Lakshman changed his tone after that, also increasing his allowance and the amount of time Memsahib could get in his official car (something he had been loath to allow her to use till then). Mia's 'Chini Auntie' had been roped in to take her for holidays and some weekends and that also lightened the mood at home. Lakshman had somehow managed a truce, but inconveniently for Neeti and the kids, had died prematurely, making everything topsy-turvy.

The old rules just didn't apply anymore and no one knew what would take their place.

Because things changed so dramatically after the Big D, not even the bond of a lifetime with Gautam Bhaiyya could help Maya-no-longer-Mia. She refused to respond to her own name and started acting out; it didn't take long for the new head of the household to come to the obvious conclusion: she didn't owe Maya anything.

'Little bitch of a girl, nothing but trouble,' Neeti had confided in her childhood friend. She couldn't bring herself to tell anyone besides Romila, who knew about the quasi-adoption, the shame of the affairs, and everything else in between. But *she* was hardly surprised by the mean streak. 'I don't know why you ever bothered with her,' Romila said. 'Blood will tell, after all.'

Neeti had flinched almost subconsciously. She kept forgetting that people knew the Other Woman. Who knew how many of her friends knew? Maybe not about all the things Lakshman had done or all the shame he'd brought to their door, but certainly enough of it. That bastard and his humiliating ways! Leaving her to deal with this alone. Mia or Maya or whoever had started looking a lot more like Usha, it was true. But it wasn't her problem anymore. Romila was right. Neeti could call the shots now, and it was clear that she wasn't even the little brat's family. The kid had been nothing but trouble since she'd been dumped here. *Not like Gautam,* Neeti had thought. *He is the good one.*

Neeti started planning to break up the little unit not long after her husband died. Stupid accident or not, she was not going to let him ruin the rest of her life. She registered her son trying to make an effort to be peacemaker—Gautam wanted to console everyone now that he was the man of the house (as Papa had told him to be), but the fault lines were clear and neither Neeti nor Mia had the time for any attempt at rapprochement.

Gautam was stuck, unable to make a dent in anything, and finding it increasingly difficult to recognise his own family. Trapped in their own emotional prisons, they were each oblivious to all else, including the burden of his self-appointed role. He couldn't afford to make any mistakes now, not at school, not with the Rishi, not at home, not if he was going to be responsible for providing for the family. There was no safety net anymore, Gautam knew.

He also wouldn't give up on his sister, no matter how difficult she became. Which was how, one fine night, he *did* break through to Maya. It was shortly after he had come back from the Rishi's special school. He saw her staring at the stars, like their father had taught her, pointing out Ursa Major, Minor, the Polaris, Orion's Belt. She had been doing this week after week, month after month. She particularly loved Orion's Belt.

'Are you thinking about Papa?' Gautam ventured to ask, breaking the bubble of silence around her, the night sky providing much-needed solace to both.

'I have no idea,' she responded. *Is it my father I am thinking about?* Maybe. After all, he used to take her out to look at the constellations. He used to tell her that the light from the stars had travelled an awfully long way to be here, so it was like looking into the past in a way. 'You've got to respect that,' he had said.

She did. But she had also been hoping that in some way that meant he could see her, somehow. But she didn't say a word about any of that. Gautam looked distraught. As an adult, she remembers clearly that she didn't know what to say then, to reassure him, and he didn't know how to deal with it on his own.

But he kept trying, even as time hung heavy in their little flat for the next several weeks. Sometimes that effort, that perseverance got through and registered with her, somewhere in her subconscious. *I am not entirely alone, am I,* she just about allowed herself to think.

Time went by as it always does, and it was enough to change everything for both the kids, weathering them a little bit, giving them a little bit more clarity and then less … ebbs and flows like the ocean. Maya still looked up at the stars, staring and staring at Orion's Belt like her father had taught her, beseeching … something.

A change … something should happen to me, she prayed one day.

Something should just take me away from here.

I don't deserve this. I don't even belong here.

Why can't I join Papa?

The prayers came thick and fast.

And one day, it was like Orion started speaking back.

'You're better than this.'

Is it even possible that I heard that? In my father's voice, no less?

'You know better.'

And the clincher. 'No one owes you anything.'

She distinctly heard Lakshman's voice.

The epiphany may have been invisible to everyone else, but there was a creeping new identity that was making its presence felt. An angrier, more aggressive one.

Gautam's love for her overpowered the weirdness, which he put down to grief. But he didn't know what to do, who to go to about the appalling things Maya had started to say, often hurting him dreadfully, though he never showed it. There were some moments of grace, though they were hard to hold on to, being few and far between.

'Why do you keep butting in?' she screamed at him once in the middle of a no-holds-barred session with Neeti.

'I'm the man of the house now,' he tried to say, but stopped. 'I want to help.'

She just screeched at him. 'It's not your business. Why do you have to jump in?'

'I have to, it's the rules,' he said. 'You're my sister.'

That calmed her down, touched her in a place she didn't know still existed.

He started playing music for her again after that, not breaking into her space so much as content to be there with her. Quietly.

It had always been their thing. He had given Mia access to his music collection—she liked Madonna those days but indulged his old-school grunge and alternative music whenever he played it. Their individual iPods and Zunes might have replaced their discman, but sometimes he'd bring the old thing out just to play their mix CDs and she would laugh at him and sit next to him, one earphone dangling as she laugh-cried with him.

Their love had always had this transformative power. Maya may not have known that she knew this, but he was an important part of the axis grounding her to the world. His love was unwavering despite the stunts she tried to pull.

'He's your protective factor,' said Gupta, writing something in her notebook fifteen years in the future. And that was the saving grace. It might have even saved her life.

~

Gautam still thinks of himself now, and even back then as a teenager, as Maya-no-longer-Mia's ally. But maybe he shouldn't have. It might have been better for her in the long run. He didn't tell anyone when Mia got all quiet and funny with all her games, for one. Nor when she started talking to herself. Or when she stopped responding to her name.

'Who? I'm Akira,' she had said once when Gautam asked how she was.

Again? he thought.

But then he had started thinking of Akira as 'the other sister'. It made things easier. Maybe not entirely seamless—it took some getting used to, but then again, she had already made everyone stop calling her Mia. And then she had created this imaginary friend when she was being bullied in school, but ... *Maybe it's a phase,* he had thought.

~

[NOVEMBER 2023]

'No one could have known what I was going through,' Maya found herself sharing in therapy before starting to feel overwhelmed, as if she was under attack again. 'Not even my brother.'

Never before had she expressed how her love for her family had turned into hatred, into dismay, self-loathing. She had never acknowledged, even to herself, the way she shut down and withdrew when she felt under attack.

Her therapist asked a follow-up question and then noticed a distinct change.

'No one had any fucking clue,' Akira replied.

A new ego state, Reena Gupta unobtrusively made a note in her file. This might be more complicated than the usual South Delhi anxiety and alienation cases that she was used to dealing with. She would need to make a referral soon.

Unlike Maya, who internalised her emotions and shut down, Akira blamed everyone else for not helping her out, for making her feel unsafe.

'I'm the tough one,' she said. 'I don't let her get pushed around.'

There would be no reliving those terrifying days when it was Maya against the world, alone and badly bullied. Even then, her family continued exactly as they always had, oblivious to her misery. (Except for Papa, who had yelled at her when she came crying to him about being bullied, but at least he cared. He had acted out a lousy mood the whole day after that, which had secretly pleased Maya-then-Mia.)

Back in the therapist's office, Maya had got an awful headache. *How long have we been sitting in silence? Look at these messy peppermint candy wrappers, ech,* she thought to herself. *Least they can do is clean up between sessions.*

'Something is triggering that trauma,' the therapist's voice echoed in her brain. 'Your memories are a road map. They're leading you somewhere for a reason.'

What if they lead to a spiritual cul-de-sac, Maya wanted to ask, but it was time up for now.

The next session, they picked up right where they had left off, comfortable with each other, even with the silences. Gupta knew when and how to prompt her.

'You had a tough time in school, you were mentioning?' she asked kindly, referring to her notes only once. 'Especially after ...?'

'Even before,' Maya interrupted.

~

'Are you poor?' a boy had asked her in middle school.

'You don't even have a real mother or real father,' another said.

'Do too,' she said, trying to stand up for herself.

'Because he's IPS, he had to take you in.'

'No one wants you, stupid. My mother heard it from your stepmother.'

'Even your brother is so ashamed.'

That one got her in the gut.

'Did your stepfather kill your father?'

'What!' That enraged her and she tried to fight back, but by then it was gang warfare.

One lunch break, the boys and some older girls stuck her head down a toilet and flushed. She couldn't even look up for the rest of the day.

'Eew, don't sit next to me.'

'Yuck, so gross, yaaa.'

Even the maths teacher couldn't help but notice her sorry condition and excuse her from class so she could go change. She had zero friends. No one came to talk to her, so afraid the taint would spread.

You have no control over anything, she learned, and tried to put up with everything in silence. But things got worse. Her support system conked out too.

'No one owes you anything!' It was one of the few times she remembered her usually indulgent father getting angry with her, when she complained about how unfair life was.

'Stop it! Stop whining. God, why can't you be more like ...' He had stopped himself from finishing that sentence.

Like who? she wondered. *He must've meant Gautam.*

'Listen. If you think you deserve something, you jolly well go out and earn it,' Lakshman said. He didn't sound like Papa, or 'stepfather', as the kids on the bus had started saying to make fun of her when Gautam wasn't around.

Maybe he was also getting tired of her.

On the upside, she did have the epiphany: no one owes you anything.

It was a wonderful life lesson. Stands her in good stead even now as an adult. *It's every man for himself,* she knows.

That's despite Gautam. After the Big D, both of them had lost their faith in stability. In themselves. In the rules. And that was when Akira arrived again, coming and going as she pleased.

Not that Maya knew this.

'Everything is so fucking grey,' Akira told Gautam one day.

Gautam winced each time his sister used this different voice but didn't know who to turn to. Who was left? It was he—the man of the house—who should figure things out, surely, so he didn't say anything to his mother about how weirdly Maya was behaving. Anyway, Neeti was already on the warpath.

~

'How serious was it at this stage?' Reena Gupta prompted after a pause.

'She was a mess and a proper target. She was skipping class and getting picked on a lot. She started thinking of harming herself.' It was Akira calmly responding. Gupta made a note. 'She really did need my protection.'

~

Maybe she's letting off steam, Gautam had thought and kept making a huge effort.

'He defended her, you know.'

The therapist wrote this down too.

~

Gautam had had a huge row with his mother, who was talking about changing things. Neeti had vehemently refused her parents' offer of a refuge back home in Allahabad, saying that she would stay put in the small flat that her late husband had bought. But that was when she had started thinking about who would stay with her, and her decision had really not been a surprise. She had the pension, she had her independence, *she* made the rules.

Gautam tried to ensure that she waited till after the exams, but his mother didn't have the patience to wait. 'She goes!' Neeti screamed. 'And that's final.'

It was the first time he saw that other side of her, the side that Maya-then-Mia encountered regularly.

Meanwhile, Maya had spent days sobbing in her bedroom, scared witless that she would lose Gautam as well, crying so hard that she was sick. Coughing fits, throwing up and then whimpering herself back to sleep. Things only turned a nice grey when she filched some pills from Neeti's room.

Gautam kept the music going and at some point, that did the trick. Even after everything changed, including the music of the day (they had *Empire State of Mind* and *Boom Boom Pow* on loop for a month, she remembered), one day he dialled up the nostalgia, singing to her the lyrics they had changed in a vintage song back in the day. It brought back a younger, more innocent age.

'... where the girls are green and the grass is pretty,' a younger Mia and Gautam had sung, cracking themselves up with their subversion of the old GnR hit.

It was shorthand for so many things about their childhood; she couldn't have changed all that much, surely?

'... Where the girls are green,' he sang as he knocked at her door.

It had been an opening, like a stopper had been released. She had burst into tears and couldn't stop. It was the first time he had seen her cry so much since she was a kid. Hours after that, she told him in a scary monotone about wandering about in school, after school, not wanting to go home or anywhere, not wanting to field any questions from anyone or do anything. She regularly spent up to three or four hours in a park near school, sitting on a bench, avoiding the couples and trying not to note their ever-more ingenious ways of engineering some privacy with a dupatta here or the back of a tree there. They were not thrilled to have this random voyeur around, but she never cottoned on. Maya didn't get hungry or thirsty, she wasn't tired or not-tired. She just was. Stoic. No idea where the time went. Never sure how she got there, even.

'Spacing out?' he asked, remembering how she could be as a little girl. She just shook her head. She didn't even daydream anymore, she told him. She wasn't sure where the time went, but she usually came to around 5 p.m. or 6 p.m. and headed home.

Gautam had known better than to tell his mother, who was increasingly quiet around the two of them. He had overheard some of the conversations she had been having with Romila, who had said it was high time for Maya's real family to step in. He didn't know what to say, not that anyone was asking him, but he knew for sure that this wasn't the right time to highlight Maya's worrying behaviour.

Instead, in a clumsy attempt to be helpful, he chose to say, 'This too shall pass.'

It was the 'Suck it up' sort of tone that got to Maya.

That was that. It was back to square one.

'We said nothing about it, of course,' Maya remembered in therapy. 'We all had these issues, but everyone was trying to act "normal" for what it was worth.'

Except me.

'I don't know how long we've been doing these damn therapy sessions, but as long as I get to talk more this time, it's fine,' Akira said languidly. 'What possible reason can there be to remember any of this?'

Reena Gupta wrote this down, smiling at her client as she did every week, working to create that safe space for trust to flourish.

Maya shared more in her sessions, her tone warming. 'It was Gautam who came to the rescue, inevitably. It's not his fault he didn't know what to say to me, not really … But he knew I needed something, some love. We couldn't reach Usha, but tracked down my aunt, Chini Auntie, who was more than prompt in landing up at home and telling Neeti what was what. They started out politely, but neither could bear the other despite both hating one person: Usha.'

Usha was one thing, but Chini couldn't believe the nastiness of this woman, Neeti. How could she plan to throw someone out midway through a school year, with the least regard for her future?

'Anyway, she's too good for you,' she told Neeti bitingly as she walked out, unaware that Maya, hiding in the room next door, had heard her.

Maya treasured that memory, clutched it to her heart for comfort in the bleakest of times. Someone cared. An adult who didn't have to, cared.

~

The next session was in a different gear.

'If you're comfortable, tell me more about Usha,' Gupta prompted, only to be met with a stony-faced silence.

'That's okay, whenever you're ready.'

Maya had followed up on her appointment so that the almost-forgotten pain and hurt would stop. In fact, she would have preferred a little pill to make her forget but had sensed that would not be forthcoming this time around.

'Why don't you tell me what you're thinking of,' Gupta tried a different tack. 'And how you all fit ... together.'

'Ohh, a family tree?' Maya made a face but gave it a go.

As Gupta noted, Gautam and Maya had a strong sibling bond. He was a protective factor. Maya sometimes referred to Auntie Chi and Uncle Pi as almost-parents and Lakshman as Papa. Usha, or the Pahaari, was not to be called Mum, and the very absent Mark was not to be called Dad. Neeti was always 'that woman' or some expletive.

~

Gupta had consulted a psychiatrist for next steps, having made a note of possible trauma-linked Dissociative Identity Disorder, but she didn't want to spook her client with a premature diagnosis. Her notes indicated that maybe the personality had started as a coping strategy to deal with a major trauma, just like in other cases.

Maya had already shared some bad experiences with the shrink of her youth and received multiple diagnoses including multiple personality, borderline personality … But this went beyond labels, Gupta knew, and shared this belief with her client.

While the main trauma seemed to be two-fold, the initial abandonment by a parent and then the death of the other parent had led to many subsequent, actually even prior, mini-traumas and crises that made Maya slip into the sort of refuge that Akira provided. Many psychologists didn't entirely believe in Dissociative Identity Disorder, seeing it more as a motivated defence mechanism, Gupta knew, but in this specific instance what mattered was her client's story and case—why and how was 'Akira' still around? The question also arose whether Maya was aware of this other aggressive but protective ego state. She didn't seem to be, but Gupta wasn't one hundred per cent sure.

~

'So … I didn't actively remember this till your questions last week, but Mia's supposed "real" mother did visit at least once. When I was about fourteen or fifteen or so. Some annoying in-between year. It was definitely after Lakshman the cop had passed away. And after I moved to Chini Auntie and Uncle Pi's house. Usha would have been what? Pushing forty? It wasn't the first visit. Apparently, she would come by the house every couple of years to meet Mia, even Gautam, but never me. Not that I wanted to meet her. Bad news, that woman was, I knew it and Chini Auntie knew it. She even said as much.

'When I was fifteen though, or sixteen or whatever it was, I came home from school to find this attractive, well-dressed lady in the sitting room talking to my aunt. I pretended not to recognise her and Mia felt worse and worse about her when she asked if we wanted to move. I don't remember much else.

'I said something about exams. And that I already had a family.

'"More than your real family?" the lady asked.

'And then I saw dear old Chini Auntie straining to smile. So, it was finally happening. Mrs Bad News was back on the scene. Poor Mia-Maya. I had to take care of it for her.

'Both the grown-ups presumed that I didn't recognise Mia's mother. Because of her prolonged absence, I guess, neither realising that I knew her the moment she walked in (thanks, Mia, for these stupid shared memories) but decided in that split second that I wanted nothing to change.

'Why should Mia or I upend our perfectly cosy life here? And go from being treated like a little princess to ... God only knows.

'This was the same woman who hated babies, remember. She had made a fine art of locking Mia in a cupboard to keep her quiet. I'd like to see her try that with me! But I didn't say much.

'There was an awkward silence at first when Chini Auntie stepped out, ostensibly to make cocoa, telling her estranged sister on her way out that Aki (only she called me that!) loved stories and was partial to specific food ... hot chocolate, yes, but also boiled eggs of all things, as well as banana bread and peppermint candy.

'She was wrong about the banana bread, but I didn't correct her. That was Mia's favourite.

'And then, before I knew it, Usha decided to tell us a story.

'About a woman with a golden heart, I remember.

'"A long time ago, there was a woman everyone loved," Usha said. They said she had a golden heart. She was gentle and kind and beloved by all the children and grown-ups in the city. Oooh, look at her and her golden heart, they would say, she makes everything so nice.

'She was so admired and so loved and so happy to be loved that she kept trying to make everyone happy. But, whatever she did, they wanted more. And this woman loved them so much, she always tried to give more. More than she had, sometimes.

'See, that's proof of her golden heart, the city cooed and cried. We love her so much. We love her heart.

'Now this woman, she had nothing left but this great love in her heart. She wandered about the world, always trying to come home with more and more and more. And the good folks of the city took all she had to give each time, egging her on, driving her to push harder and harder.

'She got tired, overwhelmed even, but she couldn't stop. She really loved making them happy. And she didn't care how she did it, she took something from her own sis ... her own family, if it meant making other people happy.

'She loved it. She loved making them happy, so much so that one day, finally, she cut out her heart and offered it to them on a plate.

'"Like a boiled egg," Usha said, looking me square in the eyes. "And they ate it."

'Mia's face lost all colour, though to her credit she didn't move a muscle. We never ate a boiled egg again.

'No one would believe that conversation, even if I told them. Of course, we've never met the supposed mother alone since then. There's been no need.

'Mia and I didn't tell anyone, not even Gautam, about our decision. But then he heard from his mother (ghastly woman!) and said in passing that he was glad we weren't leaving them all to follow Usha to the house in the hills near her ashram. And then, we were especially grateful for having stayed put when the dogs in the neighbourhood started dying. We were the only ones to notice and nurse their litters back to life. Only Gautam and I knew it was Usha's fault. We had heard Auntie Chini and Uncle talking about her, calling her a bitch, and then of course there were the neighbours' whispers about the Pahaari being a witch.

'Mia started writing in her diary again, to try and track her visits, but what was the point when we just wanted her out of our lives?

'Speaking of ...'

Akira trailed off, saying nothing further as the appointment wound down.

After a few minutes of silence, Gupta gently brought up a referral. 'Before we end for the day, I think you might also benefit from seeing a psychiatrist.'

'What?' Maya interrupted. 'I don't want to see a psychiatrist. Are you trying to palm me off to someone else?'

'No, no, not at all. I would want to continue our sessions too,' Gupta said kindly. 'But let me ask you something. You've mentioned "losing time", as you put it a few times. I think you recognise that you're slipping away, maybe as a way of coping with the traumatic things that have happened. And it must be helping you cope.'

She paused.

'I don't ...'

Maya couldn't finish her sentence, her thoughts frozen as she started to panic.

'It is helping you cope, but you know, it can also be scary, not knowing. I think you might benefit from seeing a psychiatrist. It will be a safe space.'

The therapist's voice was calm and soothing, but ... but Maya couldn't go back to that. The way things had been. She said she would think about it, but she was not convinced.

Sure enough, the following week, Maya cut off.

'You know, actually, I think that's enough for now,' she told Gupta on the phone, after ignoring a few WhatsApp messages. 'Thanks so much. The sessions have been really helpful.'

'What about a virtual call?' Gupta said. 'I really think there's something you need to work on. I'm concerned that we don't have a handle on things yet. In fact, I was thinking that a referral to Dr Sen would do some good. Do you remember we spoke a little bit about starting a low-dose medication after a referral?'

'I don't remember that, no.'

'It's to make things easier. We should at least meet again to talk through some of this.'

'But there's nothing you can do for me right now. I need a break. I'll call you again soon,' Maya said, and hung up as politely as she could.

All that dwelling in the past was well and good, but it's done, Maya thought. *There's no chance I'm going to get into what's going on right now in my life.*

Maya recognised her triggers now, she felt, and would not discuss the symptoms for the hundredth time. The moment the lost time came up, she knew what would follow. The looming presence. The migraines, the stomach doing backflips, the heightened vigilance, the panic attacks. That sense of impending doom.

She needed a break, she knew it.

In fact, she called a timeout in toto.

Announcing it—where else?—on social. What she didn't say was that she knew Worse was coming. And then Better. But she had to survive the Worse first.

PART TWO

5
Best Friends Forever ... or Not

[End-December 2023]

'My best friend has left the building.'
'Life is short, before you know it, time's up.'

It's hard to know what Maya's friends really think of her status updates before she locks one of her pages and makes another temporarily inactive. Hard to know because no one writes what they really think on social media—what is it, 2010?

The non-indifferent ones rate her as lame for thinking of herself as her own 'best friend', and who can blame them. Best friend, worst enemy, take your pick. Sometimes it's all in the mind. Quite literally.

No, Maya's friends have no idea what she is up to because they think of her privately as 'too intense', 'definitely weird', 'so high maintenance', only one of them thinking, 'God, I wish she knew how much I cared'. Okay, make that two.

For the most part, her old friend Farhan keeps his feelings to himself, having been painfully embarrassed by them for years. But there's the new, almost-significant other. *Didn't we decide that we would be together?* Karthik wonders. *Or have we kept it too ambiguous? Where has she gone?*

It's been a few days since her last post. Who knows, if she hadn't signposted this need for attention, they may not have even noticed something was wrong. But now even the friends who know she likes to test them—the ones who are used to her mood swings, her high-energy and low-energy phases, her different tests and complicated games, 'her phases like an on-off button', as Megha tells Farhan—are a bit concerned.

'She may be a weirdo, but she's *our* weirdo,' Farhan says fondly.

~

Tucked away in a little flat, Maya isn't thinking about Farhan or Megha, or even Karthik. She wouldn't be too surprised by what her friends think of her—she's been indecipherable to most since adolescence; at least since her father died. *When no one understood me or even tried to,* she thinks, before shaking it off.

A little too old to believe that someone else could fix her, she had nonetheless thought her last relationship would do the trick, but she had chosen the wrong sort of boy for that. Enough with the drama, though. Twenty-nine pushing thirty isn't young anymore, she knows. She has had that first glimpse of old age, clocking the changes in her body, noting the fatigue and slower metabolism and multi-day hangovers.

And then there is the gynae she's seen off and on for the last five years. 'Have children. It's time,' the doctor chides at each checkup, her assistant not as kindly.

A visiting fertility specialist tries to reassure her, saying, 'Don't worry, there's loads of time yet.' But she would say that, wouldn't she? She's not going to say 'geriatric womb' like the magazines do, though she might as well.

Maya's head is a swirling cauldron of thoughts. Most days she goes where they take her, but some days she just gives up. She cries when she needs to (most disconcerting for fellow passengers on the Metro, but often ignored by her Uber drivers who just want to get to the next destination and the next and can't these women hold the drama, do they not understand how many trips have to be made to just break even these days?).

Anyway. *That's enough,* she tells herself.

She has given instructions to Mishraji, taken the keys from her beloved Chini Auntie, who's off on one of her regular trips to Landour, and that's that. At least going off the grid will buy her some time away from the everyday banality, away from the madding crowd.

Some recent changes—starting with another breakup and culminating in a new 'friendship plus+'—are what she needs to think about in her own safe space. That's what she would like to think through. But the descent into ancient history via therapy has left her feeling uncomfortable, triggered even. There's something she can't put her finger on, something lingering from her childhood.

None of her friends would get it. The less said about them the better. *I've never liked them much,* she thinks.

They're so empty, so shallow. If nothing else, the pandemic had given her this terrible clarity. *We're not missing much there*, she tells herself. But apart from friends she's not sure she likes, who else is there?

No parents—ha, Usha's definitely not calling any time soon. Maya laughs at the thought of it. And, of course, her father Lakshman (she still considers him more her father than Usha's husband, Mark) ... *well, Lakshman is profoundly unavailable, isn't he, having been dead these past fifteen years?*

Maya still misses him, feeling his absence as a profanity. It's just as well he's gone, though. No way of knowing how he would have reacted to her lousy taste in boys, her naïve belief in the redemptive power of love, or her wallowing. 'No one owes you anything' and all that.

Her brother will undoubtedly miss her if she goes off the grid *achanak se*, as they would both say, she thinks quite cheerfully. (In fact, her brother is picking up his phone to call her from a picturesque house in the hills as she thinks this.)

Much as Maya tries, she can't help thinking of her 'special friend'. It was this friendship after all, a strange friendship that kicked off in an ashram, that gave her the courage to end that last toxic relationship. It was this series of events which propelled her to the psychotherapist, who has been helpful in her own way, Maya will admit. *But we're done with that now. Aren't we?*

All of a sudden, almost too much seems at stake. It's a sun-drenched winter afternoon and she is feeling undone by the dusty branches of the gulmohar tree right outside the little flat.

That's it, she thinks, taking out her phone and opening the messenger app.

She puts it down again, almost immediately. She's content now—why spoil it?

She can't help but smile, thinking of her new friend Karthik. *He's quite unflappable,* she thinks.

He had been prattling on about energy on their last WhatsApp call but had stopped short when she butted in to ask about his position on 'starting afresh', as she called it.

Surprisingly, he did not take as strong a position against it as she would have thought. But then again, he believes in reincarnation.

'Maybe it's what you *think you* need,' Karthik told her. He was finding himself increasingly incoherent and tongue-tied as only the newly love-stricken can be, but pushed on, 'A fresh start. But … you should wait for a while and then see.

'Things inevitably get better,' he said into the silence.

Hadn't they had this conversation, or a version of it, before? He sounded like he wanted to say something more, but Maya beat him to it.

'No point,' she told him. 'My soul is tired now.'

Having realised she was (just) heartbroken and unable to see it, Karthik tried to power through analytically.

'A fresh start doesn't mean undoing everything,' he said. 'It's also a symbolic move.' She listened to him, but he felt he was working himself into a right mess since he didn't want to mention the heartbreak or the ex. And being a fairly new friend, he especially didn't want to tell her this soon that he saw the two of them together for all eternity.

We create the reality we want, he remembered being told. *A dream or a nightmare, it's up to each of us.* He wasn't about to follow that thought through, given his waking nightmares. He was also not ready to mention the visions. Not even to her.

'Just wait a while,' he told her. 'You never know what's around the corner. And anyway, what if our journeys are meant to overlap?'

'Overlap?' She gave it a split second of consideration.

'Everything happens for a reason, right?'

'Fine. Fine!' she said, agreeing to hang in there a little longer. But only because he'd been such an important part of her spiritual journey since the ashram.

'It's more than that, Maya,' he told her. 'You're on the cusp of something ... big. Something bigger than us. You'll realise that as your quest takes off.'

She was quiet and thoughtful. She hadn't yet told him that she felt she was probably beyond salvation. She'd known that, sort of, hadn't she, since her father died? She still thinks her father's death is her fault, being a 'witch's daughter'. She'll never really know whether she caused it; she'd been surprisingly angry with him the night before the accident, cursing him in her mind for snapping at her for some small thing. *Why does he care what I say to Neeti,* she had wondered. *He has no idea the horrid things Neeti says to me when he isn't around.*

She had cursed him in her head, hated him all night, and the next day he was gone. *Black tongue.* She's heard of this concept, this supposed power to make things happen by just uttering them. With her luck, she probably has it, too.

The guilt has been unmanageable. And unmentionable.

But still, every night (and I find this oddly moving) Maya stares out at the stars, specifically Orion and his belt, like her old man had taught her to. Often, she apologises to Lakshman while she thinks her complex and sad thoughts.

What's the point? she wonders sometimes.

(There is no point, not really, I'd say, but it's still quite a thing of beauty. Though I can't say anything yet, can I? She hasn't entirely come to terms with me and this new life stage. In fact, I'm not even in her tapestry yet, so I stay quiet, more or less, much as I'd love to help.)

If I can't get out, I can at the very least unplug, Maya thinks. Going off the grid, such a luxury to have this choice, such a privilege. She wants to just draw it all out a bit.

I'm content. It's a calming of the energies and the thought that comes to a more rational part of her brain—the part that clocks the gulmohar, that intuits the strong feelings Karthik harbours, that feels herself feeling happy, or at least curious about life, and isn't that the same thing at the end of the day?

It's a huge step forward.

The phone rings.

She ignores it.

It doesn't stop.

She feels it vibrating from across the table. *Fine, fine, I'm coming!*

Who's leaving all this damn candy all over the place? she wonders. *Such a mess.*

She shoves a bowl of mints aside and picks up the sleek instrument without checking who it is, answering with a curt 'Hello.' It's Gautam Bhaiyya.

And about time too!

6

Social, Anti-social

Much like Maya's mood swings, one of her social media pages has taken a melodramatic and then decidedly unpleasant turn. It escalates quite quickly from there on, from the usual 'Where are you, baba?' sort of messages to 'God, I'm really worried now, Maya, and why is your phone off???♥'

Someone posts, 'You gaizzz do you think Maya's ok?!?!'

Somebody using the handle BhaktofGod writes, 'We can help, Maya. You're not alone.'

This is followed almost immediately by 'Where's the party at?' and 'I'm coming too!' by two other users.

But it's the next post with an '#IamMaya' hashtag that triggers the furious comments from her friends Megha and Farhan.

'With you, Maya!! #IAmMaya,' BhaktofGod writes.

#IamMaya some other acquaintances chime in, because everyone loves a hashtag. No logic required.

'What the ...?' Megha WhatsApps the friends' group.

'How shady is this?' asks Farhan.

'It's some sick joke,' Megha says. 'Aren't these the hashtags they use for victims?'

Akira is not too worried, sitting in her silk robe at her table, a bowl of her favourite peppermint candy in front of her. It's like watching a show. She smiles as she scrolls down the TL. Her own profile is on another page, of course. She's got her own friends. *Whatever, Maya.*

Farhan gets agitated. 'WTF? Who are you?'

'Why?' BhaktofGod asks Farhan, proclaiming that he/she is her friend too.

That's smacked down with the brutal 'Oh really? Never heard of you,' from Farhan and 'Just who the hell are you?' from Megha.

'#Soultwin,' sums up BhaktofGod, going for a second hashtag along with #IamMaya. He's hit a nerve.

'Just super weird, man!' says Farhan on WhatsApp.

'I'm calling the cops, you sicko,' Megha writes. 'You better not be a stalker.'

'+1' is Farhan.

Megha decides to call Farhan to talk through what they need to do.

'Who do these guys think they are?' wonders BhaktofGod halfway across town and starts a furtive check of their socials.

Meanwhile, back in Gurugram, Farhan is fuming. 'We can't ignore this bullshit. Who the hell is this chap?'

'Must be some rando she met, yaar,' Megha drawls. 'He probably has nothing better to do than sit online all day. Loser.'

'I've never heard of him.'

'Well, you know what? I think it's that fellow she mentioned once? From work? Or somewhere?' Megha starts thinking, taking too long as usual.

A slight pause as he digests this tidbit, but then Farhan says, 'A new friend? … Is he her …' His voice is a croak at this point.

'What? What?' Megha asks. 'Oh God, not you too!'

It's a good thing he doesn't see her rolling her eyes.

'Not that it matters,' Farhan snaps a little, surprised at her condescension and that 'you too'. *Is ka kya matlab*? Uff.

'What do we do now? What if something is seriously wrong?'

'Don't be ridiculous. She's fine. Let's not jump the gun like this psycho,' Megha says, though she's sounding increasingly unsure of herself.

'I wonder if Maya's brother has seen this.'

'Her brother, man. Shit!' Megha hadn't thought of that.

'What should we do? We should take it down, we should totally delete these posts, don't you think?'

Megha says, unnecessarily, that they should add Rohit to their chat, in case he has an idea. Though she knows he doesn't.

'Let's add him,' says Farhan.

'Yeah, typical,' Rohit says on the phone, which isn't particularly helpful but sort of telling in its own way. 'You know she loves the drama.'

He sends Megha a quick text on the side saying that she owes him a 'b00ty call', anytime next week, but that's just his general vibe.

'Let me hang up and try her again,' Farhan says.

'I've already tried, from the landline even. Not just the cell. There's bilkul no reply,' Megha responds, though she's starting to get annoyed. Maya's always such a buzzkill.

Maya's socials have become a matter of much curiosity within her circle. The comments keep coming, though no one has a clue as to what's happened to her.

Well, her brother does, but one, he's gifted and two, he's also managed to reach Maya, though there's no way for her friends to know that.

Halfway across the city, the boy who goes by the moniker BhaktofGod starts typing, then deletes the words. His handle isn't ironic or post- or meta- or anything. Since he created his original handle, he's quit the Guru he worked with and lost God. But he can't be bothered to change his name on social, that would be too drastic somehow.

Having lost his newest and brightest friend, Karthik is feeling particularly bereft. He starts to type again: 'Death was in the building because of me. You won't understand, none of you know anything of reality.' Thinking better of posting that rant, he deletes the lines.

She knew the absolute futility of everything, he knows in his bones. *But didn't she see things changing? Weren't they looking up?*

He's not even sure why he's convinced she's dead except for her morbid conversations, slight depression, four days of unanswered texts and phone calls and subsequent lack of online activity.

That and what he calls 'the Cab of Death'.

Maya did take two rides in one of the fancy family-owned taxis, the Audi and the Benz, no less, as Karthik remembers darkly. He thinks back to the night she skipped out of his house, when was it, a month ago? Happily accepting a ride from the head chauffeur K, who drives the car Karthik refers to—with no real basis in anything remotely empirical unless you count dreaming (can you count dreaming?)—as the Cab of Death.

'I should have stopped her!' He would have stopped her too, but she had laughed off his theory. Karthik's father also tends to laugh derisively whenever he brings up the subject of negative energy. Not quite able to articulate his Cab of Death theory, Karthik had mentioned it to his father hurriedly and then gone on about bad mojo and tantric tricks.

'Hundred per cent sure that's not his real name even,' he had said about 'K', as the chauffeur had started calling himself.

His father would have none of it. He declared that Karthik was only welcome at their Greater Kailash home if he left behind all that nonsense he had learned from the fraud godman, who incidentally owns half the posh fifteen-crore-rupee flats a stone's throw from their home.

'Seven years,' Karthik's father sputtered, working himself into another rage. 'Seven years you wasted there.'

This was bad form since Karthik had swallowed his pride and returned home after the decade-long stint only at his mother's insistence and 'God promise' that he wouldn't be tormented about this phase.

'Bas karo,' Garima had stopped her husband. She couldn't bear to lose Karthik again. Not after all they'd been through! She still remembered—and never ceased to remind her husband—how Karthik was nearly blind at birth and got his vision back only after a miracle blessing and surgery.

'Only a second miracle brought him back to me after all that hera pheri,' she told her husband sharply. 'We can't count on a third.'

So it was quite clear that there would be no insulting the holy men who had held Karthik in thrall since childhood, she was quite firm on the subject. That didn't stop his dad from mocking him. A little lighthearted taking the piss never hurt anyone, right?

'Wake up, kiddo. These are luxury cars, top of the line, and only for a very exclusive clientele,' Karthik's father told him with a hint of a wink. 'You can take your special friends out once in a blue moon.'

'Argh!!' His father knew he had very few friends, let alone 'special' ones.

'But who, after all, would say no to a free Beemer or a Benz?' His father couldn't help rolling his eyes. Apart from this boy of his, that is, who had become a total head job after his years in the ashram. Till date he had steadfastly refused the Audi and the S Class. His father had earlier thought it was because these were increasingly common cars and was amused, but then learned it was because Karthik was obsessed with some weird death theory.

Doesn't this Maya episode kind of prove it? Karthik asks himself, on the verge of losing himself again in thoughts of destruction. He reaches for his phone to send one more text, one last attempt at being lighthearted.

'*Ki haal*? Wanna meet?'

Desperate though he may be, he needs to play it cool. She mustn't know—if she's still around—that he's already a little panicky. He's grasping at the remnants of a connection but is starting to realise now, in this very moment, that he never fully penetrated Maya's universe, doesn't know all that much about her, and wouldn't know how to go about reaching her, not to ask her out, but in case of an emergency.

The important stuff, they never talked about. *Where the hell does she even live?* he wonders. *How did I share so much and yet not figure out anything about her beyond the weird stuff?*

'I was born with my eyes open … Even in the ultrasounds you can see it,' Karthik had told Maya in one of their last conversations before her 'disappearance'.

'That's odd,' she replied quite matter-of-factly.

'Very odd. Considering the amniotic fluid itself would have blinded me. You would think. Then again, nothing my mother ever told me turned out to be true, so maybe I should check with someone else.'

She laughed, and her hand brushed his, making his heart lurch just a little. They'd slowly started talking about the deeper things in life, the little victories and the big losses, the searing absences, the holes inside, missing pieces, and how little everything really means in the end. And how much the little things mean day to day.

It was enough for him.

Hard to believe their association started at an ashram, with that godforsaken Guruji who turned out to be just another charlatan. (Karthik isn't sure why he's surprised or why he's still so angry, but he had spent the better part of a decade in service to the man.)

'Life isn't worth its price tag, it's the worst deal in the world,' Maya had told him on their fourth or fifth not-date, full of that melancholy that he associates with her. 'I think we should figure out an exit plan.'

'It's almost tempting,' he had laughed and agreed. He had secretly wanted to say something completely the opposite of that, something romantic, perfectly on cue. But of course, he never managed to. All that spiritual know-how and dollops of sincerity, but he couldn't manage to tell her the one thing that drove him these days—the thought of spending more time with her.

But weirdly enough, despite themselves, they stumbled upon this, their own version of intimacy. Neither was actually deep-down convinced that the other would do anything other than wait to see what might unfold.

We were connecting so well, weren't we? he thinks. It's hard not to question everything, especially now that she seems to have vanished, disconnecting from everyone. *Or is it just me?*

Maybe she's still texting and hanging out with her other friends. *How would I even know?* he wonders, suddenly jolted to the core by insecurity. It's not like she ever introduced him to anyone.

Why couldn't she just give us more time? He has so much to tell her, so much to share. She seemed so interested when he promised to walk her through his reincarnation theories, partly to make up for the let-down at the ashram.

'We'll do yours next,' he had assured her, 'I know some really good people you can trust.' She had smiled brightly. 'Fine,' she said. 'Sounds like a plan.'

Wait, why hasn't he ever met any of these supposed friends of hers, again?

Karthik is brooding and spiralling, feeling more than a trace of her melancholy. He lights a cigarette and skulks through her photos and her friends' lists to see what they share, making mental notes along the way.

Mental Note: Farhan, hedge fund manager. Hundred per cent jackass.

'Photos of him in Greece, is it? New York? London?' Karthik tries to identify the cities, speaking out loud.

'Oh ho! A cover photo with Maya, very fancy, eh?'

He obviously has a thing for her, Karthik concludes, and despite a twinge of jealousy, proceeds to dismiss Farhan as a moron after reading some of his painstakingly long captions. He keeps scrolling, losing track of time, barely registering that his blood pressure is rising because of all the photos in the casually elegant places that spell big bucks. *What is with these champagne-glass toting, duck-face pouting jowly boys and booby girls anyway?* he wonders.

He clicks on a photo of a rather square-jawed, muscular specimen.

Mental Note: Rohit, spoiled rich kid, part-time actor, full-time boring.

'Looks rich and acts it too,' Maya had said about Rohit affectionately after they bumped into him at the fancy mall she sometimes wanted to go to. He scrolls past the photos. It's such a shallow game, this life. And he really feels it too—it makes him a little hollow. He's always been a little 'too intense', people have said, or more cuttingly, 'Chip on the shoulder, the fellow has.'

Maya would never say something like that, she was always easy to talk to, surprisingly easy to relate to, despite what he had presumed to be her silver spoon existence. Actually, that was possibly the only time she had snapped at him. 'What the hell do you even know about me?'

Poor fellow, he had no idea about her childhood at all and was quick to apologise, internally a little deflated at how she never took the trouble to share anything about herself, her world.

'How would I even know? It's not like you tell me anything!' he had wanted to say but held his tongue.

Maybe Maya had a parallel life that she was happy to keep separate.

Judging by the Insta posts, she's definitely hanging out with the Richie Riches, he thinks, feeling belatedly justified for making that earlier assumption. A little unfair that she had snapped then. *There's no way our worlds would ever have collided except for the ashram*, he thinks, eyeballing Maya's friend list and spiralling further.

He's not sure what she even saw in him after he quit the Guru she so adored. What could she possibly like about him, with his painful middle-class aspirations and fear of failure, his late-night panic attacks about financial solvency. Based on the way Maya spoke about people, her attitude and general worldview, he figured they were worlds apart.

Little as he knows about Maya's provenance, Karthik is almost equally clueless about his own family. He knows precious little about his father's work and life, having checked out mentally long before he left the family abode, convinced he was meant to be a monk. He would probably be fairly surprised to discover that his family is better off than Maya's. Maybe not old money like the good old Delhi blue bloods she seems to hang out with, but who cares in the twenty-first century, right? That's what Maya would tell him, without a doubt, if she knew what he was thinking.

'C'mon!' he could almost hear her say. (Not to mention what she would say if she knew about his uncle, the Rishi, who Karthik hasn't even met yet. Ha!)

Of course, Karthik is painfully self-conscious because he's developed feelings. Although, their relationship has started to feel more balanced. Just as Maya looks up to him for his spiritual and esoteric ways, he admires the knack she has for being comfortable in her own skin wherever they are in the city, of knowing all the right ways of being. And miraculously, somehow, they fit together—she soothes away some of his rough edges.

'What are you going to do next?' she had asked him shortly after he quit and came back home.

'I don't know. I want to teach. But Dad wants me to help out,' he told her, adding after a painful pause, 'you know we own a fleet of cabs.'

It seemed like a step down from spiritual advisor.

'They're luxury cars,' she laughed at the way he cringed. 'It's not that bad!'

'But cabs just the same,' he said, more than a little embarrassed.

'You have a family bijness,' she said, laughing again before getting more serious. 'Don't worry so much, people always respect money.'

He didn't know what to say. There were all these imperceptible differences between them. He was out of his depth.

'I know it's the opposite of what Guruji preaches ... but even with *him*.'

She had stopped short of criticising their Guru, or ex-Guru, rather, but really hadn't needed to tell Karthik, one of the #OG disciples, what the Guru was all about.

He had only left the Guru's sanctum sanctorum after close to a decade of service, after all. They didn't connect the dots, but it was a short while after Maya and he met. All of a sudden, it was as if he no longer needed to be there.

The team was most disappointed when he left, and thrown into a bit of a tizzy, not sure who else could handle logistics, VIP movement, donations, or even organise the private sessions so well, but no hard feelings, they told him. They liked him enough to lie about the Guru's true reaction.

Meanwhile, his father spent more than a few hours being coaxed by Karthik's mother to go easy on him, but eventually was only too happy to find that his son had some skills that might prove helpful with their business; that he wasn't 'just some sort of Hare Krishna'.

Their fleet of taxis was still contracted for all the VIP movement in the capital, and even by visiting business delegations from abroad, he told Karthik enthusiastically. 'We need to keep a close watch on things. You might have missed the in-between bits, but have you seen how prominent we are on the world stage? India's taken pride of place … and we should be proud to be making in India, representing India when these fellows come on their official trips.'

Unfortunately, Om P. was soon sorely disappointed to learn that his only son wanted to go off and be a teacher of all things. He took some solace in his friends' insistence that there was loads of money in education. Also, Karthik had promised to put in extra hours on the weekends to learn the business. That was all Karthik had been doing these past few months—apart from meeting Maya fleetingly for coffee and beer. He was slogging it out as a teacher at a private school on the outskirts of the city. The stint at the ashram had set him up for a potentially more lucrative religious studies position at a uni, but that would only be possible next year.

At this rate, I might not even be in one piece by then, he thinks, quite miserable about his dear friend. Even in his solitude he's unable to bring himself to call her his girlfriend. *We haven't reached that level yet, but of course we both know the connection is solid. Right? Otherwise, why would she have spent so much time with me these past few months? Even after I left the ashram?*

Poor, miserable Karthik. Unlike, he imagines, her fancy friends, he has no one to talk to. He's lost his belief system, his ashram family and all his friends, all at once. There's no one who gets him anymore. He had tried to talk to his childhood buddy Jyoti once, when he started developing feelings for Maya, but tuned out when she said: 'She sounds a bit hi-fi.'

The implication that Karthik is a simpleton in comparison wasn't lost on him. He laughed it off but didn't want to speak to Jyoti anymore. She'd changed completely, anyway, transforming from his supposed best friend into a typical 'auntie-type' with her two children and beloved husband, her inordinate preoccupation with picnics and family holidays, in-laws and vegetarian recipes. All within the span of a few years. And had he imagined a slight cooling off after he left the Guru's sanctum sanctorum? He might have lost his social cachet entirely.

'Oh Maya, I wish you'd waited … or at least called,' he says to his screen, going over some more of her photos. Their growing intimacy should have been a buffer for her. He gets her lows, but surely she was exaggerating the need to 'start again', wasn't she?

His mood darkens further. *What else have I been wrong about?*

Something that strongly resembles a chip does surface on his shoulder when he's contemplating her friends. He glares at the photo of the muscled fellow, as if Rohit might personally be to blame for this sorry state of affairs.

Rohit is as well off as Maya mentioned and #blessed, as he likes to post. Generational wealth has that effect. He's lucky that he doesn't have to do much and there's always way more money than he can spend in his bank account. His dad's investment chap keeps track of his portfolios and his parents are hugely indulgent, albeit in their own world. Nothing for Rohit to worry about, except life, the living of it. Not sure why he didn't want to stay at the farmhouse with them, his parents set him up in a plush pad regardless. At some point this past year, he started doing yoga and meditation, supposedly balancing out the parties and drugs, the mid-morning boozing and the somewhat skanky lifestyle.

His friends think he's very lucky and he knows that they do, but he's not feeling it at the moment. The boredom is eating him up. He's venting a nastier side of himself but only ever in private, with much younger girls who don't quite know that this is not in actual fact the way Delhi rolls. They will get their revenge, and though #MeToo may not have the same pull anymore, there will be a reckoning—where else but on social media.

But for now, there's nothing except a glinting superficiality in Rohit's life in snapshots—enough to bore Karthik, whose eyes quickly glaze over. He has to log off, remembering the work at hand, but first he clicks on the profile of someone who pops up as 'Someone You Might Know'.

Mental Note: Someone called Akira, poet and yoga teacher, hottie.

Solo photos, no connection with Maya, but finally someone who looks interesting, passionate even, and a lot like Maya! He's intrigued. Akira and Maya both seem to like the fan pages of Oasis and Madonna.

He looks up the name, thinking it's something to do with the Japanese filmmaker, but finds it has Sanskrit roots too—meaning 'graceful strength'. *Perfectly apt,* he thinks. He wishes he could meet this goddess at some point, somewhere.

This is the usual reaction men have on seeing Akira. Men, and quite a few women. She's stunning, having come from a particularly blessed gene pool. She's certainly never been accused of being un-hot or uninteresting, usually moving around with what amounts to an entourage.

Many, many moments later, he finally logs off for the afternoon. He has some serious errands to run this Saturday and wants to keep a close watch on the Audi in their fleet.

He also isn't sure about Maya's friend circle. When he'd asked her, she'd mentioned someone named Megha, but quickly went quiet. A few hours after that, she had opened up though, and if he'd thought to connect her vulnerability with his earlier question, he hadn't let on.

'There's something about being unwanted as a child that fractures the soul,' Maya had said, apropos of nothing at all. They hadn't even been discussing her supposedly devastatingly beautiful mother, who was so convinced she wasn't cut out for motherhood that she had walked off into the sunset just a few years after giving birth to her daughter.

'Once you're abandoned for good? It's like a big black hole opens up. Love, light, too much love, even? Wouldn't be enough,' Maya said that monsoon day, dangling her legs off Karthik's bed.

'Nonsense. What the hell would you even know about that,' Karthik said, laughing it off.

He can only imagine the number of would-be Romeos lurking about and trailing her practically everywhere. She has a gravitational pull that she doesn't even realise she possesses, he's amazed to discover. But no one would have guessed at the melancholy side.

Fake it till you make it, she's maintained since childhood, and she now doesn't quite know where the fake her ends and the real her begins. Her sense of self oscillates between grandeur and self-effacement. Loved, lusted after and sometimes, only sometimes, cottoning on to the power she wields.

'I love you,' he had wanted to say.

But it wasn't enough.

Love isn't enough, Maya knows. And in this case, it seems despite everything, the cracks will always resurface.

No one owes you ...

She has never discussed her own cracked foundations and their ramifications with anyone else before. Not Usha (who she barely remembers), not Lakshman (who she barely refers to out loud in public), not Mark (who's never been around), and certainly not any of the men who have been in her life. Nope, no thank you. So while she will not openly acknowledge the rise and rise of feelings for Karthik, she knows she's opened up a lot with him. A hell of a lot. She's not shared as much of herself in donkey's years. At least, not since Gautam Bhaiyya.

Or maybe, more accurately, not since Auntie Chi and Uncle Pi forced her to see a highly lauded shrink, back in high school. 'Multiple Personality Disorder,' he had proclaimed grandly, while not-so-surreptitiously staring at her newly formed breasts.

Typical male behaviour, par for the course in Delhi, shrugged Akira.

He had asked her breasts to talk more about her childhood, so she gave out some of the highlights, obviously not too much.

Triggered potentially by the loss of a father figure or abandonment?? His notes had been visible to her across the table. *Multiple personalities. Possible borderline personality disorder.*

Multiple personalities? She could just imagine being the butt of all the jokes. As if she didn't already have enough to deal with, the kids in school never having lost their mean streak. *I can't bear this,* she thought.

Maya did go for two more sessions with the shrink, enough to keep her aunt and uncle happy, with the added bonus that she got a prescription for the attendant depression and anxiety … Medication the psychiatrist warned her she shouldn't get into the habit of taking.

His leery stare had stayed with her, but she'd stuck it out, talking as much as she needed to and clamming up when she could. She'd learned her lesson. No more opening up or sharing or anything remotely morbid or non-mainstream.

And habit-forming? *Yes sir, I'll take two pills to fall asleep and thank you in the morning.*

She had told Reena Gupta briefly about that period, rather biliously, and surprised herself by giving psychotherapy another shot. 'This might be a quarter-life crisis,' she said when they first met. 'But I want to let go of all this damn baggage.'

She had sighed dramatically but said nothing about the immediate prompt, this thing that seemed to be blossoming between her and Karthik.

'I won't sabotage anything anymore. I don't want to sabotage myself.' That was how she'd played it. There was no reason to feel too unsettled about coming back to therapy—after all, more than her childhood, she'd wanted to talk about the big breakup with that jerk Roy (someone whose entire way of being seemed to encourage Akira to come out of her shell again). Maya had brought up how the last relationship, more than the breakup even, had destabilised her, but kept half an eye out, not sure why she'd been so on edge lately.

Gupta was a pleasant surprise—non-judgmental and easy to talk to. Until, that is, the therapist had started rummaging around, asking all those childhood questions.

'You've made it this far, Maya,' Gupta said encouragingly. 'And this is a safe space. Our work here should make the going easier for you, not harder.'

Gupta knew not to push when it was potentially harmful, staying consistent and steady. But she couldn't have predicted that her client would ghost her, 'performing' her self-imposed isolation on social for all her friends to see. The ubiquity of social media and the pressure it puts on people to perform their lives was something she'd discussed with Maya, including how it paradoxically makes people more exposed but less seen, more social superficially but actually more asocial, unable to connect beyond the surface and unwilling to forge bonds with those they disagree with.

'So, when you're ready we can talk about it, Maya. In your own time. I want you to look at how you're feeling and just make notes.' That's what Gupta kept telling her. She had even left Maya a WhatsApp message.

Gupta had tried to provide some scaffolding. She knew that Maya hadn't (yet) realised that nothing would ever be as bad as all she'd already gone through … nothing. But this entire exercise had felt hollow to Maya towards the end of their time.

It didn't feel safe, that's for sure. Maya was back in fight or flight mode. She deflected and talked as little as possible. The ripple effect of a traumatic childhood or not, Maya hurt easily. She did not bounce back quickly from breakups. As Gupta had gleaned, Maya's convinced she is inherently unlovable (including by her own mother, after all). Her childhood abandonment left the deepest of scars, even though surviving that experience had set her up to deal with the worst life had to offer.

'It's almost like prep classes,' Akira had joked during one session. 'Silver linings playbook.'

Akira had given Maya a wide berth lately, to be fair. She should have guessed that Maya would eventually crack again and need help. 'It's been a while,' she said to Gupta. 'I don't just come in for the shits and giggles, you know.'

7

In Over Our Heads

(December 2023–January 2024)

Farhan isn't sure why his friends are so slow on the uptake. He knows that he needs to reach Maya's brother, or someone else, to get them to lodge a missing persons complaint. It's time for drastic measures. It's been three days at least that she's been missing, if not four. There's been no social activity, no WhatsApp messages are being delivered, and he's quite convinced that shady boyfriend Roy has done something to her. Possibly in cahoots with this BhaktofGod creep who's posting dubious poetry on her TL and using those random hashtags.

He takes a screenshot so that he can show the cops if need be.

the call of the wind
the pull of the concrete the light in their eyes …
Extinguished. #IamMaya

'You can't tell me that's not fucking weird,' he says out loud to an empty room filled with gigantic screens (TV, computer screen, a second monitor of a touchscreen), but no people.

Day Four with no contact has Karthik worried too, but he's not sure whether Maya is avoiding just him or everyone. Not until he logs in to check, that is. She has 100 likes on her last update.

He posts a second melodramatic poem to go with the first.

wingless and broken
you circled the nest
yearning for an ultimate rest.

Farhan sees it immediately.

Livid, he comments, 'What is your deal?'

He switches to private message. 'I'm not kidding, buddy, I'm calling the cops if you keep this up.'

Karthik pops up in chat. 'You should have called them by now. Some friend.'

That throws Farhan for a second. 'We were told to wait. Who the hell are you anyway?'

'How does it matter to you?'

... (typing)

'And if you're such a good friend, why don't you know about me? How come I know all about you, Farhan? What, don't tell me, did you guys stop talking again?'

'Oh shut up. It doesn't matter. Stop posting your crap poetry all over the place.' Farhan is a little annoyed that Maya has spoken to a stranger about their stupid fight. She's always been immature, he remembers.

Crap? She likes my poetry, Karthik aches to type.

At least, that's what she said, he second-guesses himself. *Maybe it was just to spare my feelings.* Poor Karthik, he speaks three languages but he's most fluent in self-loathing.

Farhan waits for a while but sees no activity. He wonders whether he should block him or screenshot and then block. Thrown by the fact that the chap does seem to know Maya, he falls into his own online rabbit hole, trawling the net for clues on Suspect Numero Uno. He's also noted that there's been no activity from Roy for months. Another suspect.

If there's anything to be found online, Farhan knows he'll find it. He's confident about his domain expertise. He also knows he's got a reputation for being quite particular, peculiar even, about things online. His friends snigger behind his back, making fun of his eccentricities, 'his paranoia' they call it, about smartphones and the internet and surveillance.

'You don't need to selfie every day or "check in" at every location, for God's sake,' he'd snapped at Maya one day.

'Twitter's okay?' Maya had asked sweetly.

Seeing that he was losing it, she added, 'What's wrong with you today, baby?'

'You guys are mad. It's a fucking stalker's paradise out there.'

'Oh ho.' She tried to downplay it but noted his concern.

He tried to calm down. 'Just don't live tweet your locations all the time, okay?'

Anyone would tell them the same, he knows, annoyed at how blasé they all are even as they slam him for being a drone, focused only on making money. It's true, he works like a dog in fintech, but all his peers do too.

You don't become a crorepati sitting on your ass, he wants to say. 'But what do they know?' he asks aloud. They haven't had to work for a living, cushioned as they are by big money and school ties. They barely care about anything going on around them, not the cauldron of hate, not even the social churn … It's all changing, as he has all too painfully realised.

We've changed.

He's become one of those people too; the ones unfriending each other because of their politics and religion. Any topic is a potential explosion—alleged fake encounters, the eating of beef, the drawing of cartoons, for God's sake. Even more unnerving are the jokes about his religion, the strange comments at work from time to time about 'These *Mozzies'* and 'Who's going to put them in their place?'… conversations that strain into silence when he arrives on the scene.

What more do you want from me? he wants to yell. He used to be forced to disclose his loyalty at every cricket match, back in school and college. *Nothing can touch me on that front,* he had thought. *We're beyond this,* he had thought. *We've moved past all that immature, jingoistic bullshit.*

But it's back.

Of all their friends, he could only have these honest conversations with Maya, at least sometimes. He could explain to her why he had to try so hard, harder than the others.

'This is what it's come to,' he told her after *the* election of their generation. 'I never felt like a minority before.'

She was silent.

'Even if you lucked out and were born into the creamy layer, or even right below it. Even if you were born into a supposed post-caste world, this country would never be post-religion,' he said.

'Could never be,' he added after a pause.

'Actually, we'll never be post-caste either,' Maya said, 'Just look at the battle for quotas. Or fuck that, look at the matrimonials!'

She went on for a while, till he butted in.

'But it's not just that, Maya. We've been sucked right back into it, all of us. And all of a sudden, it's fine, it's perfectly okay, it's expected even, to show your biases,' he raged.

'This is the new normal.'

Megha or Rohit would never let him bring this up. '*Arre, chhodd ya,*' Rohit had said at the last party. 'Why get into this intense convo?' Megha had giggled and rolled her eyes.

They could afford to ignore everything, of course, money and majority rule.

'Fuck them,' Maya had said. 'Fuck tribal identities. We're your tribe.' Naïve but endearing.

'Cheers to that.' He always indulged her, knowing that despite all her talk to the contrary, she had her own bubble to hide away in. How he pined for her though, how much he loved her. Except for that one patch where she hadn't wanted to talk to him or anyone. He had been a bit too honest in his opinion of Roy and what sounded like a shameful scheme to pimp her out.

'You're debasing yourself.' He had tried to tell her she deserved more, that she was the centre of his universe, or would be if she'd only allow it. But that was not how it came out.

'Listen.' Maya's temper wouldn't allow it, her pride wouldn't allow it, and she eviscerated him. 'We don't all fucking hide our lame feelings online, okay, Farhan? Get used to the idea of how things are, how messy things are, right here in the real fucking world,' she had said icily, not even raising her voice.

That had shaken him up more than he cared to admit. *Lame feelings? So she knew how he felt? And that's how she had reacted?* He'd retreated and made very little effort to see anyone, taking the blow to the gut. He'd tried to hide the hurt, of course, and acted all breezy when she started messaging him again, never referring to their blowout. He didn't trust himself around her, though, and limited his interactions with her to tame comments online here and there. It may have been self-preservation, but he'll never be able to explain the rest of it. None of that really mattered when push came to shove—his feelings were there all along, after all.

He may have hidden his hurt and rejection and bruised ego all too well, but all that masking also meant he never acknowledged what was going on with her. He nine hundred per cent knew something was wrong, as he told Megha—those mood swings, the phases where she answered the phone in a different voice, cut off conversations. Something was wrong, and he had let his pride get in the way of being helpful. Pride, and well, his day-to-day life was just so hectic. Easier these days to send a quick WhatsApp or like a post and have that easy-breezy friendship that everyone else had.

'You know how she is,' Megha would always say in that tone of hers, understanding but biting. They all brushed away her 'weirdness', laughing it off.

But now he's agonising over the fact that he might have been the best friend she had. And the only one who cared enough? Maybe he should have heeded some of the warning signs. His brain is whirring, going over all of them—her withdrawal, the bubbling-under-the-surface depression, that old (sometimes annoying) childish reference to herself as a goddess, or in the third person in conversation, sometimes under another made-up name, which had earlier sounded like a bit of sexy role-playing till he realised she wasn't into him.

He had told her to go to a counsellor, but of course she hadn't, not that he knew of, at least. Maybe he should have just taken her. *God, when did life get so complicated? And friendships?*

That Roy must have pushed her over the edge. And this new creep. He will do his duty this time. He won't give up on her, not in this shark pit of a city where anything could happen to a girl.

He messages Megha and they decide to escalate things.

The interaction at the police station is typical.

'*Haan, aapka complaint kya hai?*'

'Missing person *ka case hai*, sir, *hamari* friend, Maya Varma *teen din se missing hai*,' Farhan starts out.

'*Accha. Family kaun hain? Kiske saath rehti thi?*' The police officer's tone is undecipherable.

'*Matlab?*' Farhan tries politely.

'*Matlab? Kiske saath rehti thi? Aapke saath?* Family?' The cop and his colleague are staring at them. Who did she stay with?

'*Ji nahin. Akele rehti thi.*' She lived alone.

'Akele.' The tone doesn't change but the atmosphere seems to have.

'Haan.'

Megha is glaring, but Farhan tries to be as calm as he can, for all their sakes.

'Aap ka naam kya hai?' the second cop asks suddenly, eyeballing Farhan in a none-too-friendly way.

'Sir, Farhan.'

'Farhan.'

The cop pauses just long enough for Farhan to hear each syllable linger in the air and it doesn't strike him till then that maybe they're thinking that he's somehow involved in this disappearance. *But then, why would I bother to come to the station,* he thinks, starting to sweat nonetheless. *Maybe Mother is right and I should have kept a low profile.*

The first cop asks, *'Yeh aap ki girlfriend hai, beta?'*

Farhan shakes his head, miserable.

'Chalo, aur details toh bataiye,' the second cop says, adding in English for the deracinated kids, with just a hint of judgement in the last word, 'share some details, where was she living?'

'Sir, yahaan pe, aas paas, paanch minute door police station se, mall ki taraf.' Just nearby, five minutes from the police station, near the mall.

'Hm. *Kahan?*' The cops exchange a look. Silence for a few ticks of the second hand. Enough time for Farhan to remember that there is a giant jhuggi near Maya's DDA flat and wonder, *Should I bring it up? Or is that classist?*

He holds his counsel and shows the address saved on his phone, which they note down.

'Ladke ka chakkar toh nahin hai?' the first officer asks, rather knowingly. This isn't about a boy, is it?

'Uhh …' Farhan isn't sure how much to disclose. *What about Roy? What about that weirdo online?*

Maybe a good time to mention … 'Sir,' he starts.

'Tchah! *Nahin, aisa kuch nahin hai.*' Nothing like that. Megha jumps into the conversation, already irritated with their tone. She doesn't bother with the 'ji' or any such honorific, completely unaware of how out of their depth they are here, all their snobbery, sophisticated airs and designer bags working against them every second.

No response.

'Megha, let me speak to them. You know how it is,' Farhan says in a harried aside, worried that the girl will piss off the cops. As it is, they seem so out of place, the cops will probably judge them or use it against them. Without access to power or even someone to call on their behalf, she seems to not know that they are nobodies here.

'Sir, aisa kuch nahin hai, hamare bachpan ki dost hai,' he tries. She's our childhood friend.

The police officer isn't mollified and glares at Megha. But he isn't completely dismissive either. *'Suno, ek doh din aur wait kar lena,* ninety per cent of the cases, the girl will show up.' His English surprises Farhan, but he tries to ignore that.

'But sir?' he tries again.

'Worry not, I'm telling you.' The cop smiles a grim sort of smile. 'Come back if she doesn't return in two days.'

'Full name aur details de dena, description vaghera …' Leave the full name, details and description. That's the

second cop again. *'Aapke full naam aur address aur number bhi.'* Also, your names and addresses and numbers.

The cops aren't sure what it is about these spoiled kids, but they make a note of the phone number and the name and last-known address, making a show of taking down the contact details of the friends as well. You never know.

That's normal, Farhan tells himself, staving off some amount of panic. *How else will they contact us?*

They leave the police station after giving the police Maya's full name, age, phone number, and other details. Brown hair and brown eyes, 5'5", not the most unusual description for Delhi, but it'll have to do for now. Farhan and Megha feel strangely deflated, not sure whether the visit was of any use, not sure if they were supposed to have given some money *chai paani ke liye*. Farhan had tried to use that time-tested phrase, but the cops pretended not to hear him.

'It's possible they want major cash,' he says in an aside to Megha. 'There's no goddamn way of knowing.'

He lights a cigarette and starts talking about cellphone triangulation to calm himself down. 'The least they can do is ping and pinpoint her last-known location,' he says, wondering out loud whether he should go back and tell them.

'There's no point, you know that,' Megha says. She's miffed at the tone Farhan took at the station but she's also decided not to talk about it and definitely not to text her husband Himanshu about this whole thing. She can imagine what he'll say. 'See? Even the cops think she's a goodtime girl.' He'd used that phrase about Maya last time and Megha hadn't even known what to say. It had sounded apt then.

Back inside the station, the police officers are mulling things over. '*Ajeeb parivar hoga. Is liye ghar se bhaag gayi hogi,*' the older officer says and feels suddenly very old and very tired. Maybe she ran away from home because she has a weird family.

He takes out a well-worn photo from his wallet of his little girl. She is no longer nine years old like in the picture, and altogether too hi-fi and modern for her old man. He smiles, thinking of how she's grown so quickly, now a mature young lady ready for the world. The world, though? He shakes his head. He's seen too much to be entirely comfortable with the prospect. Thumbing the photo, he puts it back in his pocket.

The police do take the complaint seriously, following up the very next day with a routine check at Maya's apartment building. They speak to the neighbours and to the society guard, who comments on her coming and going quite frequently. No real help there. But there's also no sign of foul play. From outside, the flat looks as if someone had just locked up and left. The guard seems to remember her taking a cab out a few days ago, but he wouldn't have been on shift that evening and can't remember if it was this time or the last time. She was obviously a very social girl, the cops conclude.

They track down her part-time domestic help in the society and ask him a few questions, putting the fear of God into him. He hasn't done anything to worry about, but his wife wordlessly packs a bag for him to go back to the village for a few days, just in case ....

The cops have already taken his details and could have told him they doubt he has anything to do with anything, but then why would they do that? He's a good backup to have. You never know with cases these days, the media sniffing around every PYT who goes missing, slamming the cops and society at large for their lack of empathy. Especially when it comes to women.

This city, the older cop thinks, *isn't a fit place for anyone. Especially not girls*. While he's convinced there's a boy angle, his gut tells him the girl will turn up, he tells his junior officer. '*Phone pe dial karte raho*,' he says.

'*Agar do din main wapas nahin aayee to us ladke ko utha lenge*,' the second cop says, somewhat ominously for Farhan. We can always pick up the friend for questioning if we need to, in a day or two. *Could be some inter-community love jihad angle*, he reasons. *It's happening everywhere*.

It's the fifth (or sixth) day after Maya goes MIA, and Farhan has no way of checking on the police. Have they searched for her call records yet? Should he recommend it? Who should he talk to?

His parents think he should stay out of it. 'You know how the cops are,' they say.

'Do you really want to be involved in a criminal investigation?' his father asks, in a world-weary tone. 'Do you know how it will impact your work, your reputation?'

His mother shudders. 'And we have to be extra careful these days,' she adds, not needing to explain why. No matter how well-cushioned they are from the day-to-day, there's the insecurity.

Farhan doesn't quite know what to say but feels some of his resolve melting. He sits in his computer room, glaring at his laptop screen. Hah! At least that worm BhaktofGod has fallen silent.

Halfway across the city, Karthik hasn't been able to sit still for the past day or so.

'I should go to the cops,' he tells himself, but isn't sure if he'd be of help or a hindrance. *It's quite possible that her friends have already gone to the police.*

He opens the messenger window and rather impulsively sends Farhan a private message. 'Have you gone to the cops yet?'

No reply.

'I will, otherwise, np.'

He gets an instant reply. 'Yes. But go. No action yet.'

'Actually, don't get involved,' Farhan starts typing—all Karthik sees are the three dots that let him know that a message is being composed—then quickly deletes the message.

Actually, get involved, he thinks. *Then the cops will be on to you.*

The three dots disappear. Karthik rolls his eyes. *Who knows what that fellow wanted to say.*

He takes out his beads for the first time in weeks and starts to count them and pray. One hundred and eight beads plus one, a one-line chant.

And again.

And again.

And again.

He loses track of himself, his overbearing worry, and corrects his breathing automatically. But in twenty minutes—or is it two hours—he resurfaces.

Oh, Maya. Where have you gone?

And why?

Part of him is wondering if he should get his father's lawyer on the line and talk to the cops. *But what if that ends up making trouble for her? What if she has actually just run off and is chilling somewhere?*

'She's totally the kind of girl who would run off to some hidden getaway,' he tells his mother forlornly when she asks him what has happened to his pretty friend.

His mother gives him a knowing look but doesn't pry. Garima had been quite happy to meet her son's friend briefly, the night of the joyride. They had finally gone out in one of the cars that made up the 'family fleet' as his father put it. But a hundred metres was as far as they got before they learned the Bentley had a flat.

'Does that even happen?' Maya had giggled.

No choice but to ask for a quick replacement. In no mood to hide his glee after all the crackpot theories his son had been parroting, the old man pointed to Krishn, polishing his silver car. Karthik had hesitated.

'It's not worth it,' he said, frowning.

'C'mon Karthik, we have to!' Maya's enthusiasm was infectious. 'You promised! India Gate and ice cream ... C'mon!' She practically skipped out, and he had no choice but to trail after her, hoping that nothing would go awry.

Later that night, he scribbled: Death sat next to her, smiling. At her naiveté, her energy, her exuberance.

'Look at K sitting there smiling,' she had whispered to Karthik as they left the house. 'You always make him sound like such a weirdo!'

Their conversation had spiralled into a strange space that evening, but she'd chattered on happily, stopping every so often to massage her stomach, moaning about bloating and PMS-induced headaches and the inevitable cramps, but quickly moving the conversation along after a few seconds.

'Do you bleed shapes?' he asked her in the same tone in which he had just asked her whether she dreamed in colour. (She couldn't remember for the life of her.)

'Shapes? No. Nothing like that. Just blobs,' she said, 'it's quite gross actually.'

'I'm sure it feels like that, but it's not gross.' He reached for her hand and smiled. 'I think it's the most natural, most beautiful thing in the world.'

'Eeew.' She grimaced. 'You deal with the cramps and the grossness.'

'You're blessed, you really are. You can give life.'

She looked at him and for once didn't indulge in a whiplash retort. *He really means it,* she thought. 'Well, but ... yeah, I guess you're right. Anyway, let's get some chocolate type of thing into my system.'

There was nowhere for that conversation to go except into silence. After they got their ice cream, she noticed him admiring her from the right.

'What are you staring at?'

'Your beauty.'

A big smile was his reward.

'I'm taking in your beauty.'

'Haha, quit that, you weirdo,' she said, but laughed quite happily.

She'd never actually thought of him as a weirdo, he knew that. At least, he thought he did. But he hadn't yet told her about his recurring dream and was afraid to do so, even though they had become so close so quickly. The dream got darker every night. *No, there's no way I can talk about that.*

'What are you thinking about anyway, all of a sudden?' she asked after a bit of silence. 'You seem so serious, so solemn.'

'Nothing. It's just that, well, once you get bored of sleeping, you're in trouble. There's nothing else in this life.'

'What are you talking about?'

He didn't say anything, so she filled the silence. 'You hardly sleep, for that matter, you insomniac ... you know you can take something for that?'

He laughed. *Take something for the pain, something for the insomnia, something for the weirdness. Where's the pill for being normal?* he wanted to ask.

'Life is a waking dream, if you think about it,' he responded.

Maya had found herself drawn a little further into his web. She loved how he was equal parts profound and awkward around her. Smiling to herself, she looked out the window only to be confronted by a jarring scene. They were passing a group of people on the left, cars slowing down as drivers and passengers gawked at a man crouched on the sidewalk, holding his head in shock.

A woman's body had been flung from the scooter they'd been riding on just moments ago. A car stood nearby, its fender bent; there was smashed glass on the road. A gaggle of men was pushing a teenager around. Evidently, he was the driver who'd done the damage. The mob started hitting him in slow motion.

This, too, was par for the course in Delhi.

'Was he drinking?' Maya asked, her voice small.

'Does it matter?' Karthik retorted.

He didn't think of getting out to help. Someone there must have already called the cops. There was blood, a slick, red patch of blood that no one could do anything about. A flag almost.

'It doesn't even look real,' Maya said, feeling infinitesimally small and alone.

Karthik leaned over to hold her hand in both of his. She looked pale, and miles away. He cleared his throat and told the driver, '*Chalo, ghar le chalo.*'

K had that weird little smile on his face.

That was the first time Maya and Karthik slept together. She was in no shape to go back home, she said, and asked if they could just take it easy and whether she could spend the night. One thing followed another and they were mutely astounded by the chemistry. Neither worried about protection or registered any concerns, not in the moment or its afterglow. They revelled in the warmth, sensitive to each other's needs. They enjoyed holding each other in silence afterwards. It was the first peaceful sleep Karthik had had for as long as he could remember, waking up only around sunrise when Maya prodded him, saying she needed to head home.

They both felt mellow, at peace with the world, not anxious for once. She didn't message Karthik when she reached home like she'd promised, but sent her brother a quick text, 'Boo', before passing out and sleeping peacefully right through the morning.

Karthik didn't sleep for hours after that, or text her, though he was dying to. He'd decided not to message for a while, just to play it cool, but then got upset that she hadn't bothered either. At that point, he put off his WhatsApp and internet altogether for a bit. When he finally woke up and got back online, that initial moment of bliss and wonder faded and turned into a thought spiral.

Oh God, I don't want to lose this.

What if she's got bored and tired of me already?

The gloom that enveloped the room was palpable. He went back to bed and slept a fitful afternoon sleep, dreaming again of an apocalyptic clash, the end of the world, no less.

The poor boy dreams of annihilation every day, bringing it forth every night. Waking dreams, recurring dreams. And he's powerless to stop it. Every night, thanks to his imagination and what some might call a gift—a little extra from the universe—he unleashes the terrors of the world on himself. The question isn't whether he does so in reality, Karthik will learn later. Rather, which facet of reality?

He's witness to them all ... the nine-headed dogs of fury, Yam-raj, Jörmungandr, and worst of all, the nameless, shapeless wraiths that walk among us, who plague him even in daily life. The Shades. Not even his father and the fleet of death can stop them. While he feels terrified, powerless, watching waves of destruction, he's even more worried that he's the one pulling the puppet strings. *What does that make me?*

He's not yet aware of exactly what he's doing—just that he's wracked by these dark, deep dreams of death, destruction, suffering. He has no words. Often, he wakes up with the hammering of his heart the only sign of panic.

Better I don't sleep, he thinks, hoping that it's just the stuff of nightmares and a creeping dark that exists and manifests only when he's unconscious.

No sleep ... he really tries to pull that off but frequently loses the battle around the witching hour—three a.m. and he's out like a light.

Om P., looking in on his son every so often, is equally at sea. *There's something a bit odd,* he feels, but doesn't want to admit. This strong feeling, which is possibly triggered by Karthik's obsessive chronicling of accidents and chance encounters; his Cab of Death theory. Even for a cynic, Karthik can be quite convincing. Or is it just plain chance? The boy's found out that three people from three different delegations who had contracted their services later lost a close friend or relative in some sudden death. Unrelated to the car or travel, Om P. notes, but it's uncanny. *Isn't it? Or am I becoming superstitious, like the rest of them?*

Both parents are a bit worried about Karthik's mental state these days, especially with what sounds like night terrors every so often. Should he talk to someone, they ask each other in whispers, but are too afraid to rock the boat with their newly returned boy. Is it the girl, do you think? Or worse?

'She's been coming over for a while, he seems happy,' Garima says. 'But who knows?'

Deciding to cover his bases without fully trusting Karthik's intuition, Om P. quietly keeps a close watch on his senior-most driver, K. It's a pity that it's the same driver who has a reputation for being courteous, efficient and fuss-free.

Another day, another conversation about their son thrashing and yelling gibberish curses at night and stumbling around like a zombie in the day.

'Was he brainwashed at the ashram?' Om P. asks his wife. 'Maybe that's why he's obsessed with all these things.'

Garima isn't sure if it's that simple. Hadn't she been told years ago, by a palm-reader no less, that her son was special and in need of special guidance? It was something that Om's brother, the Rishi, had echoed. But Om had scoffed and she had refused to part with their beloved son, not even for training, ignoring the kernel that was planted then and is sprouting now, decades later.

They have to make things right, though.

'Let's talk to the Rishi,' Garima says, ignoring Om's eyeroll.

'No.'

'I'm telling you.'

'No.' He thinks he's being adamant, but she knows her work is done. She has seeded the idea.

Should we really tell him about some of this? the old man wonders. He hopes to build up to a second-level conversation gradually but can't bear the thought of losing his son to more mumbo jumbo, not after the ashram. Best not to rock the boat, he decides.

Maybe he'll take to the family business after all, Om P. reasons. No need to bring in the spiritual and esoteric and that Rishi of a brother. Only the one son, after all.

There's nothing to be gained by rushing things, he tells himself, just the way he lectures his son. In his own way, he is trying to protect Karthik from the Unknown. But there's only so much he can withstand with Karthik's theory approaching epic proportions and his own concerns kicking in after hearing his son yell out in the night.

'Isn't he too old for night terrors?' Garima asks.

Om wonders. He finally puts in a quick phone call to his brother, the Rishi, who's supposedly doing some important work 'next door', which is to say, he's in Bhutan.

'Listen, he's an old soul, like me,' the Rishi says, laughing at his brother's worries.

There's a moment of silence when Om relays the Cab of Death theory, the nightmares, and the boy's babbling. Then the Rishi starts laughing again. 'Is that it? Is that why you've been keeping him from me?' More laughter.

Om is quiet for a while. 'I want him to have a normal life. We just got him back from that ashram, and I only see him worrying constantly, obsessed by death and all kinds of strange things. Why can't he have a normal life now?'

'Ahh, Ommm.' A long sigh. 'You know you can't protect him from what's in his stars, right? You can only equip him.'

The old man tries not to look for hidden meanings, a lifetime of conditioning kicking in, and yet his worry is palpable.

'Don't worry. A friend and I will drop in and make sure everything is alright,' his elder brother tries to reassure him.

Om feels unexpectedly lighter. And grateful. Like many parents, he worries about the damage the world might do to his son, rather than vice versa.

Back in his own head, Karthik's replaying the last several conversations with Maya.

'Listen, my dad and mum. They're totally superficial, but a total blast,' he had told Maya before her first visit to his home. 'Don't expect anything profound and you'll be fine.'

She looked at him funny. 'How did you end up the way you are, then?'

'God only knows!' Karthik laughed. 'Maybe it's a good thing I found Guruji, after all.'

He had told Maya very little about his life and was certain that he shouldn't bring up the pending apocalypse, his heightened intuition, or even talk too much about his theory about the cabs. He did mention it once or twice but always lightly, with less weight than he wanted to. Today, with her missing, he wants to kick himself for not having warned her. *What if it would have helped?* he agonises, falling into a restive sleep.

It's a weird moment. Weirder than most.

A stranger enters one of his dreams. He looks so familiar, Karthik tries to puzzle out who it is and what he's doing here.

Far away, Gautam has felt a tug and decided it's time to go check on his little sister.

He replies to her 'Boo' message with a couple of 'XXs' but knows that she needs to chat with him. Sir won't mind, he knows, as long as he's on call and available when needed.

8

Hiding Out

[January 2024]

O*kay, rules are rules. No Facebook, no WhatsApp, no Instagram, no Twitter, I mean X.*

Five minutes later: *Scrolling through comments can't hurt, though.*

Heheh, look at these guys! Maya is most amused, and even drafts a status update that she's very tempted to post.

'Maya's MIA, baby!' She says it aloud.

That used to be her childhood pet name, Mia. Rolls off the tongue nice and easy. She laughs out loud. She holds off on posting the update, then discards it altogether. She can't bear the thought of a conversation with anyone right now. *Anyway, don't I have to prove that I can outlast my own timeout?* She needs to prove it to herself at least.

Maybe next week. I'm sure people are still feeling their holiday hangover.

It doesn't strike her that her friends are super-stressed about her. *They'll be relieved when I pop back up*, she thinks. *No point being 'always around' anymore*. Her ex's harsh words have left their trace.

'What was he like?' Reena Gupta had asked in that therapist's way. 'And by that I mean, how did he make you feel?'

'Well, it was a disastrous relationship,' Maya said.

'Why do you say that?'

'I mean, it started out fine, but we jumped into something too intense and well, then, that's when he started saying shit like that … That I was always around. That I tried too hard.'

Her voice had become smaller somehow. 'That I was too intense.'

'That can't have been easy for you to deal with.'

'Well, maybe he had a point.'

Maya thought about how if it hadn't come to a head and the relationship hadn't ended, maybe she would have remained stuck. 'If he hadn't been so horrid about my whole time at the …' The words stuck in her throat. She wasn't sure how much to share.

'At the …' Gupta prompted. 'Keep going.'

'Well, maybe I wouldn't have found the ashram and Guruji and … Karthik, I guess.'

'What about your other friends? Did they like this ex of yours?'

'Oh God, no.' They don't even like Karthik, she didn't add, though to be fair, they'd never met him.

'That's usually a red flag,' Gupta said.

'The truth is, they're all leaving her knackered,' Akira said after a pause. 'All her friends have become so predictable and square, and not even good for her. She can't bear them anymore.

'But you know her problem, right? All she's ever wanted since childhood is to be like them—to have the right clothes, the right fit, the right skin, the right life.

'The elegance of the thin, perpetually lounging Megha, with her easy laughter and dimples, the fun they all have without a second thought, she yearns for it, for their grace of being, even Farhan, who's a worrywart these days, but is so smart and always solid company. Rohit has still kept some of his charm intact, and his wit and one-liners, I mean, he is a flake, but ... all of them are something, they have something Maya will never have.'

Gupta was quiet for a bit before prodding. 'Which is?'

The answer didn't come out loud, but it was definitely about their comfort with themselves, of being in their own skin, a security that Maya would never have.

~

It was another session, but Maya was finally talking about her friends a bit.

'You know,' Maya picked up a cushion and sat with it in her hands, 'I've just been thinking about how high maintenance this group is. They're also so insulated from reality, I don't know. It's not like my friend Karthik, whom

I met at that ashram. He's more like me. He's edgier than them too, more authentic.'

The others don't care about real things, things that she's started to feel so strongly about, like social justice, human rights, and why the hell can't they have those kinds of conversations too? Only Farhan joins in.

'Karthik, he's so deep, so authentic,' Maya had tried to tell Megha, but saw the incomprehension in her eyes. All her friend had wanted to know was what had happened to that loser Roy, and didn't Maya want to take a break? Also, which part of town did Karthik live in, and had he also fallen for that Guruji?

How dull, Maya had thought even then, but it's not as though she's ever been picky about her friends. Earlier, anyone would do. Some sort of security blanket was better than none. She would make friends with anyone, craving that absolute, deep sense of belonging that came so naturally to some people. She never wanted to be on the outside again, no out-groups for her, not after her growing-up years.

She had a rough time at work too, no mentors or 'uncles' like her other colleagues.

'I worked really hard to be a certain way, especially at work, you know, more professional. I was good at work but non-threatening, even voted "most efficient" and "most popular" at the team bonding sessions,' she told Gupta. And yet, she couldn't avoid the MCP-ness of your regular Delhi office. 'A sexy piece of ass to boot,' as her charming boss put it, in his wife's hearing.

'It was back in the summer that I felt I'd had enough, you know,' she told Gupta. 'Summer this year.'

'Come over for a single malt one of these weekends,' her boss would keep telling her, trying on what he thought was his most winning voice. 'We have so much to catch up on.'

'I don't think so. Ugh.'

She laughed with Gupta a bit about how this was an occupational hazard despite all the HR guidelines.

'Rinki will be out next weekend,' he had insisted that last time, slipping his hand to the small of her back. She must have made a face. 'Don't be so uptight, my dear, that won't do. Not if you want to get ahead,' he said and laughed. 'Advertising isn't an industry for the uptight, doll.'

'I tuned out. *Ugh*.

'And then, just like that, it's an office party and I'm skulking about the bar, trying to avoid the boss, when I meet Roy. The handsomest man in Delhi, I thought. Popped into my life at an office party like it was no big deal.'

She lost herself in her memories. Not entirely sure how much she should share ... none of it was pleasant to go over, to be honest.

'Haven't seen you around here before,' she said, coyly, 'I'm Maya.'

'Roy,' he grunted, giving her an appraising look, not once letting his eyes drop from her face which, as everyone knows, is unusual for men in Delhi.

'I used to work here ... before your time, I guess,' he added.

'Oh? It's such a lovely place. Great vibe,' she nodded enthusiastically, looking around, wondering what to say to sound impressive.

'Bunch of idiots, the suits … but yeah, it's alright.' He looked away, took a swig and said, 'Going out for a smoke. Do you wanna join?'

'Sure!' she trilled, though she had promised herself that she would quit smoking (again). This would be the fifth time, so she had been unsuccessful and remained a smoker, yes, but she consoled herself that at least this way there'd be some amount of detox.

Plus it was a great way to avoid the creep who she pretended not to notice was walking towards her right at that moment. She turned and let Roy guide her to the balcony.

'So, what do you do now?' she asked, leaning against the balcony railing and then wondering if that really was her most flattering angle. (Her left profile was better than her right, she'd discovered.)

'My own thing, as far as I can … Working for a living is so overrated,' he laughed.

'Wow,' she said.

The vodka had clearly gone straight to her head because she could all of a sudden feel her heart hammering away in her chest. *Good looking and authentic, what are the odds?* She scrambled to find something intelligent to say to fill the vacuum, but needn't have worried. He was quite enjoying the way the silence spread. It was a warm space and the girl was pretty hot too. 'What about you?' he asked.

'Oh, I sold my soul a loooong time ago,' she stretched out the words and managed to get a laugh out of him.

'Bet you a whole bunch of bucks that you got a raw deal.'

'Yeah, well, I've never had that one great passion, you know? I don't even know what my supposed skill set is.'

The boss came up to them then, to say something inane. 'God, Maya, you clean up good. How sexy is that dress.'

Roy gave her a look and buried himself in his drink.

She laughed ruefully and looked away, wishing she could disappear. Luckily, her boss had a short attention span.

'Oh, there you are!' A drunken colleague had walked up to them, checking Roy out and laughing a little too loudly at the boss's come-on to her.

'I'm so out of breath from the stairs!'

'Oh, hi Riya!' That was Roy.

'Who is this? Not Roy the famous ...' Riya giggled and gave him a huge—Maya couldn't help but notice—tight hug. To her relief, the boss just grunted at them and moved on.

'Where have you been?' Riya squealed. Never her favourite at the best of times, Maya wanted to kick her. *Ugh*.

'Just *yahaan pe hi*, madam,' Roy said with an undercurrent of something Maya couldn't quite place. *God, what am I thinking? I don't even know this guy*, Maya tried to shake herself out of it.

'Accha, will you get me a drink, pleeeease. G&T. I need to talk to Maya for a second.'

'At your service, as always.' He loped off, pleasantly aware of Maya's eyes trailing him.

'Arre, what are you doing?' Riya's screech jolted Maya back to normal. She was a bit piqued that Roy hadn't offered to get her a drink and unsure that he'd even return to their cosy little corner. 'Don't you know who he's with?'

'No, I just met him. Who?' Curiosity got the better of her, but her survival instinct was strong enough to ensure she played down the attraction. Twenty minutes in and it was already a full-blown crush.

'Geetu, yaar, you better not fuck with her.'

Oh great, the #2 in office. 'They're seeing each other?'

'Married, darling. Married.' Riya paused. 'Actually, maybe separated. But they came together tonight, so you know ... You'll thank me later.'

'You're mad. We were just having a smoke and a talk, that's all.'

Just my luck, Maya thought, but acted sanguine and went in to get another drink. Riya made a half-hearted attempt to follow her but was side-tracked quite quickly when another friend stopped to give her some gossip.

'A vodka tonic please,' Maya told the suddenly crusty bartender who had been all smiles for the greying gent in front of her just moments ago. He didn't approve of these fancy girls with their cigarettes and alcohol and terrible clothes. She knew the type and made no attempt at conversation or challenging the misogyny. She turned to survey the room—there was not one person here that she was interested in talking to. Well, just the one, but apparently, he was out of bounds.

Possibly unaware of his change in status, he appeared out of nowhere, at her elbow. 'So …' he started, tapping her on the shoulder. 'What say we blow this joint?'

'Um, well, I was just getting my drink,' she said.

'Um, well, you can just drink that down and follow me out the door. You know. If you're in the mood for anything this side of drop-dead boring.' He smiled at her, challenging her, almost. 'Or do you want to wait for your boss to hit on you again?'

'Ugh.'

'C'mon. Let's cut to the chase.'

She just looked at him.

'Bottoms up, babe.'

'I hate that word,' she said, her voice like a pistol whip, the sudden change almost throwing him off balance.

'Oh, no worries, I use it lightly, your most respected loveliness,' he flirted shamelessly, letting his eyes run over her beautiful chest as he emphasised the last word.

She smiled, unable to help herself.

Game on.

'Eh, what did you have in mind?' she got out. 'Nothing too sketch … I mean random, I hope.'

Why did she say sketchy?

He looked offended for a second but hid it quickly. 'Just a drink, ma'am, just a drink. Let's get out of this fishbowl and get a drink.'

He smiled because they had started that slow dance, the rhythm taking over, enticing them to the only natural conclusion. He walked her down the stairs, was guiding her to the parking lot, with her looking like she'd trip on those fancy boots of hers, when she turned and kissed him.

It's the little things.

'It was so organic, the whole thing,' Maya told him the next weekend at a wine and cheese picnic at one of the historic parks of the city.

'Not in the least,' he wanted to say, but he was delighting in her laughter, her enthusiasm, her adoration, for now at least, so he said nothing. 'I mean, she's super sexy,' he told his friends, boasting as always about his conquests, like they were back in college. He did not acknowledge that she was a bit intense, not at first.

Maya didn't register his mean streak for quite some time. To be fair to Roy, it didn't surface for a few months, but by then she was driving him insane. That's sometimes the problem with intimacy. It accelerates the journey, opening your eyes to everything unbearable about each other.

'You're like two different people,' he told her and was met with another fucking meltdown. So much drama. Roy had enough on his hands with the divorce proceedings. *This chick is too clingy, what the hell.*

'You try so hard all the time,' he started to tell her when she made the nth plan in as many days. 'I need some space.'

(And Akira had stirred.)

But then, when she did something sweet or thoughtful or super sexy, he forgot about the annoying bits. The sex was usually pretty great too, he had to be honest, and he liked the dedication with which she went down on him. Not like his ex, who gagged each time.

This chick, though. He thought he'd made it clear there was to be nothing resembling a commitment.

'You do understand that I don't want a relationship, right?' he had asked early on. And like every woman of a certain type since the dawn of time, she had said, 'Of course!', hoping secretly that she would change his mind by virtue of being her amazing self. *One day he will realise*, she had thought, *what a great deal he has*.

Maya's friends had all said she was too good for him, noting between themselves that he didn't seem to care about her much. She'd ignored them. *What do they know? Nobody understands me anyway*!

'It's too one-sided,' Megha had tried to vent to Farhan, not sure why he was always seething these days.

After meeting them all at a party, Roy had started the litany of complaints, not worried about being too insulting.

'You're too flakey these days.'

'Just give it a rest!'

'You're always around.'

Maybe the meanest was after she'd talked about emotional eating. He drawled, 'Yeah, that's true. You're getting fat.'

Maya didn't say much anymore, but she cried a lot, her enormous eyes welling up with tears, red and puffy almost every evening. She was constantly wondering what to do after having moved all her stuff over; she had been convinced this was it, surely, the normal way forward? A steady relationship at last. (It wasn't just that Roy mocked her, he'd also laughed about the fact that she'd never had a long or stable relationship. 'Really? By this age? I mean …')

She'd thought it was the men, but now she began to think that maybe it was her.

'Yeah, what's up with that?' Roy said, 'Maybe you should think about that sometime.'

Worried that she was not measuring up, she tried harder.

'You're exhausting, dude,' he said. She'd changed too drastically, he argued, telling her quite brutally that all her flighty silliness was an attempt to be liked.

But he still reached for her at night and she rationalised it all. *The sex is as passionate as ever, so this must be his real self*, she told herself, *that's how he expresses himself … forget the verbalising. The number one sign of a relationship in trouble is in the sack, all the magazines say it. So we must be okay. The sex is still fine, that's his love language. I can deal. I can try harder. Happiness is worth chasing—all the Insta love gurus say so.*

So she'd sucked it up. But then, one day, she couldn't deal with all the negativity. And, she realised, it must be her. Of course she had caused all of this. She blamed it on the boss at work. He was constantly in her face and she couldn't navigate it all much longer on her own.

It's too much, she decided, *I've had enough*. She quit her job. No one warned her that by quitting she might just drown in her own solitude. It made her inarticulate, it gave her palpitations, this staggering awareness that she was essentially on her own and might have single-handedly torpedoed her career. She moped about for a few days but didn't reach out to any of her friends. They'd all been acting a bit forced since she moved in with Roy.

But it's okay. Maybe I need to put in more effort and spend more time on what's important, she thought. *I can try harder, right?*

'Quitting the job was a demented idea,' Roy told her. 'I don't know why you didn't just sleep with that fucker and get it out of the way.'

He started to get a real kick out of insulting her. A kick out of listing all the things that were wrong with her. 'You're boring yourself, you're boring me,' he said. 'You know that, right? You try so hard, God!'

~

Gupta jumped in here. 'Listen, I don't know how you decided to quit the job but this bit, this is classic, this is emotional abuse, to be honest with you. I am not one for quick diagnoses, but he sounds like he has a narcissistic personality disorder or something like that.

'I wish we'd been in touch back then, and I know it's been really hard for you to go through but also to share all this with me so openly. I appreciate that. We'll unpack more the next time, just to make sure you're aware of any patterns you may repeat or any residual trauma you want to deal with.'

Maya nodded quietly. She didn't want to share any more.

Roy had just gotten more and more … himself. Almost daring her to stay. He started calling someone else daily and fucking off straight from work. 'It's nothing,' he said. 'But she does give you some competition in bed, darling.'

Maya remembered being very still, not reacting. Roy was impressed that she finally looked like she felt hate towards him. 'Attagirl!' he battered on. 'Don't be a pussy about this, babe. It's how the world works.'

Ugh.

'We never said we should be exclusive, man. You're just … God, you're always around.'

She started crying then.

'Oh, cue the drama,' he laughed, oblivious now to the sight. 'Who lives like this? It was bad enough being married, man, this has got to stop.

'And you know what, babe, I'm going to tell you something none of your little friends will. You have no real personality. It's why you can't sit still, it's why you keep flitting from one thing to another.'

Ironically, it was her latest fad, the one that he mocked the most, that allowed her to get out of the relationship. It was his joke about her discovering the ashram and Guruji (and Karthik, who Maya had never referred to, though he had begun taking centre stage quite quickly in her waking thoughts). It was Roy's mockery of something that had brought her some much-needed calm and peace of mind that somehow also gave her the spine to stand up for herself.

(That, and maybe Akira made a quick reappearance.)

9

The Ashram Diaries

[Flashback: March 2023]

Maya had discovered the spiritual side of her nature almost by fluke. It was one of her ex-colleagues, Seema, who helped usher in this new chapter in her life. The banner near their old office had proclaimed that salvation was at hand. The message was simple enough.

'Guruji in Delhi … Join us for meditation and prayer sessions. Satsang on Mondays, Wednesdays, Saturdays, 2.30–5.30 p.m. 1 April onward.'

Seema had been looking for someone to go with.

'I need this, Maya, I need your help. I don't want to go alone.' She'd connected with this same group online during the pandemic but wanted company to go IRL.

Maya had agreed to go, only learning later that it was all an exercise in creativity.

'Well, you use what you can,' Seema told her. 'It didn't work for me, but I did get to write some killer copy!' She linked to an ad for a winter getaway. 'It totally helped. You totally helped.'

Maya had laughed it off but was a bit thrown. She definitely did not divulge that she was all in. She'd end up attending prayer sessions every Saturday for several months. From then on, in fact, she was never quite the same. She'd found what she had been yearning for. Community.

Over the next few months, she chanted, gyrated, prayed. Daily. She promised to fundraise, proselytise and, surprisingly, learned to stand up for herself. She started yoga and talked about finally feeling at peace.

In a while, she felt more peaceful than ever. She dropped the cold war and hate she had been harbouring against Gautam Bhaiyya's mother Neeti, and even drafted an email to her (that she didn't send).

She didn't grudge Gautam Bhaiyya for being out of the country so often, or for living his life without much interest in hers (a mistaken presumption, she belatedly realised). She *knew* he loved her and was there for her, somehow. Contact had been sporadic but irregular texts had made way for regular video calls, eventually settling into a pattern of photo upload–prompted mini-conversations.

Guruji preached love and freedom from the negative, so she lowered the barricades and learned to manage her feelings. And her expectations. She learned to put herself out there more … authentically.

She messaged Gautam to reconnect, following up with a phone call, a video chat, even an email. She went right back to a core she had forgotten she had—friendly, energetic, passionate even.

Guruji talked about the need to be free in all walks of life and Maya warmed to that message, feeling that it shed a glow of light on her adolescence and young adulthood.

Perhaps I wasn't so far off the path. There was nothing really to be ashamed of, she thought. *I just didn't know it was the path.*

'You are all part of something bigger,' Guruji preached. 'Your pain is my pain. Your losses my losses. But there is also so much more.'

They paused to sing a bhajan or two together.

'Your laughter is the key to the universe. The light of the Almighty shines in all of us, we must learn to recognise it.'

Maya nodded and sang, swayed and prayed to something bigger than herself. And when they passed around the donation box, she brought out ever-bigger amounts to contribute.

All this while, she'd felt burdened by something she couldn't explain. Not just the grief of losing her father. It was her old self weighing her down, choking her, something she could never slough off, not even in her relationships, she realised.

'You,' Guruji had pointed to her in the front row after her fifth or sixth time at the ashram.

Every prayer session, he called up a limited number of people for a quick one-on-one and this was her (first) lucky day.

'You're not well inside?' he asked, still beaming, as she sat cross-legged right in front of him.

'There is a sick feeling,' she admitted. 'The things I have done, the things I let people do to me, or the way they treated me.' She couldn't bear to continue.

Guruji patted her on the arm, and she felt a transfer of energy.

The next time she went for the satsang, she smiled throughout. She wasn't lucky enough to be in the front row for another two months.

'You,' he pointed to her and three other participants, once again smiling.

'You feel the beauty of the universe?' he asked her this time. 'We are all connected.'

'Yes, Guruji,' she acknowledged. 'But Guruji, when I leave, I feel the same emptiness, the desolation.'

He nodded solemnly but then raised his palm in benediction. It was a signal for her to go. No answers this time, no transfer of energy.

While getting up she added, 'But I still need help, Guruji. Till I came here, I didn't know it was possible. I started to feel parts of me flying off, I kept losing myself … with each person, each relationship. There's someone else.'

She couldn't be sure how much he was willing to hear.

He stroked her hand and spoke a little more about the universality of things. 'Love is free, love is pure,' he assured her, 'There is no need to feel shame. What you are is as you have been made.'

'But … Guruji, I'm worried … there's nothing left.'

'This? This is not nothing,' he said, gesturing more forcefully. 'How can there be nothing left? Something has brought you here, something bigger than you, isn't it?'

A slight pause, while people around them nodded vigorously. 'A great cosmic consciousness. You are part of it.'

He nodded sagely. This was another signal for her to leave.

He half-turned to the next disciple.

'Yes, Guruji, but I feel just … shame.'

There was an abrupt silence. Was she imagining some negativity? (Then again, she had hogged more than her share of his time.)

'There is nothing more divine than communion with another,' he said. 'I feel you are not grasping it …'

He turned and crooked a finger at a young man in maroon robes behind him, whispered something to him.

'Go with God, sister,' Guruji said. 'Have faith and all will become clear.'

She was dismissed. With finality this time.

The young man in the robes looked no more than twenty-five, but he was quite grave. He motioned for her to follow him and led her to a small anteroom where several other people were seated, waiting for something.

She wrote down her name and phone number on a small chit of paper and gave it to him as directed and was waved in the direction of a nondescript plastic chair.

She sat, noting that he hadn't yet said a word. *Maybe he's differently abled*, she thought. *I wonder if it's easier to feel good when you're forced to be quiet.*

Maybe it's easier when you're not constantly chattering, faffing.

They say it's easier to see with your heart than your eyes. I wonder if …

Her rambling thoughts were periodically cut short by a young lady with a chic haircut and a maroon sari who came in from the main room, calling out names from an iPad.

Whoever she called followed her—sometimes in twos and threes. Maya wasn't sure what to expect, but her name was finally called out an hour later. She walked into an inner chamber and the young lady did a pronounced namaskar.

'Call me Monica,' she said briskly. 'That's Karthik,' she pointed at the young man in robes who had accompanied Maya from Guruji's satsang.

'You will be needing some focused sessions,' Monica said. 'Chakra re-centring, healing, group prayer.'

'Um. Okay.'

'You will be needing to do some intense meditation to prepare.'

'Okay.'

Maya couldn't help thinking her friends would probably have been laughing at Monica's accent and demeanour by this point, but then again, they'd probably be laughing at her if they knew.

Not to mention Roy.

God, I'm just not going to tell anyone.

'You will be needing to do some breathing exercises for seven to ten days first.'

'Umm ...'

The scepticism leaked through. Maya was beginning to wonder if she was being silly and being taken for a ride, but the next few minutes put her somewhat at ease.

'Guruji is not prescribing these for everyone, but he is believing you will benefit.'

'Um, is he?'

The girl was brisk and all-business. 'That will be fifteen thousand five hundred rupees, plus tax, hundred per cent in advance. No refunds. Thank you.'

'Hang on a minute, are these sessions with Guruji?' Maya asked but was already scrabbling in her bag to get her wallet.

'Some senior disciples.' Here Monica nodded at Karthik, who was looking peaceably at Maya. 'Sometimes Guruji.'

Maya handed over her debit card.

'Sign here please.' Monica indicated a disclaimer form of some sort.

'When can you start? Next week? Saturday?'

'Umm, sure.' Maya was still feeling quite vague.

'It is good, you will feel better.' Monica smiled encouragingly.

'Please bring a yoga mat, water bottle, identity proof, two passport photos, no phone. Also, any contribution is welcome.'

Apart from the 15.5K? That's pretty steep, Maya couldn't help but think.

'It is salvation,' said a deep voice.

Maya took half a second to trace it back to Karthik in the corner.

Did I say that out loud? she wondered, but was fuzzy.

'Doesn't come easy.'

He smiled.

She was hooked. 'It's a community,' she wrote in her diary that night, 'a safe space for me to heal. I never want to feel that desolation again. No more dark days.' She underlined this last bit and shut the notebook.

Never again, she promised herself before going to bed. *I'm not going back to the darkness.*

She clasped the little booklet of the Gayatri Mantra that her fifteen thousand five hundred bucks had earned her and fell asleep, dreaming of another audience with Guruji.

Young Karthik led the group sessions. Seven to a group, but he gave everyone individual attention. Delighted with Maya just for her name to start with, his enthusiasm rubbed off on everyone.

'You are all meant to be here,' he assured them on Day 1. 'You are part of the cosmic pattern. It was inevitable that you would come to seek out Guruji. You will go far.'

They chanted together and took turns leading the hymns. It seemed to be a non-denominational sort of belief system, taking the best of all schools of thought, Maya noted.

'Maya, it is important to stay focused,' Karthik chided her once in a while when she spaced out.

'But I'm thinking,' she would say, unable to add that she'd been thinking about how she might have killed her father—being the last person who saw him alive, the last person who spoke to him, not just the last person to curse him in her head. *What gall. Who was I to tell him to take off? And why had he listened? … Could he even have heard me? Who knows … I have the genes of a witch, a black tongue, presumably …*

Karthik would bring her back to herself.

'Yes, you have been awakened, it is true, this is your calling'—his voice itself was so reassuring—'but that's for the time of intense personal meditation. This is the time for community singing and giving.'

She took to Karthik slowly. He had been a disciple of Guruji's for seven years—seven is a magical number, he told her—and was convinced he'd been reincarnated several times.

'This will be the last,' he laughed.

'How do you know?'

'I just do.'

She could not get enough.

'Help me meet him again,' she would whine and plead, hoping to inveigle her way into the inner circle.

He was used to this.

'All in good time, dear.'

'Why can't we see more of his sessions?' she would ask, deflated. Guruji, or his immediate support staff, had capped the number of sessions 'special' followers could attend to one a week.

'You know how it is, there are always too many … too much demand,' Karthik would explain patiently, quite taken by her intensity. He didn't have the heart to tell her that paying more would get her much farther, much faster. Perhaps it was not the heart, per se. He knew he didn't want her to stop talking to him. He'd lost track of the last time he felt a connection with someone.

'But surely, no one will know. I mean, just me at the very back. I need to have darshan!'

'Are you trying to say you want to break the rules?' he cut her off sternly. 'Do something wrong, for the immediate pleasure or satisfaction of your impulses?'

She went mute.

'You have to wait like everyone else, my dear. It's part of the process.'

'What, like to see if we're worthy?'

'Not worthy, but ready.'

'I know I'm ready!' she exclaimed, but resolved to be more patient.

What is she hoping to learn? What is she hoping Guruji will reveal? he wondered. Even she wasn't quite sure.

'Don't worry, it will be fine.' Karthik had such a calming voice. It felt like he could reach right into her mind and slow it down, soothe the agitation.

She said nothing, but he knew he was getting through to her.

'Till then, you've seen the YouTube videos too, of course?' he lobbed her an easy one, trying to get her to unruffle her brow.

'I have,' she conceded. 'I'll watch again.'

Karthik smiled. 'Do your meditation daily and come back for next week's group session.'

It was time to go.

'Can't he bless my beads at least? Can I leave them with you? Please please please, c'mon, no, please please.'

He laughed at how childlike she sounded, but nodded, accepting them and then bowing at her.

~

Whatever it was, she was getting there.

It came to her gradually, dream-like at first, that she didn't need to be with this mean SOB Roy.

She realised it not long before the episode that she pretended to Farhan was Roy's request to 'pimp her out'.

It wasn't a pimping request, but she'd been too ashamed to tell her friend what it was.

She'd actually walked in on him laughing with some friends about their pal who had roofied an acquaintance at the last office party. He pretended to her later that she'd misheard. 'Stop being so dramatic, hon,' he said, condescendingly. 'You're always imagining things.'

But Maya had better game by then. Not as dazed anymore, not as self-doubting. She might have been too embarrassed to talk to her friends honestly about this Roy fiasco, but she was getting a lot of comfort from her meditation circle. Not to mention the feeling of belonging to a community. No one there knew about this other side of her and it was refreshing to reinvent herself. Looking at Roy a day after that overheard conversation, Maya couldn't remember anything of significance they'd done together, not their travel in the early days, not the endless faffing.

Mindless.

Why is it such a chore to be happy? She'd always been good at putting in the effort, rarely admitting defeat, but looking at the back of Roy's balding head she thought, *This is it.* She took one deep breath and then released.

She didn't want to be rude, not even now. But her life was passing her by, and no one else even seemed to notice it.

Well, that was not true. Karthik did, but he was too nice to say it. In fact, Maya was never sure how he started getting her to open up about her disastrous relationships, intimate and family, or even her light-weight friendships. She had lost track of when their conversations had spun off into longer and longer sessions, but it had helped ease the weight. That existential loneliness was held at bay, at least for a while.

Roy, meanwhile, was a study in contrast. Watching him dispassionately as he speared his kebab that evening, Maya realised she was not even attracted to him anymore. No stimulation of anything, not physical, or sensual, or spiritual, or intellectual even. She sighed.

No big deal, she reminded herself.

'I'm going back to my own place,' she said, very quietly, almost to herself, as she started thinking about her ashram routine instead.

And with that, she finally got Roy's attention back. *Is it possible we're on the same page at long last?*

'There has to be more to this life,' she said.

'Amen,' he replied, also half under his breath.

~

That is the conversation that will come back to prick Roy for half a moment when she goes 'missing'. Did he let her down by not trying hard enough?

But she has everything so easy, he wants to yell when he hears from her worried friends. *Fucking drama queen!*

'What the hell would she go and disappear for?' he asks Farhan when the boy finally gets through to him, 'Except attention, as usual?'

'I think it's more serious than that,' say Farhan, a tone of superiority in his voice, 'which you would know if …'

'Are you guys mental? Whatever she wants, she gets. Money isn't a problem. Men aren't a problem. She's just a bored chick, yaaa. I don't have time for this nonsense.' Roy hangs up and hopes he's out of their lives for good.

Maya had been reluctant to talk about the ashram with her friends—she didn't want to contaminate the experience with their world-weary cynicism or even share too much of herself, her need for that sense of belonging. When she did finally let a few hints slip, she was surprised that they were not entirely sceptical.

'I mean, after all, my brother is also so spiritual,' she had reminded everyone, though she'd never been remotely interested in her brother's work, or Guru, or anything to do with that all that.

She was convincing though, so of course her friends agreed to hold off judgement. To be fair, they'd only voiced their concern when Maya disclosed that after a burst of euphoria in the first few months, she'd started to feel sluggish.

She was not alone in this. By then she'd met a couple of Guruji's followers from the private sessions, who said they felt the same way, though they all wanted to say that they were feeling better several months on. *They had been re-energised at first, hadn't they?*

'Must be something in the prasad they give us at the end,' Maya said and laughed it off. (But started to worry after hearing from someone the theory that all prasad is cursed.) She didn't tell Karthik anything about this of course, and then for good measure, decided against mentioning him again in her friends' circle.

No more prasad though, she decided. *More likely it's drugged rather than cursed,* she reasoned. *Highly avoidable either way.* She also decided she needed to put more of a lid on how much she shared with people. It was, after all, the only real way to deal with things.

The good thing was that by now, she'd learned some grounding and other techniques from the therapist she'd started seeing regularly.

I can do this, she wrote in her diary, underlining the words again for good measure.

10

The Other Sister, Other Secrets

[January 2024]

Akira hasn't surfaced for a long time, not since that last therapy session at least, but she does pop in sometimes to 'help Maya out', as she puts it. Especially when Maya finds herself getting overwhelmed.

'I do know more about love and about life,' Akira would say if you asked her, 'not to mention how to fake it till you make it.'

Maya knows none of this, though something niggles at her in the dead of night, something about the bad times and the lost time. But in any case, Maya is coming into her own finally, no longer living in fear that the cracks will surface and that Everyone Will Know that she's a weirdo and that she's vulnerable and that she just does not fit in.

She's processing her big life lessons and thinking her big thoughts and feels like she deserves this timeout. But while

Maya's busy manifesting her zen and what-not, there are all these weird comments floating around and friends acting strange, which makes Akira secretly suspect that:

1) Maya needs her, as always.
2) More crucially, Usha is back on the periphery.

Akira can't explain exactly why, but trouble always follows that woman. That enigmatic lady who had made it clear close to thirty years ago that she wanted nothing to do with her daughter. That lady who was never to be addressed as Mummy or Mum, who clearly had no maternal instincts whatsoever. That lady who may or may not have traumatised Maya-then-Mia by locking her into a closet (Akira can't remember anymore if that was from a movie she'd seen or a real-life memory), who had definitely chucked out her own daughter and vanished before ghosting became all the rage.

'You go and stay with your father,' she had told Maya-then-Mia when she was four or five, having palmed the child onto a family with no thought of the fault lines that lay exposed. No one said it was weird that she meant Lakshman, not Mark, but then again, no one talked about infidelity in those days, the less said the better. Don't ask, don't tell.

Maya doesn't remember any of this, of course. Nor does she remember the effort her biological mother tried to make later … it was too little too late.

Shortly after Lakshman died and his wife Neeti made it clear that the 'bastard child' was no longer welcome, Usha did come back and make a small effort. But it wasn't very convincing, if you ask Akira. The hero who saved the day was actually Gautam.

Gautam, who felt that he was betraying his own mother, but still made the SOS call to Chini Auntie that probably saved Maya. The shame Gautam felt, for his own mother, for Maya's shame and humiliation, feeling unwanted like that. It's surprising she doesn't remember any part of it. But Akira does. She remembers Usha as well, quite well.

'I have no time,' Usha tried to explain once. 'And I want you to be happier than you will be with me. But if you're okay coming back with me, away to the hills, I would like to try ...'

The rest was left unsaid, and the offer so flimsy as to not be registered by the child. Her complete lack of interest was palpable, the adults felt. It was obviously not Maya's fault, her aunt told her, and so did Gautam, dearest Gautam who had heard his mother and father back in the day, talking about Usha's 'deal with the devil', as they put it. The kids presumed that made Usha a witch and they operated on that assumption all the way into young adulthood. Nothing could ever be normal growing up with that kind of background.

Maya has forgotten that incident, and even the story of the Egg, and Akira's not going to remind her. Or tell her that she turned down Usha's attempt to bring Maya home that one time. *(One time means nothing, after all.)*

Also, they've all but forgotten it, but Akira would rather not relive that one escapade. It has been years since Maya went off on a wild goose chase up to and through the hills, down south to the famous ashram, unable to track down the woman they called 'the Pahaari from the city', unwilling to let go of the belief that her mother would come back into her life if only she got to know her better now, as an adult.

No such luck.

Anyway, around the time Maya was coming to the realisation that she was chasing a chimera, she was punched by a drunken lunk and robbed blind, and worse, left stranded. It was momentary, but Akira had had enough. She took over, managed to charm a rest house owner into letting her stay on a few more days, no charge; his wife could glare as much as she wanted, but he said it was fine.

In a strange twist of fate, it was Gautam who found her there, of all places. He took care of her somehow, getting her in for a checkup there, in the hills. She wonders if she ever thanked him, but somehow knows that she doesn't need to say the words—he understands.

More than a decade on, even if Maya is hazy on the details, she knows he still does understand her, even when it feels like he doesn't. She has been making a little bit more of an effort of late. Then again, he doesn't get *everything*.

'There is this Guruji,' Maya had begun one conversation.

It had started out serenely enough and Gautam Bhaiyya had asked all the right questions. But when he heard more about the darshan and the inner committees and the amount of money changing hands, he got a bit more wary. And judgmental.

'What the … it's like one of those spiritual ponzi schemes,' he said. 'Be careful now, don't fall for their bullshit.'

'Bullshit? What, just because you've found the Rishi, you think ...' Maya didn't finish the sentence, remembering the damage that can be done with words. And didn't Guruji preach universal tolerance?

'Not everyone will understand your mission, your path,' he had intoned.

Maya cut off without saying much else.

When Gautam hung up, he felt a bit deflated. But also startled. Surely, she wasn't comparing their journeys? He was working on spiritual development holistically, in an integrated fashion. They thought through and tried to apply the principles of compassionate capitalism in keeping with the teachings of the Buddha, but tied to ground realities. Not this *phoo-phoo* stuff half the godmen were preaching, tied to obscene bank balances and ever-larger requests for donations.

Does this have something to do with your mother? he'd wanted to ask, but held his tongue.

But still. Was Maya blind to all the sex scandals that were starting to come out in the papers? Or worse, was she being inculcated into the inner circle that way? He couldn't say any of this to her, because sometimes Maya was ferocious and he was scared of alienating her further. Not after they had finally bridged the gap of years. So he bided his time and made a point to check on her subtly and to stay in touch. Maybe he would ask the Rishi for some time off to go take a closer look at what was going on.

A bit wary about sharing too much, shouldering an even bigger fear of being judged by her one close relative, Maya didn't tell Gautam when she outgrew her attachment to the Guru or when she started to develop feelings for his disciple. (She wonders if Gupta would consider all of these red flags and decides not to bring them up even if she does go back to therapy, an idea she's toying with again.)

She got more and more secretive. For months on end, she used those group sessions as an excuse to make her own plans away from her friends. Plans that included an increasingly besotted Karthik, who was finding it hard to maintain his legendary calm.

Akira's all over this. She won't take darshan, dubbing this chap, Maya's Guruji, a charlatan. And knowing all the superstitions since childhood, she warns all her friends against eating prasad from temples or pujas, *especially* not from pujas.

'It's cursed, don't you see?'

She has offended more than a couple of people over the years with this pet theory and certainly doesn't get called to any 'traditional' events, not that it bothers her. 'The bad mojo is transferred onto the prasad and given away—bad karma for the passersby, good karma left for the rich who sponsor the pujas,' she tells all of them. 'It's foolproof.'

Luckily, by the time there are front page headlines from an investigation based on a whistleblower's claims that there are steroids being pumped into the prasad across places of worship, Maya has stopped taking the offerings.

Forget all that now, Maya thinks. *I need to re-centre, rebuild.*

Akira fingers the bracelet her aunt has given her, a good-luck charm if ever she did see one. An elephant with trunk outstretched dangling from the blue and white beads of the amulet.

It's Maya's turn to be quiet.

Akira, meanwhile, thinks her third eye is tingling.

It must be that woman. She's back, Akira thinks.

Maya can't talk to anyone to check, though—not even Mark, obviously. Though she keeps a quiet watch on him and his doings from afar.

Even after all this time, she thinks, marvelling at Mark's capacity for love, at his stamina and endurance. Unknowingly, he's set up all the young men Maya will ever know. None of them have been able to match him in his everlasting love—how could they? Unconsciously judging them by this most impossible of barometers, willing them to pine for her, as Mark pines for Usha, turning cold and distant when she finds that they are simply incapable of such a feat. Turning cold and distant when she finds the one (or two) that do. (It'll take much more honesty in therapy to recognise some of these patterns.)

None of these memories or thoughts are the point, though. Akira needs to figure out exactly what's going on—with Maya, Usha, all of it. She knows she can talk to Gautam about some of these shadows in Maya's brain.

Maya's been thinking about Gautam Bhaiyya as well. He's been planning his visit and she cannot wait. She's been flashing back to childhood so much that even though they've not been seeing eye to eye of late, she can't help but feel the strength of that connection. How had she not realised that he'd also had a rough time? He'd always had the time of day for her, right from their childhood when they could hear almost all the conversations taking place through the thin walls, whether it was an aunt consoling a little girl whose mother had left her, or a father telling a little boy that he had to toughen up.

'Man up, son!'

That's the only time they heard the phrase till adulthood.

'You've got to be a man, the man of the house, little fellow!'

'Suck it up!'

We had sympathised about so much as kids, she reminisces.

Oh, and his music! Always a soundtrack to the drama and the memories.

Cue: *Bittersweet Symphony* (old but gold).

'You are never to call us Dad and Mum in public, do you understand?' The ghosts of an early memory come back to her.

Cue: *Paradise City* (with their own special lyrics).

'If only we could go!'

'We will, one day.'

Gautam Bhaiyya used to tell her it was just as well, saying that she would never have got to hang out with him as much otherwise.

Cue: *Empire State of Mind.*

We're all connected through the most improbable links, she thinks. There aren't enough mix tapes in the world for what's coming next, but there's no doubting those connections.

Grabbing her phone from the side table, she dials his number. No answer, and a strange ring. She disconnects and decides to WhatsApp him instead.

'Boo, you okay? Just checking in xx.'

Two ticks but no blue ticks, so he isn't online then.

She doesn't have anyone else to talk to, that's the problem; she's cut them all out. The last week or so, she's been feeling surprisingly wiped out.

~

Meanwhile, just under a week ago (and the timelines are finally syncing up) …

'*Kuch ladke ka chakkar toh nahin hain*?' It's not about some boy, is it? The cops Maya's friends had spoken to at the nearest police station smirked. They'd seen their share of young people in this city, after all. '*Chalo, beta, ek doh din aur wait kar lena*. She'll show up.'

'If not?' Farhan was not looking himself that day. If Maya had seen him, she would have called. Dark circles under his eyes, lines creasing up his forehead.

'Then you come back,' the cops said, 'and we'll lodge an FIR.' The senior officer was kinder than his cronies. He ended the conversation on a positive note, almost. They came to the perfect compromise—which appealed to no one—that they follow police advice and wait.

~

Before deciding on a timeout and the need for a dramatic going to ground to sort out her own feelings, Maya had needed to see someone (and not just for the keys to her hideout). There was only one person who wouldn't judge her (at least, not to her face). *Chini Auntie was always such a support, full of laughter and affection, even in the tough days. Almost always*, Maya remembers, but forces herself to skip over the difficult bits. That's not what matters here, she knows.

After the Big D that knocked them all out, Maya had got a full-on second shot. She didn't think there was anything more or less unusual about her situation, except she knew (and the others didn't) that life was full of terrible surprises. She didn't think too much about anything and certainly doesn't remember any of it now, but the children in her class had taken to calling her a 'bastard' and 'an orphan'.

She didn't respond, but looked it up online later, trying to find some loopholes at best, or even other examples of people like her. Of course, her classmates were mistaken, she had parents. Papa might be gone now (her heart still broke to think of this) but she had parents, Mark and Usha. Just that they didn't live with her for some reason.

Just to be on the safe side, she had quietly asked her aunt one day.

'Oh baby,' she still remembers how Chini Auntie swept her up in one giant hug. 'Of course you're not. You had Dad and Mummy, who is on a … uh, let's call it a holiday. And you have me and Uncle Pi. And you had Lakshman, didn't you? And you have Nan, even though she's sometimes busy. So actually, you have all of us as your parents, you're even luckier than the luckiest girl in the world!'

'Luckier?'

'Because then who would give you double, triple presents? Or all the chocolate and candy you can eat? And love and hugs, hmm? You mustn't mind what people say.'

'Even Mummy?'

'Ha,' her aunt laughed. 'Tricky tricky. Now off you go, sit in the fancy chair and let me make us some hot chocolate.'

As a child, Maya delighted in hearing her aunt laugh. It was her favourite feeling, her favourite sound in the whole world. She adored being around her, her aunt always exuding a faint aroma of cinnamon mixed with traces of talcum and sandalwood. An unlikely combination, but one that would come to define kindness in her head. She sniffed around people sometimes but rarely found that particular blend.

[December 2023–January 2024]

The scent is a little faint now and Chini Auntie is older but still happy to see her niece. 'And finally you come to see me, you minx!'

'Chi Auntieee,' Maya squeals. 'It's been so long! I've missed you!'

'Well, you should stop by more often then, I always say!' A big hug and her aunt beckons her to sit down at the kitchen table. 'Why, if you'd told me in time, I would have baked your favourite banana bread. Let me see what I can rustle up.'

'What? No, I'm not hungry at all!'

'Ha, not hungry. You're so skinny, it's like you've never had a proper meal in your life,' Chini Auntie kvetches. 'Any news from that no-good sister of mine?'

Maya shakes her head.

'Ah well, good riddance! No news is good news and all that.'

Maya smiles politely. It's still a bit of a twinge for her, but it's likely just scar tissue at this point.

'I wish you had told me earlier that you wanted to stay here. I would have called Meena to be with you since I'll be out of town the whole winter break. She still asks about you, even after all this time,' Chini Auntie keeps going.

'What? Meena-di? She never comes over, I even told Mishra-ji the other day.'

'Ah, you know how it is, we're all getting old. Her daughter's working at a website now, on the content team, can you believe it? Meena comes to give me updates every once in a while.'

Maya smiles and flits to the next thought.

'Oh wait, I brought you something, where is it? Hang on!' She digs out a beautifully wrapped gift from her bag and hands it over.

'What's this? Youngers aren't supposed to give gifts to their elders, you know that!' Auntie is blushing almost and smiling at the same time as she tries to sound stern.

'Open it, open it! I think it's perfect for the season, but I hope you like it.' Maya has gone to the swishest store around to pick up a beautiful hand-embroidered stole for her favourite person on the planet, the only person she will probably ever love to this extent and feel secure in loving. (Well, her and Gautam Bhaiyya.)

As her aunt oohs and aahs, Maya walks out through the new screen door to the extended balcony, passing a laughing family as she does so.

She smiles and waves at the little girl and her father, oh wait, that's Uncle Pi! She smiles again, as she strides towards the kitchen garden, marvelling at her aunt and uncle's ingenuity. They could always make so much out of so little. *I wish I were more like them,* she thinks.

They had taken her in unquestioningly, treating her lovingly and spoiling her, not changing one bit, not even in the tough teenage years.

And then, of course, the déjà vu hit.

She knows hazily in the back of her mind that she's seen this scene play out before, it's like the softest outline of one of the shadows in her heart. A puff, a mere wisp of an outline. She looks again from the dappled balcony. Adjusting her specs, she can just about make out her uncle and a little girl smiling at her. Well, to be honest, it's only the girl who's smiling. Her uncle simply looks a bit stunned in the distance.

She remembers being here before. *Home. This makes me so happy.*

~

'Your house makes me so happy.' Maya is back and talking to her aunt, who's looking at her as fondly as ever, albeit grey-haired and slightly more stooped. *Her heart is made of something else altogether,* Maya thinks, reminiscing about her unusual childhood, wondering at the scenes playing in her head like they were freshly cast. How exactly do the memory clouds know when to immerse us in their cotton-candypuff selves?

'You know we never wanted to move, or have you move out. We wanted you to have that stability,' Chini Auntie says. 'We didn't want you to feel—well, none of us like to feel that we don't have roots, right?'

'You've always been my roots, Auntie Chi.'

'Hahah, child, child, that's the smart and sensible person Uncle Pi raised you to be,' her aunt says, trying to laugh but launching into a coughing fit.

'Here, Auntie, you sit for a bit. Let me make you some hot tea. Some honey in there will help,' Maya volunteers. She's never been this attentive to anyone in her life, but sitting here, looking at her aunt and feeling such an outpouring of love, she can't imagine being any other way. She can't imagine telling her how topsy-turvy her own life has been. *Though there's something positive on the horizon,* Maya's starting to feel it.

'How is Gautam? Are you in touch?' Chini Auntie asks and her eyes narrow a bit when she notices that Maya seems a bit lost. *Hopefully not back in her own head?*

After her transplantation, Maya's worst fear was quickly allayed. Gautam Bhaiyya made it a point to visit almost daily and quickly became one of her aunt's 'kids'. *Auntie certainly knew how to handle the abandonment,* Maya is thinking. *They always put me first,* she thinks, amazed that they would do that for someone else's child without any agenda. *They always thought of what I needed and worked it out.*

Her uncle and aunt had taken it upon themselves to make sure that the transition was as smooth as possible. They went to her school without Mark or Maya the first time, to complain about the appalling fashion in which a schoolteacher had taken it upon herself to shout at a child about fees. That very morning, they came to an understanding with the principal. From then on, Mark was regular with the money he sent for Maya's tuition, food and board, like a guardian in absentia. It was her uncle and aunt who attended annual days and school fetes and parent-teacher meetings, if and when required. The principal was to keep a kind eye out for the little girl, who everyone acknowledged was a bolt of sunshine. Except when she dipped into one of her moods, then she was to be given a wide berth.

It was understood, though never discussed aloud, that her mother was 'disturbed'. And that was certainly not the child's fault. That was that, there was no judgement, no name-calling, at least not in front of her. Nan had once or twice tried to say something, including that she believed her daughter had taken sanyaas as her only letter home indicated, but she was shushed by her younger daughter before Maya could ask what sanyaas was and whether it was like taking saans *(a breath)*. Nan had often told the child to breathe deeply in the hope that it would calm her down. In with the universe, out with the universe. *Ommmmmm.*

Maya can never hope to aspire to the delicacy and tact with which her aunt and uncle navigated these facets of reality, not just her mother's absence but also Mark's utter despondency in those early years. At first, he did try to visit as often as he could, but was simply too broken-hearted most of the time to be able to spend any time with Maya without triggering a tsunami of grief in both of them. It was kinder all around, her aunt and uncle decided, to taper off the visits till he felt better.

Mark also gave his daughter a generous allowance, which her aunt decided to split—surreptitiously, at first—stowing away half of each month's allowance in Maya's young savers bank account. When Maya was eighteen, she told her about the savings and that she must never worry about money, but could do worse than to learn the saying 'Enough for my need, but not my greed'.

Maya took that to heart throughout college, belatedly spoiling herself in her twenties and beyond, after realising that the money in her savings account kept multiplying, with the old man still making regular deposits. She isn't entirely sure what he's up to these days. *Does he still have a practice? Should I check?* She doesn't bother. What's important is that he doesn't pry. Except for one awkward conversation back in the day—he told her he wouldn't be sending her any more money until he heard from her doctor that she was going regularly for her sessions and taking the medication. If she started going again, he had made it clear, the bank transfers would restart. She did, and so they did.

Mark isn't a bad sort, just bruised, she reflects. He still doesn't have the heart or emotional resilience to see Maya more than once a year, usually around Christmas, preferring to stay for stretches of time in exile, overseas or in far-flung Tier 2 towns, doing penance for God only knows what imagined sin. The best they can do is a phone call a couple of times a year and emails to make sure neither drops completely out of touch. It's the only tacit agreement they have, apart from not mentioning her mother (sorry, Usha, she corrects herself automatically).

She remembers that she wants to talk to him about the old flat, wondering whether they can do it up and rent it out as a sort of fresh start, now that she's almost done with this phase.

'Maya, Maya?' Chini Auntie is calling out to her.

'Sorry, sorry, I spaced out a bit there,' Maya laughs. 'Such lovely memories, Auntie. I love you so much.'

Chini Auntie smiles and hides the worry, enfolding it into her big heart. 'You just make sure you come and visit more often,' she chides. 'Especially when I'm back from Landour. And stay as long as you want. This will always be your home.'

11

Karmic Mysteries

[December 2023–January 2024]

Meanwhile, across a border, in the Land of the Thunder Dragon, an incomprehensible conversation is playing out.

'It's the same chap,' Maya's brother Gautam tells his mentor. 'They're calling him Guruji, but he's the same one we called the Crank. The one with the gout.'

'Mmm,' says the old man with a long beard and funny accent. 'And so he resurfaces, what is it, ten or fifteen years later. Mmmm.'

'Has it been that long? Since we lost the Pahaari and him?'

'Yes, indeed. Time is flying, my friend. And so should you.'

Gautam tunes out the terrible wordplay these days. But he marvels at how fast this century is zipping by. 'That long since Rishikesh!'

'Hmm. And we find him in connection with young Maya, that is something beautiful with the universe. No?'

The old man's mind is far away, back in the day, sitting on a hill and listening to the gushing of a river. At the time, distraught over a young devotee's corruption and exit to the tantric brotherhood, he had barely registered the disappearance of the beautiful sadhvi they called the Pahaari. Or so he claimed.

His youngest disciple had come up to give him the news. 'Er. Sir. Ji. We tracked her to the rest house, sir,' a young and abashed Gautam had said. 'There's no sign from there on.' He had stopped, anticipating the Rishi's legendary volcanic rage (outbursts that mellowed and eventually faded entirely as his spiritual practice took hold).

What followed was ten times worse. Silence, punctured only by a deflated, 'It will be as it was meant to be.'

That was all the Rishi would say, but he was so knotted up, it was days before anyone heard him laugh again. He was one of the few people Gautam knew who laughed from his belly, and they used to say you could hear it all the way in Vaishnodevi.

The thrum of the universe in sync.

Today the Rishi is in fine form, eyes twinkling he looks at his favourite friend and assistant. 'Gautam, stop dreaming and pack. You'll find there is a lot waiting for you to clean up.'

'But sir, do you really think we might find Her?'

Ah, the enigma of the Pahaari. She has quite the story. But the Rishi doesn't share all of it with anyone.

'Who knows, babu,' is all the response Gautam gets. 'But your sister can't wait.'

Gautam's eyes narrow. He still can't believe his sister has fallen into the grasp of that charlatan of all people. Something about an ashram, a breakup and a new friend. He was annoyed enough to let it show, but the Rishi had just laughed and pointed at himself. 'Pot, kettle?'

'But, but. Surely my own transformation is anything but mystical!' Gautam expostulated. *There's another person comparing the two journeys when they're nothing alike!* 'He's an absolute fraud!'

Look at our work, grassroots, actual work on the ground, he wanted to tell Maya. There was a lot of physically demanding activity back in the hills, a small gurukul where they taught some of the kids, special classes for the 'gifted' ones. Gautam felt such satisfaction from his job that he couldn't imagine anyone confusing him with a wide-eyed disciple.

'It's the difference between spiritual authenticity and the fly-by-night shucksters and con artists,' he tells the Rishi.

'Of course, now it's all in the branding,' the Rishi laughs, but only half-jokingly.

'It's not at all the same thing, nothing mystical about it,' Gautam says emphatically.

'Not any longer at least,' his Guru says, chuckling. Gautam can never tell if the Rishi is making fun of him or trying to teach him some sort of lesson in humility. There's no way of knowing.

'I'll go and check on them, sir, the Guru and, well, the boy,' he says. 'Though I doubt there will be any hera- pheri as such.'

The old man just chuckles again. 'Once bitten …'

'Anyway, I'm going down to keep an eye.'

'Your sister?'

'I worry. There's something I'm not able to put my finger on.'

'Of course, go on, go on. You'll be back soon enough.' The Rishi is quite equanimous, as well he should be at seventy. (No one knows his real age, as he's always been around. Seventy? Eighty? He laughs whenever Gautam asks him. 'What is time, after all, if not stretchable?')

Stretchable indeed.

'Check on that rascal too.'

'Sir?'

'The filthy rascal, capitalist.'

'Your brother, sir?'

'Hm. Yes. He'll make sure you have transport, it's the least he can do.'

'Will do.'

Gautam goes online to arrange for his travel. Luckily, he's not too far, despite being in another country—it won't take more than a couple of hours by flight. He packs neatly and concisely, stopping only when he chances upon an old framed photo of his sister. *Who is this strange new friend, this boy from the ashram his sister has been speaking of?* His hand hovers over her face and while he's not yet tingling with the connection, he finds himself drawn to thoughts of a young man possessed of a peculiar personal intensity.

He thinks back to his last conversation with his sister.

'What is it about Guruji's preaching that's made such an impression?' he asked her, expecting her to be hard-pressed to answer.

'He is light, he emits such great vibes, such great energy,' she started, unaware of the slight scepticism on her dear brother's face. With the momentary blurring depending on signal and bandwidth (though it's supposedly 4G), their WhatsApp video calls don't catch all the features.

'He's always so happy and laughing. It's like seeing pure love in motion. You feel blessed, truly blessed, to be around him.'

She had waited hours to see Guruji again after her last darshan, she told Gautam, despite the ashram rule book. There was no chance of meeting him offhand, though. She would have to wait to get to the front row again, sit in front of him, have him see her, bless her.

'I wish he would shake my hand next time,' she told an increasingly surprised Gautam, 'I wouldn't wash it for days, if he did. My friend Karthik said he tried to get me another audience but I should just … do the work.'

He had laughed at her then, not with her, but had to admit to himself that she seemed so much better, so much happier than he'd seen her in a long time. He'd had an inkling of Maya's deep-seated loneliness since childhood, but hadn't known that she felt such an acute need for healing from a sickness he didn't even know she had.

It's a spiritual cleanse she's after, he reckoned. For the first time in a long time, she had started to let herself be, to feel happy. She hadn't even registered it herself, but she had mentioned her new friend Karthik several times, always with an animated smile, and Gautam had quickly realised Karthik was very much a part of the 'awakening'.

Before he leaves, he has to workshop the Rishi's speech. He tests it out on an audience on their YouTube channel, a shorter version going up on their other social accounts.

'Time is running out. This could be your last chance to seize the moment, live the dream, be the person you had always hoped and imagined you would be. Isn't that what you're told? Often? With just an edge of hysteria or panic? "Life is short! Live for the Moment! Carpe Diem! Make the most of today because who has seen tomorrow?"'

And on and on.

It's feeling a bit manipulative, no? He decides he'll make some changes.

~

Gautam is probably online, Maya notes as she watches a reel and likes a post just as it pops up in real-time. She scrolls on and then leaves a question mark under his second comment: *Some of us have seen tomorrow, we just don't talk about it.*

He's spun it out into a blog post, which he directs her (and anyone else interested) to.

'Some of us have a lot of time, like seriously, light years on our side. And not just astronauts battling the gravity fields of other planets either. It's like spinning the wheel—and not a rigged game. But you don't get to choose. We never do.'

She smiles, remembering full well his earnestness.

'Who knows what hand you're going to get? Some of us are Laika, some Neil Armstrong, the rest are mostly in between, having to make do with a regular handful of years when we peak, spending the rest of our lives trying to live up to that one grand moment, while being made painfully aware that the rest is nothing but a hollow echo.'

Ahem, she writes, not entirely sure how to react. *Do check your Whatsapp when you get the time! Smiley winky face.*

She's forgotten how Gautam sometimes talks to himself. Oblivious to whether he has an audience, he acts like he is on stage.

Maya and he used to daydream about possible futures, parallel universes, what they would have done if they'd had a shot at doing things differently. Gautam had got into Stephen Hawking at a young age and would fascinate her with tales of black holes and imaginary time, parallel universes and wormholes, though they hadn't realised he was slipping in healthy doses of science fiction as fact to buttress the theoretics that were out of reach for a pre-teen.

Right now, one of Gautam's chat windows is open and he can see that Maya's furiously typing away.

Such a beautiful, gentle girl. She didn't deserve any of her childhood, he thinks. *And whatever else, she didn't deserve Usha.*

Then again, he does have a younger disciple who believes children choose the families they're born into, to work out some sort of karmic kink. 'Even our siblings,' he'd pontificated, 'are long-lost enemies born into the same family to work out karmic residue.'

That's what some people say, but Gautam isn't sure.

He finds his mastery of the arcane to be slipping and good old-fashioned emotions emerge when he contemplates the Pahaari. His blood runs cold when he thinks of the impact her antics have had on Maya. It's fuelled his quest all this while, ever since he's known, but definitely since he 'rescued' Maya, or Akira as she called herself then.

Without a thought to her own safety, Maya had dashed off on her loony quest, convinced she would find her mother and be able to bring her home. Gautam had found her delirious and penniless at a random shack masquerading as a rest house outside Manali. It was he who got her some food, a checkup, put her on a bus, and promised to make the quest his own.

He had been enraged then at the callousness of the Pahaari but also the unfeelingness of the Universe.

He'd been sure to pencil Maya in for a quick checkup, as much for his own peace of mind as for hers. 'Medical and spiritual,' he had said as he led her to a surprisingly ageless old man with a long beard. (The Rishi's youth had been spent training to be a doctor. It had lent more credence and credibility to his 'special school' for the gifted back in the day.)

'No scars or internal bruising,' Maya had heard a figure in the shadows say quietly before she passed out.

'Gautam,' the Rishi had said, trying to placate him, 'she'll be fine.'

'She does have her mother's looks, eh? But her father's eyes,' the Rishi commented to his forlorn disciple. 'And how about his compassion? That would stand her in better stead.'

Gautam had tried to be matter-of-fact. 'She has it. She goes on her aunt. I mean, the aunt is practically her real mother, by now—' He stopped for a second. 'I didn't know that she would still be looking.'

'We're always looking,' the Rishi said, patting his favourite disciple on the shoulder. 'Don't worry so much.'

It was a pretty foggy memory and Maya's never discussed it, not quite sure she didn't dream up the whole thing.

Needless to say, the Pahaari was nowhere to be found. She hadn't wanted to be back then.

~

It's been—what? A decade and change?—but Gautam still worries about the trauma his adoptive sister has been through. He can't find the right way to raise the topic from afar and she keeps telling him things are fine. So he says nothing. *Maybe it's not my business,* he thinks, a bit forlorn.

Though, these days, he should be happy that she's at least sharing more often. There's her message from some weeks ago, for example.

'Hey. Where are you?'

'Dying to chat.'

'I want to tell you about someone and (also, you were right) the ashram.'

'Oh, and there was this drama with the ex, I guess.'

'Seriously. So much to catch up on! Hope you're doing great!'

'I know you're out of the country but come back soon!'

He'd had to postpone his trip and instead they'd had a long video chat ('Video chat, imagine!' he'd laughed gleefully). *He's so old-school like that,* Maya had thought, oblivious to all that was going on around her, oblivious again to her mood, to Akira bubbling up.

Today there's a simple ping: 'PS I'm pretty sure the Witch is back.'

An instantaneous reply. Only Gautam would reply without any questions, just with a succinct: 'On my way.'

~

He's not going alone, after all. It is pretty funny how the universe works. Call it the steamroller of karmic realisation. After some viral YouTube video, the Rishi has been invited for a talk in Delhi by the same movement that runs the Crank's new outfit. It's the perfect re-entry. And he'll be following Gautam in just a day or two.

He makes some cryptic remark about how Gautam should be ready for another big revelation. 'It's the way of the universe,' he says, without elaborating.

~

'It's the way of the universe that you're born, you die,' the Rishi says in almost every talk. 'The beat goes on.'

He always earns rapturous applause with that one.

Gautam is working on updating parts of his speech for the Delhi sojourn.

'The inevitability of death was never in question, yet it's always been quite astonishing to see how many people are surprised by this,' he writes.

'Death is always a part of the deal,' Gautam says out loud and can't help but smile.

'This is the way.'

He's been trying to colloquialise the Rishi's vocabulary for the past decade or so, to make him more relatable. It seems to be working, judging by the number of applications they have for internships at the ashram-that's-not-called-an-ashram-anymore. The website, YT channel and that TedX talk in Banaras had clearly helped.

And there were always the pop culture references. *Winter is coming,* Gautam remembers they'd used on the last trip when the show was such a hit. The references ease things with the younger lot and even those of a certain vintage. Some of them have started following him around the same way he used to follow his mentor, making note of where he's scheduled to show up, leaving comments for him on their social pages, audio and video messages, both.

It's funny that he's more or less come to terms with what used to upset him earlier—the inevitability of things. *Do what you want, but what's going to be will be, apparently.* It used to make Gautam edgy at first. Like knowing that doomsday is around the corner.

'But it is!' the Rishi told him, smiling. 'Every culture has its version, but they all have it. Like Ragnarok.'

Gautam had looked it up and was none too thrilled by what he found of the crux of Norse mythology, the apocalyptic ending.

Nonetheless, no question that he's come a long way since, incorporating it all into the Rishi's speech, updating his notes.

'Winter is coming? Always.

'Some of you have heard of Ragnarok or Kalyug, as the ancients had it. Some of you think it's the End of Days (we've seen the hashtags).' That always gets a laugh.

'And you think like the preppers you can prep your way out of it?

'Will it really help us to predict an apocalypse? How does it help us if we don't change in the here and now?

'Seriously, how does it help you to know that things are ending? Does it make you more desperate or less? Anyone adjusting their attitudes? Learning from the perspective?

'Remember what the pandemic taught us? Remember the blue skies, even in Delhi? But here we are, right back to the same old, predictable pollution, environmental degradation. We haven't learned, we don't learn. We don't change our behaviour. We don't change in accordance with our beliefs. And unlike the squirrels, we don't store food for the harsh times. Even if winter is coming.

'So the question is, can you train yourself to do better? To make your spirit more robust? Yes, actually, more's the pity, because no one thinks to do that. But how else does it help to know the pitfalls that await all of us? That we don't think about. And then time ticks on, inexorably. Or does it?

'No way of telling objectively, even the scientists agree with us on that. Space, time, all these are constructs, my friends. So what are we to do? That's what we are here to discuss.'

Gautam wonders if his sister will be in the audience this time, given her recent interest in the spiritual side of things. Will she find it all as profound as the others do?

The Rishi walks in to see Gautam deep in thought. 'Arre, shouldn't you get going? Don't worry so much. I keep telling you.'

'Sir, this guy, the Crank. I can't believe he's back on the scene.'

'Oho, that's the way of the world, no?'

The Rishi is always finding these things amusing, Gautam thinks, leaving his postscript unsaid. *I wonder if the Pahaari is with him still.*

'The world is a village, baba,' the Rishi usually says. Not this time, though. Maybe he notices that Gautam is stressed. 'Baba, he's a charlatan, but he's harmless these days.'

Gautam had told him about Maya going to the satsang, about her theories on the prasad, but the Rishi only rolled his eyes. 'Lucky for the public then that we will be headed there so soon,' he said, promising to sort it out once and for all.

'I thought you said there's only a series of ripples; that nothing is forever,' Gautam lobbed back, though he knew his teacher was just trying to reassure him.

The Rishi had laughed. 'Touché.'

'So, my speech? It's done?' the Rishi says now.

'The speech is done.'

'Arhm,' Gautam makes some weird throat-clearing noise.

Unusually diffident, he asks, 'Sir, once we sort out the collections and the payments due, we'll be pretty much done, right?'

'Yes. Indeed,' the Rishi says kindly. 'And you must take some time off. Time for a break. Time to be with your sister. Take some good amount of time.'

That could mean anything, a week, six months. A pause.

'Take your time and then come back here.'

Gautam smiles, reassured as he always is, but then his mentor pauses and articulates what's really been bothering him. 'What's creating a bit of a hiccup for us is young Karthik.'

'Her friend? What, you know him?' Gautam is startled. How does the Rishi know the boy haunting his sister's dreams?

'Well, yes, I've been watching him his whole life, you could say,' the Rishi says, smiling. 'There are connections, my dear boy. The world is a village, you know.'

'Connections? Maya?' Gautam's brain is racing.

'Yes, I thought she would add some meaning to his life,' is the cryptic reply before the interminable pause the holy man is so famous for.

...

'But something's not right. I feel a tug that I can't quite explain away.'

...

Gautam waits for more.

'Karthik got away from the Crank, it's good only. But I wonder if the destruction he keeps dreaming of is already done.'

What is going on? Gautam wonders. *What is the connection?*

'Why does it matter? Maybe it's a coincidence, sir,' he proffers, unable to make much sense of this. 'He's an outsider, no?'

'Hardly. Karthik is hardly an outsider, baba,' the Rishi says, not unkindly. 'He's my nephew, after all. Though we haven't spoken since he was a baby.'

'What? Your nephew?' Gautam stops. He wonders just how much he's not been privy to; how much he doesn't know about this man he's been following around for the past twenty-odd years.

The Rishi just smiles at him benevolently.

'Uh … sir?'

'Hmmm? Yes, yes, he's family. Tribe.'

…

'Not to worry, I think we have some time with him.'

Gautam doesn't know what to say or think. *What should I do now?*

'Oh ho, I keep telling you, don't fret. In fact, you'll see those beautiful ripples, no? That Usha might yet play a role in all our enlightenment, baba.'

'What? But how?' Gautam is thrown. *So the Pahaari is back on the scene?*

'Hmmm, yes. Yes. That is the problem. How … Even a contract signed in blood seems to not be worth the parchment it's written on these days.'

'What?'

The Rishi can see Gautam's in no mood to joke around, but starts laughing nonetheless. The boy's expression is priceless. 'I'm kidding—no blood—you know the tribe accepts digital signatures these days!'

It's that booming laugh that the disciples are always reassured by; the bass forming as one the thrum of their heartbeats in their ears, the thrum of the universe, Gautam's always secretly felt. Something about the pitch.

But all of a sudden, he's feeling a bit unbalanced by all this new information. As usual, he's not privy to half of what's going on. *Perhaps best not to think about work for a while?*

The Rishi isn't done.

'So! I come with you. I'll leave today instead of tomorrow. What shall I pack? What's the fashion?' the Rishi asks. 'You know me, I want to be stylish.'

Gautam smiles despite himself, though his heart's not entirely in it.

'I think I'll go with the saffron robes this season.'

'Nice, very restrained halo-chic,' Gautam concedes.

'And we'll fit right in.'

That booming laugh, that all's well with the world.

But is it?

~

Not long after, Gautam's thoughts are drawn back to Maya and her new friend, this dark and tortured Karthik, who has turned out to be the Rishi's nephew, of all things. This time, he focuses his attention on a photo of the Crank's original disciples and manages to get a reading.

Well, well, what do we have here?

Trust Gautam to feel no qualms about travelling a few moonbeams into someone else's dream. Entering Karthik's, he's overwhelmed to find the annihilation that abounds. The love is clear, surprising that Maya didn't mention how deep their connection is, but the rest is disturbing.

PART THREE

12

Seek and Ye Shall Find (Yourself)

[January 2024]

Walking back up some grungy steps, Maya can't help but stop and think of a childhood memory. The older, beautiful lady. *How did I not know my mother came to check on me?*

Could I have stopped her? Made her stay?

Didn't I know at some level?

How did I blank that entire episode out?

She shakes her head. It had come up again in her last therapy session. Reena Gupta taking notes as always, looking warm and like she was on her side. Maya's side. *(Until she spoiled it all by trying to palm me off onto a psychiatrist.)*

'You remember this visit? She was a beautiful lady, you said last time.'

'Yes. Usha,' Maya said, and Akira stirred.

'I'm not sure if you mentioned that it was her by name.' Reena flipped through her notes. 'No, no, you didn't.'

'I'm not sure I remembered it *was* her,' Maya said and then paused. 'That's odd.'

What was that about dogs? Maya-then-Mia had never believed it, remembering how the scary lady had helped nurse a little bird back to life, just because. Maya still has a soft spot for crows.

~

There's always something we don't yet know, she thinks.

So many things she can't remember these days. Actually, it's always been a problem.

Gautam used to laugh at her 'memory holes'.

'Convenient,' he'd say.

But now, she's tired of all those different times, those different ways of being. *There's no need to be so strained and stressed, is there? Maybe I will see the psychiatrist Gupta refers me to.* Scary thought.

~

No crows now, she notes. Today, it's just the pigeons standing sentry. This is after all their house, though no one seems to have told the new tenant. Despite having moved in just a few weeks ago, she has already ruffled their feathers. Around this neighbourhood, everything is under observation. Not least from the ghosts of the abandoned lot next door. It's only the people who walk around, oblivious.

This dull, grey Delhi afternoon, there's absolutely no question of anything remotely interesting happening. But Maya's barely taken one flight of stairs when she notices the birds flying low en masse. *Uh-oh. Lucky I don't have to go anywhere*, she thinks. *Birds flying low means rain*, she remembers from reading *Asterix* as a child.

Sure enough, the thunder starts, followed by lightning. It's as if the dark clouds roll in within minutes. Then, sheets of rain. *Phew*. She's quite pleased with herself for being safe and dry and, to be honest, staying out of circulation seems to agree with her.

The tube light shines extra bright before short-circuiting itself. *Zzzzpt*. Lights out.

She keeps walking up, smiling and talking to herself. 'It's going to be all right,' she tells herself. 'Nothing to worry about, love.' A minute later, she cocks her head, as if listening to something.

It's been a few weeks since she noticed that her old knack of hearing thoughts has resurfaced.

'Nothing to worry about,' she chants as some sort of mantra as she huffs and puffs her way to the fourth floor, and sure enough, the lights come back on with a bang—wait, that's just the window that's blown out from the force of the storm. She fumbles with her key and makes her way into the dark, empty house.

'Oh,' she says, spotting the figure in the corner. 'It's you.'

It is indeed.

Gautam Bhaiyya is sprawled out on the sofa, looking exhausted.

'Murukku, murukku,' a pigeon trapped in the kitchen gobbles at them.

'Ech.' Her brother can't help himself.

She giggles but shares her thoughts. 'South Indian pigeons, I reckon. Urbane, non-aggressive, unlike most of our neighbours in this city.'

Gautam is unable and unwilling to mask his disgust. 'You know how I hate pigeons! I hate the noise, but also the shitting, the constant shitting.'

Maya doesn't want to stop him mid-flow but can't help herself. 'This is spiritual training? I thought you were learning to be Zen?'

'Zen is one thing. These winged rodents are another. Gawd. They're so annoying and also pestilential, you know.'

He gets up and walks towards her for a hug.

'So how are you, my dear? Wait, don't tell me, let me guess, feeding pigeons, hiding out, waiting for Prince Charming?'

'Will you quit being obnoxious?' she asks.

It's a long, warm hug.

He's in protective mode very quickly, especially upon spotting an ashtray half-full of cigarette butts.

'Sister dear, this city is a gas chamber. I mean, do you really need to be …'

'I know. I know. Actually, I've quit.'

'Hrmph. You should come and stay with me for a while.'

She laughs again.

'I'm serious! It would do you good!'

'Oh c'mon … And what will Mishraji do then, hmm?'

'I don't even …' Gautam laughs. 'Mishraji, wow. I can't wait to see him!'

'Stick around for a few days,' she says, smiling. 'Also, Chini Auntie asked about you the other day.'

'Haan, she sent me a mail. Off on holiday, she said?' He doesn't mention her postscript request that he check in on Maya. They're used to each other and this rhythm.

'Yes, it's all actually been perfect for me,' she replies. 'You know, a lot of these flats are empty right now—more space for me.

'There's an urban legend about an infamous murder and subsequent haunting, otherwise this might just be coveted real estate. Anyway, this is only an interlude—the place is undoubtedly going to be sold, bought up, demolished, broken down, and built up into a swanky apartment block at some point,' she says, in a pragmatic tone.

'Why are you staying here again?' Gautam snorts. Though there's no denying how well she's looking. How happy he is to see his sister! He was worried something serious was going on again. She had once cut off contact with him for six months but on resurfacing to find him in an utter panic, had promised to never be that drastic again. He wishes it were easier to be helpful, to be 'there', and sighs, his father's constant refrain from their childhood still with him: 'Go easy on her, don't pick a fight.'

And his favourite: 'She's not … feeling herself.'

Their father used to tell him that once a month, on average.

'She might never,' Gautam had replied once. He would never forget the look his father gave him for being cruel; knowing it was true, but unable to fathom what to do next.

One minute a ray of sunshine and laughter, the next thunderclouds on the horizon. They understood that these weren't moods. They were precisely her, feeling 'herself'. Little Mia, quite the Eeyore of the family. *Dad dying devastated her, but she never understood how it affected everyone else as well, the ripple effect*, he thinks.

But hang on, she was a bit Eeyore-like way before, to be honest.

'The thing is, in the books, all his friends just accept him the way he is, no questions asked,' Maya would have replied if he'd ever voiced his Eeyore theory.

He never did, not after Chini Auntie told him about the therapy, the diagnosis, that Maya was on medication and preferred not to talk about it. Sometimes he saw traces of the old her and tried to engage, but she'd shut him out quite successfully, sticking to the superficial. Until recently. Until the Guruji saga.

'Waise, you know,' Gautam starts, 'it's not the worst idea in the world. Upping sticks.'

She smiles.

'But if you don't want to be alone, you know, if you want more than pigeons for company, you could easily move into mine?' he starts off, with a nervous laugh. 'Or mum's, rather? She's making the most of it since I'm hardly around. But it's quite lovely.' Gautam comes to a dead stop. His sister still has that uncanny knack of eyeballing him, almost daring him to continue. He does keep an eye on his mother this way, he wants to say, but drops it before he even starts.

'I don't need anyone to keep watch on me.'

'I wasn't suggesting that. Anyway, I'm going to see her later, if you want to come.'

'No, no thanks,' Maya says, and while her tone is cold at the mention of Neeti, she makes it a point to smile at him to break the mood.

She pulls out a jug of nimbu pani from the fridge, grabbing glasses for both of them.

He looks at her and pulls a wry face. 'I should've brought you something. A gift! I have a book somewhere; I'll just find it.'

'No need, no need,' she trills. 'I'm famished, I just realised, you must be too!'

She's already brought out a pizza box, humming her way to the microwave. It's only then that Gautam realises that it's not that his sister is feeling 'herself' for a change, despite the hiding out. He resolves to wait patiently for her to spill the beans.

She's never learned to cook for herself. I wonder …

'Oh, I can cook well enough, brother dear, I just don't have the time.'

'It's back?' He smiles. 'Glad to hear it. Though it's not thaaaaat impressive that you can read minds, when it's just me!'

He laughs at her.

She'd forgotten how he used to tease her.

'It's not …' she stops midway. 'It's not entirely clear with you, Gautam, there's a huge ball of wool stuffing something up in the middle of your head!'

'You always said that, ya lizard brain.' He laughs and walks to the window to check out the scene. He turns back.

'So,' he begins.

'So … I thought you were resolved to wait patiently.' She smirks at him.

'Patiently till I'm done with this pizza, for sure,' he laughs. 'Pepperoni works, it's been a while.'

He's trying to remember what he has told his sister about his 'job', or apprenticeship rather, and his rather unusual decade-long quest to find the enigmatic Pahaari; the side project that he's been obsessed with ever since he was a teenager looking out for Maya-not-Mia/Akira.

'Tell me about you?' she asks.

'More of the same,' he grunts. 'Spiritual cleanses and meditation retreats. Though now we're in Bhutan and working with some of the groups out of Paro. It's beautiful. You should make a trip.'

'I must!'

'But,' she ventures after a short pause, 'doesn't it get lonely?'

It's his least favourite question, but her smile disarms him entirely.

Gautam grins. 'Who's got the time?'

A pause for chewing. 'And you?' he asks, wondering if she'll tell him about her love life.

She sighs but doesn't sound too upset when she says, 'Nah, a pretty disastrous last one, but my recovery time is getting better!'

He has his reassuring face on.

'Actually, though, I did meet someone nice.'

She puts her hand on her stomach and sits down near her brother. 'But you know how it is, I don't know about this whole love thing. You know?'

He nods at her. 'Sure do. Whatever will happen, will happen.'

She smiles at him. He hasn't changed after all.

'And work? Still glad you quit?'

'Super glad. I'm just relaxing for the first time in ever, it feels like,' she says. 'You should try it.'

'I might just,' he says. 'I'll join you.'

They stare out the window for a tick.

She asks him so casually that he knows it's actually been bothering her, 'How come you got over here so fast?'

She doesn't want the tremor in her heart to come through in her voice. He can't know how close she'd been to the edge again. Though all the grounding techniques have been keeping her calm, there's something just beyond her line of sight, she can feel it.

'Oh, you know, I haven't seen you in ages!' he says, aiming for a chill vibe but not quite pulling it off. They try to skirt around their actual worries.

'Plus you did mention She might be back?'

She nods, shrinking into herself. 'Just a feeling, but you know how those are.'

'Do I ever,' he says. 'I'm glad you told me. I think we may finally have a lead, and somehow … somehow it connects back to your old ashram.'

'No way!'

'Yes way,' he laughs. 'Did you know that the Rishi knows that Guruji of yours?' Out of respect for her feelings, he doesn't tell her they've dubbed him 'the Crank'.

'What?!' She's as surprised as he was to learn of this development.

'I'm pretty sure it's all going to tie in somehow,' he says after a minute.

'You know what? I think you're right,' she concurs.

Gautam doesn't know why he's hesitant to talk to his sister about Usha, considering they both saw her as kids and whispered about her all the time. The estranged mother used to be enough of a topic of discussion back in the day. He figures he'll just mention it.

'Actually, the Rishi also wants to check out whether Usha is in town … and check out the ashram.'

She raises her eyebrows but says nothing.

(Akira knew she'd been right to come back.)

He's not sure why he doesn't want to say any more about his suspicions, that Usha's been even more connected to the Rishi and the Crank than they know, potentially even to Maya's new friend, Karthik. He doesn't bring up the fact that Karthik is the Rishi's nephew, not just yet. Does it matter that there are connections behind connections? *We'll never know.*

'Usha has been evading the Rishi for what feels like half a century or more,' Gautam volunteers, though he can't shake the feeling that he doesn't know the half of it.

'I didn't even know she was on his radar,' Maya says.

'Tell me about it.'

They sit in silence for a bit, a companionable silence that has been a long time in the making.

Gautam clocks the pijjus on their perch, the old crow on the windowsill and the lazy cat outside. He's been unconsciously bracing for trouble, but finally relaxes, knowing that what's going to come will come. Till then, at least there's pizza and a reunion.

There's no reason, after all, to think that Usha wants to come find Mia. He turns to her as she starts to ask him something.

'Do you remember that time we met her?' she says, a vivid memory of her brother as a kid on the staircase, talking to the beautiful lady.

'Yeah, man. She got straight into my head, no?' He laughs laconically. 'Freaked me out.'

'Yup, totally,' she smiles. 'I remember her helping me nurse that little crow baby, though. It's weird, like out of time. I keep waiting to see that little bird all grown up, the stories he'd have!'

He smiles at the crow that's staring at him, beady-eyed. 'You never know,' he starts, then stops, not feeling the need to say anything further.

There's that comfortable silence again.

~

'Some weird times are coming,' Gautam wants to say, looking at his sister, reading her mood cloud—*a bit confused, yes, but is she scared and alone? Or is he projecting? Best to build up to it gently maybe, give her some space and time to come to it on her own,* he figures. *Maybe it's all just much ado about nothing. There's something else that he hasn't been able to decipher. It's new. Resilience?*

Instead of commenting on that, he says, 'What's wrong with your pals, by the way? A bit demented on social right now. Have you seen?'

'Ah, haha,' she chortles. 'They're alright. They love a little dramaaaaa!'

'Oh ho, they're the dramatic ones, eh?'

She laughs. 'But actually, now that you mention it, I've been MIA longer than I had planned.' *A couple of weeks maybe?* At least a week since that social post she shared, though she can't keep track of time anymore.

Gautam laughs at her use of 'MIA'. '"Time is stretchable, it's fluid as it flows," as we keep telling people. But yeah, maybe you can drop a message online, people will figure out that you're okay and the drama will cease.'

She nods in acknowledgement. *That's what she'll do. Maybe soon.*

Quiet for a second, Gautam looks out of the balcony at the lot next door, run-down and deserted. 'You should get an award. Quite the bravest girl in the world,' he says. 'Living like this. Not to mention, surviving everything.'

He's pleased to hear her laughter, all light and tinkly again.

'That's what you used to call me when were little. You said I was almost the bravest girl in the world!'

So much love in her voice, it warms him to the core. 'I was right, too!' he says.

'Why almost the bravest? I never thought to ask.'

'I thought I'd let you work your way up to bravest, by and by! Guess it felt more scientific.' He remembers thinking Mia had to be the most terrified girl he knew, what with her mother turning out the way she did, but ever diplomatic, he doesn't bring that up right now. *Now is the time to get her to come back out of hiding, and he's glad she's ready.*

'Now now, big brother, if your little sister can tough it out . . .' Mia laughs and takes her own time to start speaking again. She wants to explain properly. 'I'm just doing my own thing, hardly stepping out. I've been spending some quality time with me, thinking and being and not being scared for a change. I'll be out by and by, you know that, right? Also, Mishraji's around on and off, so you know, I'm all sorted.'

'Well, maybe just reach out to some of your friends,' he says, and then changes the subject as she groans. 'Yes, fine fine.'

Gautam laughs. 'You know what's funny, though?' he asks. 'I didn't even need you to tell me where you'd be. It's like you knew I'd know where you'd head to.'

Maya smiles. 'I knew.'

She continues after a short pause, 'I mean, it's home, no? And it's always been here for us.'

Chini Auntie's always been solid, Gautam thinks and tries to quash the part of him that feels bad for his own mother, always appearing petty and mean in comparison. Turfing out a child shortly after her husband died. *But what did they expect from her?* he wonders now, heartbroken though he'd been as a child. *A constant reminder of her husband's infidelity?* Ah yes, that was quite the conversation his mother had sprung on him one memorable holiday, though he doesn't yet know she's kept out some significant bits of the story.

Maya's also lost in her own thoughts and they're comfortably quiet again, in a way they are with no one else, chasing memories that are caught in the interstices of this space-time frame, memories that Gautam is worried will be lost if they stay apart too long.

'You know,' he starts, just as she says, 'Thanks for coming by.'

They both giggle.

'Of course!' he says. 'What a thing to say!'

'No, I know you're busy, Gautam, with all the work and life stuff, so I just want you to know I'm grateful.'

He smiles at her, looking quite solemn in the evening light.

'Man, it's such a bummer that I won't have much time to chill here. I have to head out tomorrow for a quick thing, but I'll be back in a day or two max.'

She smiles at him.

'You know I'm here, if you ever need me.'

'I know.'

'I wanted to make sure you're fine. And also, I've been thinking of taking a break. If you have room ...'

She says she's more than fine and of course there's always room for him. *There'll be time enough then to share. Even the shameful bits (her brow darkens as she thinks of the Roy chapter).*

Gautam knows some of what makes his sister tick, some of what makes her unhappy, and feels bad for what he considers her restricted opportunities. *She has so much potential.* He wishes things were just a little bit easier for her.

There's something she wants to tell me, he knows, just as he knows that she's going to take her time to open up about it and there's no point pushing her. *Hope it's not right before I leave tomorrow. I hope she doesn't wait till then … Or hate me for going.*

He looks up and sees her staring at him. 'It's an important job, otherwise I would drop it. I know that's no comfort but … You know how much I love you.'

'I know you do, Gautam, I know you do.' She smiles at him, a proper smile from the soul.

It's a lovely way to end the night, a freeze-frame of a memory Gautam will hold on to when he gets lost and lonely. Because, of course, even older brothers have their share of issues, even if they can't let on. He crashes on the couch instead of the guest bedroom, and blames that for the restive sleep and dreams he has little control over. A hauntingly familiar, beautiful face looks back at him as if from a little way ahead on the road, calling his name. There's something she needs to tell him. He's grasping, straining to hear, searching for something, but all it turns into is … a murder of crows.

~

Caw, caw! A beak pecking at the window.

It's morning. Maya is already up, which is a role reversal for them. *How unusual.* He's always been the more disciplined one, the early riser. She seems to be lost in space as always, in her own world, but she's softened somehow, and he knows she hasn't noticed he's awake yet.

A split second later she has.

'Let me get some adrak chai for you,' she says, turning to beam at her beloved brother.

There's a glimmer of a thought in Gautam's brain that he can't quite reach and he doesn't, not until he's done brushing his teeth, going through the motions of the early morning plumbing. It's the image of her putting a protective hand on her stomach as she bends to place the mug on the side table that brings him to a halt.

'Mia?' he asks her, in awe, because he knows.

How could he have missed it? She glows outward. It's like a physical glow, he thinks.

'Haha, yes, yes. And what's more, I think she knows you.' Mia smiles, her full-on twinkly smile. 'She kicks when you speak.'

'Is that possible? I'll have to ask …'

'Sir? Yes, I know, I know. But first let's have some breakfast and then figure out what we're going to do about all this.'

'Are you going to …?'

'Not telling anyone yet, if you don't mind, Gautam. Not till I've told the father.'

A pause. 'If I'm even going to do that.'

Why did I say that? Of course I'm going to tell him, she thinks. She knows very clearly who the father is, but she shoves that thought aside—she's not fully ready to go there yet.

'Gotcha.' He smiles at her. *Is this why she's gone underground then? Just a timeout?* He tries to shake off the feeling that she might be in danger by herself—*isn't she too vulnerable? Too isolated? Then again, there's Mishraji and the house itself, the memories—her true home.*

'It's my safe space,' Maya says. 'Don't worry about me so much.'

'Okay. You know I can't help it, though.' His voice sounds funny, older, more vulnerable.

Maya looks at him, love in her heart and only a smidge of anxiety, scratch that, fear in her soul. What can she tell him about her premonitions? *Can she tell him that death had come to her in a dream? Driving the taxi that Karthik has mentioned more than once? She had disregarded his bleak warning, thinking his paranoia worse than her own, and yet … Is it superstition? Who knows … Can you manifest your own irrational fears?*

She of all people knows the pitfalls of the mind.

'The Cab of Death? Seriously?!' She had laughed it off. And because his father was already exasperated with his son's kooky theory and the fact that the whole city had started taking radio taxis, Maya had pretended she wasn't more comfortable in an Uber, accepting a ride from the head chauffeur instead.

Well, she wasn't laughing now. *Something has rubbed off on me and Karthik,* she thinks. She wanted to bring it up in therapy just for some validation, but there are limits. (She'd also ghosted her therapist, so that was another mini-drama.)

Maybe talking it out will help. 'Something weird is going on,' she starts, but … what can she really share? None of it is tangible. *Those weird dreams,* she wants to tell him, *death, destruction. Karthik. What if it impacts Karthik's baby?*

'What is it? Something I can help with?'

'Just these weird dreams. You know my friend has them and I've started having them. But … actually, never mind, it's nothing,' she finishes lamely.

'Mia,' he too tries to start a sentence, not realising he's reverted to her pet name since coming back. 'About the boy. Your friend from the ashram.'

She stops him, her heart pounding, all of a sudden. *She doesn't want to hear anything negative.* 'I don't want to talk about all that right now. Let's have a chat *araam se* when you're back. There's a lot to unpack.'

He acquiesces. *What else can he do? He's got to go track down Usha too, after all. Make sure things are safe, no?*

'As long as you're done with that Guru,' he says. It's the best he can do for now.

'Oh God, yeah. Did I tell you about that weird prasad?'

She spells it all out and Gautam slowly breathes again. *He's been waiting to exhale, it feels like. But she's fine, she's safe.*

She can't even believe that whole phase, but then again, she did learn a lot, she says a little defensively. 'I mean, it was fine, but I'm glad I'm done with it. Not to mention that I also started therapy again, which helped. And you know what, don't worry about Karthik. He's quit the ashram anyway.'

'Well, that's a relief.' Gautam has a smile on his face.

But isn't it just a brief respite? He doesn't want to worry his sister unnecessarily, but … something is going to go down, he just knows.

'It will not end well,' she wants to say, but is able to pause there even as the thought arises. *Observe your thoughts and let them be, don't catastrophise,* she's been learning and putting into practice.

'There's worse and then better,' she wants to say. 'But you've got to get through the worse first.'

(That's the first life lesson I learned, to be honest. And I'm taking notes, you can bet.)

Maya knows that her brother is preoccupied with something, also realising that he's always loved her almost too much. She has this awareness and realises—for the first time? Surely not—that her heart feels full. *How delightful and unexpected*. Just when she's discovering she doesn't need to fake or project being anyone other than her own self. *She doesn't need to*. She mulls over the thought, almost missing out on what Gautam is saying.

'Chalo, I have to leave in a bit, Mia, but I'm here now. If you need anything, just call. Actually you can even come with me if you want a ride somewhere.'

The car is downstairs, he's got a text. 'The Rishi's brother sent his best driver, some chap called K, who was smiling the whole way here yesterday. Very un-Delhi like.'

'K?! What? How does he know this K?'

Her brother looks at her, waiting for her to go on.

'Okay, listen, just be careful. Karthik doesn't like him very much; he has some strange theories ...'

'About the driver?' Gautam smiles.

She laughs. *But wait, what?* 'The Rishi's brother sent him?' she asks.

'You mean ... wait, what?!' The penny drops.

Gautam looks sheepish. 'I just heard about this myself. It looks like the boy from the ashram, umm ... your friend is the Rishi's nephew. They've barely ever met though, I don't think ...'

Is she in shock?

'Mia?'

She's actually a bit awestruck. 'But how is that even possible? Can the world really be that small?!'

He laughs, 'I know exactly what you mean.'

He knows he has to go but doesn't make a move. 'Hey, umm, do you want to come with me—just hang out for a bit? I mean, we could just go now.'

She puts her surprise aside. *I'll process this later.*

'Oh, you big ol' worrywart. I'll be fine …'

'Are you sure?'

'Gooo! I'll see you soon.'

'Patch up with your pals! I'll see you when I'm back. Maybe even tomorrow or day after. I'll see you before you know it.' He's sounding more confident now. He takes his backpack and heads out the door.

Not wanting to let go of this surprise, juxtaposed with the unusual and magnificent feeling of fullness, Maya pauses and 'sits with her feelings' as her therapist has taught her. *What does it all mean, though? Who knows,* but she's glowing inward too.

She's not sure what to do next. But it's probably time to get back on the grid. 'And don't forget what he said now,' she says to her belly (to me, that is). 'Almost the bravest girl in the world. You'll inherit that and … well, more, from your uncle Gautam. That you will.'

(Something has changed, something imperceptible to the outside world, and it's proving to be a force for massive good. Or, at least, I like to think so. I mean, I would, wouldn't I?)

Okay, rules are rules. Digital detox. No Facebook, no WhatsApp, no Instagram, no X. But we can make a new rule: new identity, and some X. We don't want to get bored to death, eh?

'The mind is a dangerous place, but I've just come through to the other side,' @Mia1000 tweets. 'It's time to share what I've learned. (Or not.)'

She pauses and checks herself for ego.

Should she delete this? She stares at her cellphone—almost as soon as she's switched it on, there's a call.

'Hello!' she says, not recognising the number but presuming it's one of her annoying friends. *To be honest, she wouldn't mind the company today.*

'Namaste.' It's the SHO.

Quite delighted to know that she's fine but asking her why everyone is going around trying to lodge FIRs. Does she have any idea the ruckus that's been kicked off? And her friend Farhan? He's been acting a bit strange. Is she sure everything is fine? Does she know how long it's been? In fact, where is she staying and will she be there later today? He and his colleague want to come over and make sure everything is okay.

'Of course,' she says and dictates the address.

Maya feels guilty now, genuinely so. She had no idea that people would go to any real trouble for her. No idea that her friends would even bother beyond the social platforms. That makes her emotional. Now that she's online again, she goes the whole hog, and realises that her friends have really been freaking out. *How is it possible they've jumped so quickly to foul play?* It's looking less and less fun online. *Is this because of all the stuff they've seen and heard?*

Or just PTSD from life in this city? We jump to the worst conclusions, especially about our women friends.

She decides to drop a line as a status update, casually like.

Shouldn't I?

No, better to call them up and have a more in-depth chat, she thinks, *there's a lot more to share.*

But then the moment passes.

I mean, Chini Auntie knew I was here, so if they'd just reached out ...

Easier to do the quick status update, she decides, parking the guilt that's bubbling up.

'All good in the hood, if you've missed me, we'll be chatting soon♥,' she writes, a bit too breezily.

That does not go down well.

13

Are We Friends Or What, Even?

[January 2024]

It's been a few days since the news got around that Maya is perfectly fine.

First, they got a call from a not-at-all-amused (actually a tad irate) cop who gave them a little bit of hell for wasting the police's time. Then they all saw that status update.

Eye roll.

And then a group message saying: 'Guysssss, sorry to trouble you. All well, miss you, see you soon xx.'

Like that's going to cut it.

A group of friends—now down to three—is sitting at a cafe, trying to digest the message. While Farhan and Megha had roundly criticised Rohit for being so blasé and not bothering to help all this while, they now grudgingly acknowledge that he's the smartest one, not wasting his time panicking, probably because he so evidently doesn't give a shit.

'Arre, be fair,' he says, 'I only don't give a gratuitous shit.' He laughs, or rather, snorts into his coffee. 'I mean, I do care; I'm the milk of human kindness, you know that.'

This last bit said nudging Megha, who can't help but smile at him. They've been hanging out a lot more after that call from the cops—that Maya is fine and alive and in the same city but taking a 'timeout'. Of her own volition.

'What a chick,' Rohit says. 'What a chop!' He can't help laughing at these two.

They're sitting around grumbling but starting to realise that she clearly doesn't care about them. They obviously don't even know her at all, says Megha.

'I mean, don't exaggerate,' Rohit says. 'We've always known she's self-centred.'

'Koi danger hai?' Farhan had asked the cop.

'Bilkul nahin,' the officer had replied, but then made a small concession. 'Madam *ne bola ki phone karenge*.' The cops clearly think they're all too spoiled for their own good.

Now they're feeling guilty for being pissed. It's a good thing she's safe of course, but they can't help that bitter aftertaste. Was Roy right?

'Maybe it's like some sort of vipassana,' Farhan comments, ever generous and ever amorous. He's possibly also the most relieved, given how the younger cop had been eyeballing him. He hadn't imagined the hostility either. The cops had seen too much go down to put anything past anyone. They're still convinced that *ladke ka chakkar tha*, but finding a smiling and glowing Maya, with her brother in tow no less, they've been left with nothing to do but shake their heads over this one.

'*Paise-wale hain, aise hi hote hain,*' the younger cop told his senior colleague. '*Bilkul nautanki, time pass hi karte hain. Pcchah.*'

Everyone's feeling pretty much that vibe.

'What rubbish, ya,' Megha says, 'I'm damn irritated with that girl. Wasting all our time with this useless melodrama.'

'I know, she could have just said she needed some space,' Farhan says, unable to keep the hurt out of his voice.

'Uff. Whatever,' says Rohit.

'Anyway, you tell us your news?' Megha starts.

'Yeah,' Farhan tries to chime in. '*Hua kya tha?* Why were you moping? Breakup? And who the hell were you even seeing?'

Rohit is a bit flustered. He hadn't wanted Megha to know he was talking about that.

And just like that, they're back to doing what they do best—dissecting their personal lives every which way, making some effort to make sense of the world, an increasingly difficult job, without revealing too much of their own inner realities. Rohit talks to them about his heartbreak, not sharing many details, though it wouldn't take a Sherlock to deduce that he's talking about Megha herself, Megha who's been out of circulation this past month or two, no booty calls, no nothing; despite herself, she's found herself siding with Himanshu on how flakey and dramatic these friends are. 'Kidults,' he'd called them.

'So this girl, she just doesn't care, what's up with that?' Rohit wraps up.

'A married woman, really?' Megha says, eyebrows shooting up. She's not sure if he's talking about her or someone else. 'You're such a slut!'

Rohit grins. He's baaaack. Sure, he had a few moments of self-flagellation about his violent streak, but has mainly blocked it out—it was just the one time, right, or twice, maybe. And that young girl hadn't even said much the next morning or at the next party. She'd just looked through him. *It's quite possible she doesn't remember anything,* he thinks, remembering the amount of drugs and alcohol in their system. *That's cool. There's no way I'm that fucking guy ...*

Back in the moment, one of his friends is droning on in full earnest, he registers. *Of course it's Farhan.*

It had felt so good though, that's the problem.

'It's good for you,' Farhan says. 'It's not when you're happy but when you're miserable that you discover what you're made of, man.'

'Slow claps,' Rohit starts off, 'seriously, bro. Too good.' He rolls his eyes. 'Where do you even pick up this BS?'

Farhan is offended as usual; the triggers are getting smaller and smaller. 'Man, I don't even know why I bother.'

'Why are you always so dull?' Rohit keeps going.

'Oh ho, guys, time out,' Megha tries to pacify them, but is pretty done being the adult.

'Just imagine, he was quoting Rumi, c'mon.'

Rohit's having none of it, his blood already up. '*Kya yaar, apna behenchod philosophy de raha hai,*' he says. 'You talk to me, buddy, when you've scored with more than one chick in your life.'

The 'buddy' grates on Farhan's ears.

'Idiot.'

'You're an asshole. A fucking asshole.'

'Wow, that's the best you can …'

'Nobody needs the self-help guru na,' Megha tells Farhan, pouting at him. 'C'mon.'

She turns to Rohit. 'Not that you're any better. Just wallowing about. It's time to close the old chapter. It's time to rebuild, baby.'

'Haan haan, it's that easy, no?' A cruel laugh. 'How's that working for you by the way, and that jackass you married?'

'Oi!' Farhan butts in as Megha's eyes pin-prick with tears.

'Oh, fuck this,' Megha says and makes to pick up her bag to leave.

'Okay, okay, I'm kidding, baba, I'm fucking around.' Rohit grabs her hand; he knows he's gone too far.

Farhan surreptitiously looks at his watch and then looks at Rohit, who nods.

'Aaah, it's okay, buddy, you carry on to work,' he tells Farhan. 'Not to worry. I got this.'

'Hey, you guys want to hang out after, kya?'

'Hmm … why not,' Rohit says.

'*Chalo dekhte hain*. You make a plan and let me know,' Farhan says, wondering if Maya will join them this time. Should he even message her?

Too soon, he decides.

As he leaves, he hears Rohit singing, 'Time to rebuild, baby, rebuild.' He's obviously trying to get Megha to laugh and loosen up. 'Aha!' Rohit yells out when he finally succeeds. 'It is alliiiiiive, ladies and gennulmens.'

Rohit is all smiles as Megha giggles. *And he is looking damn hot,* she realises as she peers at him over her sunnies. He's just flirting for the heck of it and she's totally lapping it up. Rohit, meanwhile, secretly pokes at his own hurt—discovering almost clinically that he can tease back the rage beating through his skull. *There, see, an ache like a bruise, and then a slight pounding. He's not thought of Megha for months.*

Okay, at least weeks.

'Are you seeing someone else?' he had asked Megha the last time and couldn't bear the answer, so laughed to cover up. 'I mean, apart from Himanshu.'

She had looked at him with an inscrutable expression. 'What?'

'You know what I'm asking. You're never here overnight, you never want to make plans.'

'Oh, don't be silly, darling,' she had cooed, and got up to sit in his lap.

'I was just wondering if you have some other lover hidden away,' he said, trying to navigate away from her, aware that he sounded like an immature schoolboy.

She laughed, mocking him. 'No no, no younger lover,' she said, running her fingers through his hair, instantly affecting his heartbeat. 'Now, do you want to talk some more, or ...' She had navigated his zipper while leaning over him. He went for it, of course, knowing somewhere in the back of his brain that she'd never answered the question and was unlikely to. A few hours later, she was gone and he was left wondering what to do next.

Anyway, how does it matter now? he thinks. *We've properly broken up. I should be happy there's no drama.*

Megha's inviting him to join her and Farhan that weekend—'We should at least go see Maya once, no?'

'What the fuck?' he says. 'Who has the time for this?' *They're so weird, so wired for all of this,* he realises. 'I thought we discussed cutting out the drama?'

No reaction.

'Whatever, you guys carry on,' he says. 'To each their own, as my dad says.'

~

It turns out that Maya *is* glad to have Farhan and even Megha come over, though she wouldn't have known it. She's called them to Chini Auntie's flat and lets them look around a little bit, not sure how much she wants to tell them.

Still, some company, she reckons. *And I did promise Gautam.*

'Guys, fiiiinally. I'm so so glad to see you,' she says, enveloping both of them in a tight hug. Her eyes prick with tears waiting to be shed.

'You too, doll,' Farhan says, breathing in her lovely fragrance. It always gets him, the jello-in-the-knees feeling, every time.

None of that for Megha, who is fuming. 'What the hell happened?' she asks. 'Did you know how worried we were?'

Maya shakes her head, not sure what to say. Megha usually takes a few minutes to cool off.

But maybe not this time.

'We went to the fucking cops, Maya. We thought you were …'

'Where have you been?' Farhan butts in, somewhat more restrained.

'I just needed some time,' she tries. Ironically, she is trying to be honest for once, but no one's buying it.

'What? The? Fuck?' Megha is glowering. 'If you need time, use your damn words. What is the point of seeing that effing therapist?'

So you did go to the therapist? Thanks for not telling me, Farhan wants to say.

Maya tries to tell them she's had an epiphany. She starts by explaining how she's always been alone and a bit depressed because of all the stuff that happened …

'We know, yaa, Maya, all that shit from your childhood, right?' Megha starts and then decides to course-correct. 'I know, we *know* it's been tough, but you have to get over it, man, we're pushing thirty!'

'She doesn't mean …' Farhan starts to say, 'But you really should have just told us you're not feeling okay.'

It's not that, Maya wants to say, *I've never been better!* But one look at their faces and she changes tack. *How much honesty is too much honesty between friends? I mean, will they understand any of it?*

She takes off on a tangent. 'I just needed some time to myself I mean …' she starts. 'It's not just that,' she chooses the easiest but worst path forward, compounding the mini disaster with her friends. Maybe the crux of the problem is that she's been 'lovesick', she tells them. 'After weeks of crying jags, of losing weight, losing interest in myself, in life … it was like the bad days again. This was the worst, absolute worst ever,' she goes on, 'and like the biggest reality check. When I realised what it was, I couldn't believe it. I was just lovesick, I think.'

She laughs, inviting them to make fun of her.

They're not laughing. Not Farhan, and definitely not Megha.

'What the fuck. Lovesick?' Megha says, clearly unimpressed with the diagnosis. 'And you put us through all this?'

'What are you, fourteen?' Farhan has been trying to be nicer but the hurt and exasperation come through. *All the jumping through hoops for her, it's so typical of Maya, come to think of it.*

'And I suppose this stupid friend of yours was also in on it ...'

'Which friend?' she starts to ask, but never mind. Maya is guileless. *There's no way she's deviating from her story.*

'Broken heart syndrome is a thing. A serious issue. And I totally had it. And that's all it was,' she tells them, missing the look that they exchange.

'You know, we were just chatting in the car, forget that new weirdo, BhaktofGod, I believe!' Megha exclaims. 'Your old boyfriend, Roy? He was bang on in the end, wasn't he, Farhan?'

'Excuse me?' Maya's shocked that they had dragged Roy into this.

'We checked with him too, you know,' Farhan ventures.

'He basically said that you're melodramatic and spoiled,' Megha adds.

Akira's eyes flash, but Maya's back in control. 'Roy! Yeah, I don't know, it's been a while. I mean, I doubt he'd even care,' Maya says. 'Not that he did even back then, I mean ...' she trails off.

Awkward pause as Mishraji comes in to ask what everyone wants. He speaks gingerly, looking a bit concerned, but they wave him out for the moment.

'I guess Roy knows you better than we do at some level,' Megha says, devastatingly. 'What happened in the end anyway?'

'Just ran out of energy, no? All just a tragic farce in the end,' Maya says.

'Wait, didn't you tell Megha what he asked you to do?' Farhan says, raking up the nastiness. He's clearly upset. For the life of him, he can't understand why she even went out with the guy. *He's* always known that Roy was all wrong for her. All wrong. If he were to admit it, he's gotten a savage pleasure in her coming to that painful realisation on her own. 'You didn't tell her?'

Maya freezes. She doesn't want to get into this at all.

'Excuse me, what is that about?' Megha is annoyed that she doesn't have all the details.

This is why I needed a timeout ...

All the love in the world. It would never be enough. Maya remembers saying that to Karthik. She really needs to give him a buzz.

Meanwhile, Farhan is looping Megha in, and she looks disgusted.

Maya is watching them but also feeling these overwhelming feelings all of a sudden. Her blood pressure is rising and stress levels spiking. But she can't bear to be alone today. Or at all. She has a sudden, desperate realisation of how untenable this isolation is, even for a minute longer. *We need people. We need something solid, non-dramatic, boring even, to hold us in check, to keep us anchored in the present.* She wonders how to pull that off. *Megha would know*, she intuits with a mean after-thought, *especially the boring bits.*

But as the thrum of the conversation fades into the background, she realises she's feeling even more uncomfortable. A migraine is starting up.

Maya presses a glass of cold water to her head.

It's only a few minutes later, she's sure, that she notices the silence.

…

'Jesus. Some hostess I am, guys, tell me what do you want to have? Coffee? Tea? Diet Coke? Something stronger?'

Why are they staring at me like this? She tries not to panic.

'Mishraji,' she shouts towards the kitchen and then walks over when he doesn't reply. *'Teen coffee de dena. Chini aur doodh alag se*, please.'

She turns back.

There's a sharp intake of breath.

Wait, did I say something? Did I miss something?

Her friends are looking askance.

'So what, guys. I mean, what's going on?'

'Um…'

As Maya comes back into the living room, she notices a big pile of peppermints in the main bowl, wrappers overflowing. She grabs it and walks back to the kitchen.

'Oh, just give me a second,' she says, wanting and willing them to pretend that they didn't notice that—whatever 'that' was.

Did I say something? Did I lose time again?

...

'What was that? What is going on?' That's Megha to Farhan.

'God only knows.' Farhan tries to be reassuring, but this time he's a bit weirded out. 'We should think about getting her some serious help.'

Megha groans. 'What else is new?'

We all have problems, Megha thinks, *and this isn't the time to get into them.* Though it would've been nice if Himanshu had bothered to show some support. Instead, by way of comfort, her husband and the father of her child had said, 'She's just a bored rich kid. Don't worry, she'll be back before you know it.'

'And what's even more annoying is that he was right as usual,' she says to Farhan, adding the kicker. 'By the way, do you think she thinks about you as much as you lot think about her?' Himanshu had asked her last night.

That had cut. Deep. *Right again.*

'There's nothing more we can do, Farhan. I'm exhausted. She's already got a therapist. She's clearly got other people in her life. Like, what's the deal with that BhaktGod thing?' Megha asks, sort of to hold up a mirror but also to say she's reached her limit. She's exhausted.

'But does she? Do they really care about her?' Farhan asks. 'And have we been paying enough attention to the cries for help?'

He did not just say that, Megha thinks. 'Excuse me?'

'Shouldn't we have tried harder to get her help?'

Now that they're thinking about it, Maya hasn't been herself for more than a few months. She's been a bit low energy, a bit secretive, sort of like when she discovered that faith leader. Megha had given her a wide berth after Maya begged off the last two of their regular coffee catchups. *You can't force someone to hang out with you*, she had told herself, wishing for once that she had normal, stable friends like most people their age seemed to. *It's probably time to make friends with other parents*.

'She's just messed up, na?'

Farhan nods.

'Hey Maya,' they both call out together.

She walks in as if nothing has been going on, quickly realising from their expressions that they aren't buying it. She aims for humour, or at least a lighter tone, which falls flat.

'Well, I really hope you're not still mad at me. Apparently, it's been a rough phase for everyone, Mercury is in retrograde or some such thing, I bet,' she says.

A stony silence.

She wades on. 'I mean, jokes apart, I do think it's taken me a long time to get sorted in the head. I was just jumping from thing to thing, experience to experience. The ashram and a spiritual quest but also the Roy chapter ... I mean, I just needed some time ...'

'Yes, this broken heart syndrome thing.' Farhan is trying, you have to give him that.

'I'm so sorry it felt so ... dramatic. There's been a lot ...' Maya wants to say more but stops abruptly before she shares too much. She can't say more about what's happening right this minute (not till she speaks to Karthik), but she can tell them something, anything to keep them around.

'I'm just saying, it's never good to be with someone who always puts you down or humiliates you,' she says. She senses the hostility and tries to get more real. 'Or your friends, for that matter.'

'That's all true, but how does that matter now,' Megha asks. She rolls her eyes again. *Kahaan phas gaye,* she wonders. 'Not everything is so dramatic, Maya. You need to learn to be a little considerate.'

Maya is wounded by the tone.

'Oh really? You don't think?' She continues after a small pause, 'You'd be surprised. Not just the love stuff, but every single thing, my *dear* friend, every single thing is filled with drama.'

The dear is so sarcastic, so the opposite of what it signifies, that it might as well have been an out-and-out four-letter word.

'You don't know what it's like. And it's not just a small thing—the old stuff. It's not just that. It's also the new stuff. It's knowing that there's no one in your corner, no one who can help. That even the ground beneath your feet is insubstantial.

'We ourselves are so insubstantial. It's ridiculous. I know I'm supposed to be over all that. I know that you think it's all drama. But it's baggage, it's suffocating, it's been choking me and sometimes I need … I need it all to stop.'

Farhan is transfixed, but Megha is not as indulgent.

'That's fine, sure. That's what you are dealing with. But take a second. You didn't tell us that. You cut off completely. You scared the shit out of us. We went to the fucking police. The least you can do now is bloody apologise for all the shit you put us through,' Megha says, now really pissed off.

'And by the way, you think you only have these randos in your life, these random relationships? Random drama? What about the two of us here, sitting with you? We're always around, listening to your shit, making excuses for you. What about that?'

'Sorry …' Maya tries. 'I'm really sorry.' She bursts into tears.

'No one in your corner? Are you serious?' Farhan for once isn't falling for this, his heart catching up to what his brain already knows.

'And what is this about randos and relationships? Hmph,' he snorts. 'I should have known. That guy, online, he's your new … what, your new friend? From …'

'The ashram,' Maya says quietly.

'Unbelievable.'

No one knows what to say.

Farhan is properly miserable now. He puts his head in his hands.

Megha starts, trying but failing to sound less angry, 'No one can *really* help anyone at the end of the day. It just doesn't work that way, and it's fine if you didn't want to tell us anything, but we went to the damn cops, Maya.'

A silence falls over all of them.

'I need another refill.' Maya goes into the kitchen and walks back to an intervention.

'Listen, I'm leaving you the number of a really good guy. He comes highly recommended. I really think you should talk to him,' Megha is saying, looking very uncomfortable. She and Farhan have obviously conferred. They look like they're preparing to leave.

'For whom? Me?' Maya is surprised. Even more so by Farhan's look of concern. *Are those tears in his eyes?*

'Shit, c'mon guys, don't go just yet. I'm really really sorry,' Maya says, and now she looks like she's going to cry again.

Farhan gets up, walks to the balcony to light a cigarette and stare at some of the urban chaos on display.

'Maya, we can't keep watching you do this kind of thing. We're just enabling you,' Megha says. 'You know you need help. And we can't just stick around watching you flame out. It's got consequences for us too, you know.'

'I am seeing someone, I promise I'm getting help.' Maya tells a half-truth, but really does want them to stay, all of a sudden.

No dice this time.

Mishraji brings in the coffee quietly, as always keeping his thoughts about Babyji, her friends and their shouting, angry tempers to himself. Only his wife Meena sees how world-weary he's become these days; they both talk about the once-upon-a-time adorable infants they cared for and try and ignore the hash they're making of their adult lives, despite having so much.

'They had such a cracked beginning to their family,' Meena tells him. 'The foundation is only kharab. The cracks keep spreading underneath.'

She tries to explain it to him every so often, but he just sighs and rolls over, happy his daughter is so much more settled. She's getting her promotion soon and will let them arrange her marriage next year. At this rate, he'll be able to retire soon, after all.

14

The Pahaari: Back in Time

[1970s–close to Present Day]

Before she was the Pahaari, Usha was already a bit of an enigma, stunning and inscrutable. Back in the day, she was used to getting her own way with pretty much everyone, except for her immediate family. It was hard not to take to her, to fall headlong into pledging undying love.

'She set my heart afire,' her first—or was it second—boyfriend said, a man who proceeded to propose to her every day for the better part of a year.

An up-and-coming police officer said quite simply that she was 'a goddess'. Sadly, he was married to her neighbour, which made things complicated … But then easier, as it turned out.

And yet none of it helped.

Looking back, she knew there were many things wrong with her. She had been told as much from the time she was about ten years old. One was her *thuthuthu* beauty—*nazar na lag jaye* was literally the first thing she could remember her own mother saying, to ward off the evil eye.

Her sister had seen some family puja being done and laughed and said she was a 'manglik' and would bring everyone bad luck. And then promptly started bawling, causing their mother to come in and give Usha a tight one across the face for troubling poor little Chini. The aunts and cousins were all a bit awkward and conversations tended to come to a standstill around her. Even as a pre-teen. And then as a teenager, while she was trying to figure out what she would do with her life.

'Anything you want,' her father told her, and her mother agreed and added, 'But first, think about doing the ceremony with the tree, no, just for the old-timers' sake.'

Usha withdrew. She noticed soon enough that the boys, the men, were much nicer to her. Even among her own cousins, who hardly gave Chini a second glance and told her to ignore her little sister's nastiness and pettiness. 'She's not as good as you,' they'd say and try to 'win her favour', as they used to say back in the day. They wanted her to come out every day, to watch them play anything and everything—cricket, football, carrom.

She had a few friends by the time she was a young adult. And still she felt that something was missing.

When she got into Delhi University without mishap, her mother breathed a huge sigh of relief. Must be thanks to all the pujas, all the vigils, all the temple pandits paid, all that hard work. *Who knew what was in the stars though?*

She tied a thread to her daughter's wrist as she slept, admiring her beauty but worrying for her future, for their future. *In the morning, I will definitely bring up the tree ceremony again, it's for the best.* Usha didn't get to know directly but heard from one of her cousin admirers that her mother was planning a massive puja at the house in a few months, to time with Usha's eighteenth birthday. The gods would be propitiated, the holy men would be called, a marriage might be arranged.

And Usha would become the laughing stock of the neighbourhood.

She cried hot, bitter tears and locked herself into the cupboard to think about what to do. She knew she had to run away, but how? Where? Hard to manage without a chaperone and without money. *I can't bear to just put up with it, though; how can they do this to me? Without even letting me know?* It was like her friend who had found out that wedding cards were being distributed in her home state behind her back while she swotted for her MA exams.

A girl's lot is bullshit, Usha felt. And yet, you looked abroad and realised this wasn't the case everywhere. Flower power, trippy dippy hippy love was the flavour of the times and people were having the time of their lives. Just not here in this pokey city.

It just isn't fair.

Usha was getting fairly down in the dumps, but luckily for her, less so for her mother, the fates conspired to send her Mark.

He'd heard of the legendary beauty of North Campus, who hadn't those days! But he had decided to be impervious. He was, after all, just back from the vaunted Abroad, having studied at a prestigious medical school, and was all set to prove himself. Then, a friend of his had asked him around to North Campus and one thing led to another.

It took the length and duration of one cup—or more precisely half a cup—of coffee at the Coffee House (through which time his heart was practically hammering onto the table) for him to fall hopelessly in love. He had proposed a second cup, then a third; Usha was used to this sort of attention and paid it no mind until he gathered his wits and started to talk about his love for medicine and his plans for the future. He painted a right pretty picture to go alongside and there was space for her, she could tell, way better than marrying a tree and being humiliated by her own kith and kin.

Why not elope?

Mark was handsome and charming and clearly adored her. She was forthright enough to make him understand she would be his, but not on that date. It took a little bit of wooing, Mark would remember fondly, a lot of laughter and blushing, and that iridescent beauty, which would last her an entire lifetime, if not more.

They got married in secret, a court marriage, each with a witness sworn to discretion, at least until Usha had time to get her things from her house. She moved into his bachelor pad (they decided against his family home, given her temperament) and he got down to the business of building his own practice while consulting at a major hospital in the city.

It may have been a shock to her parents when she finally told them, but Usha carried on as usual, ignoring the family histrionics, noting that only her fat younger sister Chini was delighted that she'd left the house. She finished her degree and continued to do her thing, now less apprehensive about any supposed humiliation. Look at her suitor number one, her secret husband, who was intent on working his way further into her heart. As she eased into herself, she got more accustomed to the wild compliments and behaviour. Not everyone knew she was married and 'off limits', as she thought of it for a while.

But at some point, things began to spiral. She was getting all that unvarnished adoration and adulation and didn't know what to do with it. She had an estranged family and didn't know how to deal with that either, and poor Mark was way too busy to listen to her cribbing every day.

Her mother cried secret tears but was unable to bridge the yawning gap that had sprung up between them. Usha's father was allowed to visit her on the condition that he'd never bring the other two. He stopped telling them when he'd seen her; it seemed kinder that way. Poor man never knew what it was to pick a side, but then again, how could he choose?

He'd been one of the first to acknowledge that his wife and younger daughter had gone overboard with their secret confabulations and pilgrimages and pujas and pujaris. 'Good for you only, no?' he said to his wife. 'She's married a Christian. That mumbo jumbo won't affect him.'

No need for tree ceremonies, after all.

At the same time, Usha was enjoying her liberty and everything that went with it. 'To be young and in love, nothing beats that,' she said, plagiarising some line from some book, as she put it. No reaction apart from a wan smile from Mark, who was looking quite worn out these days. 'The world is just nicer when you're beautiful,' Usha had told this new husband of hers once. 'Beauty ... it's the gift that keeps giving.'

Mark didn't know what to say to that but continued to indulge her, burying any hint of a doubt deep down. He had to spend a couple of years really slogging it out, he had told her, and while he worried about her patchy attention span and lack of interest in both career and family planning, he preferred to stick his head in the sand. In fact, both turned a blind eye to their own internal contradictions, trying to will a happy family into being. She didn't need to work after all, Mark came from money, and he was more than happy to let her be. As long as he had her, he felt surprisingly secure, at least at first.

It was a few years of Usha doing her own thing, making a go of this domestic bliss, and then the travel bug got her, or was it the combination of travel and spirituality? She up and went to the hills and managed to find her own version of worship, she told him. 'There's peace in the hills.'

He was a bit surprised but remembered her upbringing and all those godmen about. 'As long as you are safe,' he said, and she said she most definitely was. She started going seasonally and would always bring such a blast of sunshine with her that he didn't worry too much about it. *Women need to have their own outlets,* he thought to himself. He hardly had enough time to worry about her not being around. His very capable Man Friday looked after all the details and kept things running smoothly.

Secretly, Mark wondered how they would build a life together this way. He didn't have that much free time and she showed little inclination to do anything meaningful together, but he knew better than to say anything. *Why rock the boat?* Usha had her moods certainly, and Mark ensured that he was very, very calm when she began acting strangely, but it was when she was quiet or more withdrawn than normal that he worried. It didn't help matters much, but he suggested they start socialising again, perhaps together? She had enough friends, she said, including their neighbours—a police officer and his wife, it seemed.

Mark didn't say much, but there was that worry again, worming its way to the surface.

...

And then, one day, the big news. Unfortunately, there was a huge dip in her spirits around the time he realised that she was pregnant. She visualised her brain rearranging itself into mush. Hormones aflush, she felt unable to hold a thought in her head for more than a few minutes at a time. The pregnancy also changed the frequency, or rather the tenor of attention that she got. *But it's even more than that, something insidious*, she felt. The throwing up brought out the worst in her.

'I hate this demon baby!' she yelled at Mark once, viciously pleased to see his face turn white. *This is a banshee, surely, who had replaced his beautiful wife?* He was really not sure what to do apart from taking her to the best gynae for advice (this was the pre-shrink era).

Mark arranged massages, he promised her a live-in nanny, an ayah to do all the heavy lifting. All that money could buy, he was willing and happy to throw at her. And still he hit a wall. There was nothing, no connect.

'You don't know what I'm going through,' she said accusingly.

He could only agree.

'This is your fault,' she added, which destroyed him. (It was also a little unfair, given her raging affair with the police officer next door, but he couldn't have known that at the time.)

What else can I give her, Mark wondered. *How to make her happy?* He concluded that whatever it was, he needed more resources, and threw himself into work (not that he had ever really let off). He worked himself up to a feverish pitch, a vague notion in his head that if he got more money and maybe a stint overseas, she might be happy with the change of scene.

That wasn't quite what she had in mind. She ruled out his return to London. Not with her, at any rate, she said.

But maybe he had planted a kernel of an idea.

'I need a breath of fresh air,' she told her bewildered husband a few days later, and hit the hills again, sans baggage.

~

There was no one in particular she was looking for, but she'd had a premonition that she would meet her destiny on one of those winding roads. It was just her luck that she met *that* chap, the tantric (or Crank, as we know him). On his own trip, that one. He was quite cantankerous those days, definitely not Zen and definitely upset to see this woman, probably sent there to distract him from his work.

'What do you want?' he snapped when she refused to go away an hour into his meditation.

'Peace of mind,' she said and only looked a little perturbed to hear laughter in response.

He was nothing like his friend, the Rishi, who saw past the curtain and had read all the canons, all the ancient texts and could talk you through the Sanskrit, the Latin, even the Aramaic, legend had it. Few could keep up, but most could appreciate the hint of the great grace of the universe that he held in his laughter, a booming laugh that enveloped all.

No, it was not Usha's luck to meet the Rishi. Not yet, at any rate.

Later, the Rishi would come to feel that perhaps her great beauty led others astray—so many beings thus endowed draw towards them forces of which they know nothing, forces of destruction they can't hope to control. *But isn't that another version of victim blaming?* his young disciple Gautam would wonder.

Ah, but Usha never was a victim. She herself would have scoffed at the thought.

No good thing comes of great beauty, the Rishi theorised, leaving Gautam faintly discomfited for one of the few times in their relationship. But then he looked at Maya and wondered: *Do the forces of destruction hurtle through those with great beauty, enveloping them in a trail of devastation? A twisted tribute of sorts?* He shook off the thought as barely disguised victim blaming. *It's just luck of the draw, surely.*

Meanwhile, Usha, who was desperately trying to get out of the 'normalcy' so many crave, started journeying inward more and more. Feeling lost and trapped and boxed in, she found she just might be able to do her own thing. She started visiting the Crank, this supposed Guru with gout, a bad temper, and a proclivity for the tantric arts. Perpetually losing track of the ways of the universe and feeling the weight of his years, he indulged the side of his personality that he shouldn't have and started to enjoy using his power to manipulate this beautiful woman.

To his credit, he did try once to tell her that none of it would last. 'None of this,' he said, gesturing at her, and meaning all of it, the good looks, the tough times, the pregnancy ... 'None of this will last,' he repeated. 'Not even the good weather.'

He couldn't or wouldn't impress upon her the importance of that transience. Maybe he didn't try hard enough. *Why send her away, after all?* She posed a delectable challenge and wasn't confusing the monastic life with the spiritual. 'Things should be felt in the moment,' she would reply. 'If we're not feeling them, we can't pretend.'

He had started off quietly but let himself go. *Why not?* he thought. Even though he knew that things are sometimes meant to go to shit for a while, that some things shouldn't be meddled with. He wasn't even supposed to be over women for that matter, and who wouldn't enjoy having such an alluring companion?

'Okay, let me see how fast you learn,' he told her, throwing down the gauntlet and revelling in the new-found respect.

It's not that he taught her nothing. He showed her how to centre herself, how to chant into nothingness, how to slow down time. She learned how to un-crease her brow, finding some semblance of harmony again.

This is it, she thought one transcendental morning, *this is what I'm meant to do.*

He showed her how to channel the energy of the universe and promised to show her how to awaken her seventh or Sahaswara chakra when she was ready. (He thought that for this he would rope in his friend, the Rishi. It was a delicate business.) And indeed, the Rishi (or the Kind One, as she dubbed him), showed her how to meditate ever deeper into stillness, how to remove the 'I' and how to see the universal, how to feel it.

She was awestruck for the first time in years, feeling a life force bubbling in her veins. 'It was a joyous affirmation,' she gushed to Mark, who wasn't entirely sure what she was talking about but was delighted to see her recharged.

The Crank taught her a few mantras, challenging her to increase her powers of concentration, and was pleased with her progress, he indicated after some time.

She wasn't aware of how much time had passed until one day she looked down and saw her belly fully taut. The baby had suspiciously started kicking less and less and in so doing had also stopped troubling her mother, who could no longer hear the echo of the words she had used earlier.

A faint impression made by the 'demon baby' resonated in the universe though, because alas, the words we utter all have an impact somewhere. But at least Usha was beyond that now. Or so she thought.

Reluctantly, she made plans to leave her new idyllic (albeit spartan) home.

The Crank was not sure she would come back to him, but he did ask her to, telling her that it was worth renouncing whatever was troubling her, and making a strong case for personal enlightenment. As if he needed to, with Usha. (He may have pretended later that he didn't mean she should abandon the child she was about to give birth to, but that was the message that had landed.)

Meanwhile, the Rishi knew that something was going on with the Crank, his one-time friend, and began his own arduous journey to try and bring him back into the fold. He could sense some darkness, but whether that came from, or through, the Crank himself or Usha, he told Gautam later, he couldn't be sure.

Later he said, 'You had to credit her single-minded focus to live in the moment.' Her obsession gave her amazing energy and certainly helped her to stay young, that much Gautam gleaned.

'Yes, with Usha it was almost pre-ordained,' the Rishi said. 'Even the Fates conspired to give her what she wanted. We'll see, in the long run, what she deserves.'

~

It's true that she learned more than she let on. Usha did manage to arrest Time. Long hair, clear skin and luminous eyes, she doesn't look a day older than forty-five, even today. She's also finally found her own measure, in sync with something older than time. But that was in a space she had carved out for herself.

Back in the city, back in the day, it was a different story. What was it, thirty years ago, finding her way back to the city, she had sought out her still-besotted husband Mark and told him it was time. She had banished him from the hospital after he dropped her there, saying that on no account did she want him with her in labour, but he had disobeyed her this once. He had fainted once, which the nurses had been too polite to tell Usha, who was anyway suffering some sort of post-partum depression.

Her calm gone with the change of landscape, Usha was convinced the second baby had tried to kill her, ripping her vaginal walls on the way out.

'I told you, demon babies,' she said.

Again, that echo.

Babies? Mark had wondered even then, but presumed it was a stress-related outburst and then asked what next, hoping and willing her to come home.

She shook her head. 'We're not doing this.'

If there ever was a moment for him to hold his ground as the father (as far as he knew), it would have been then. But Mark was petrified that the love of his life, his goddess, was going to leave him again, this time for good. *That would be unbearable,* he thought, the poor chap. He aimed to keep the peace and readjusted his expectations. He didn't need to know what she didn't want him to know.

Nothing would ever be the same again.

'This giving birth has got to be the ultimate deal with the devil,' Usha said. 'No one checks the fine print beforehand. But what is it but a biologically driven play at immortality?'

She eyed her infant daughter with a cold, calculating eye.

The other baby, well, the procedures were simple enough given a more-than-willing family and a wad of cash to the staff for their discretion, and their respect that the father would be a police officer.

She thought of leaving for the hills after dispatching her infant, through Mishraji, to the girl's aunt or even the father, with a warning via letter, dire and bold. She would let them/him know that she would decidedly not be around for the rearing and raising, that she was taking sanyaas.

Something stopped her then, though the idea had been seeded and lay in wait for a few years.

At that point, some sort of guilt tugged her towards the baby. 'You don't have to see all of my fight with the darkness,' she said and tried to show some of the patience, the cooing, the feeding, the love that was supposed to be coming to her naturally. It was tough. She was not sure what was wrong with her. *Maybe it was her stars.*

Mark got her to talk to the paediatrician, who tried to explain that some negative feelings were normal. 'Most mothers outgrow it, Usha, just get through these months. You have nothing to worry about.'

Understatement of the century.

'Fine, fine,' she said. But she'd better not forget to feed the baby again. Sometimes she just stopped watching her, it was so boring. But Mark said that was only natural. The ayah he hired could take care of the day-to-day stuff.

She could never be Zen like this here in the city, Usha realised, not at home. But she might as well be present and remember to feed her child while she was around.

~

It wasn't as if Mark hadn't been bracing for the worst. But he didn't know what else to do. The first four to six months had seemed okay, but by the end of the first year there had been a litany of complaints from his beloved which would have tried the patience of anyone less obsessed. He wasn't sure how they'd manage, but Usha took a break every so often.

It clearly wasn't enough.

By year two, it was a torment for both of them.

'Ugh. She's trying to take over my life.'

'She's a little monster.'

'What the hell do you all want from me?!'

Mark was worried enough to consult with a colleague, who said it was quite normal for new mothers to feel some sort of depression. That didn't help either of them. There was some cutting-edge medication available apparently, if they wanted to try.

They carried on, papering over the cracks. Who knew exactly how the next few years passed—it was a blur all around. The ayah was paid handsomely. Usha would take her breaks and come back recharged and then slowly lose everything, her energy, the luminosity. Every single time.

If only he'd been paying closer attention, he would have seen what was coming, he would think later. *If only.*

It took a few years for her to decide that she had done all that was humanly possible.

Usha had been thinking biliously of her sister, who was beloved only of children who didn't know any better. All her arcane rituals, steeping herself in mythology and superstition. Her sister, who could never compete with her in looks or talent, so made do with being as nice as was humanly possible. To everyone else, that is. And it was all fake, Usha knew, boy did she know, given what her sister used to try to do when they were kids.

But it's just as well, she figured. *Who better to take over the auntie duties?*

'Right, that's it,' she said one day and asked Mark to drive her to her sister's house after taking the baby from the ayah.

She left *him* in the car outside. The windows down, he heard a lot of yelling, some name-calling, even crying, and then an ominous silence.

She stomped out, not entirely victorious. 'So that's settled then.'

'Is it?'

'Mia will *not* be going there.'

If he was surprised, he didn't show it.

'For now, she goes to Lakshman and Neeti's. Chini may visit, and of course, you can go see her whenever you want. Will you drop me to the bus station tomorrow?'

'Lakshman, the cop's family?' Mark asked, unable to meet her eye.

Maybe he doesn't want to know, she thought, and spared him.

If he was confused, he didn't show it. And that was that.

She left as soon as she could, coming back once a month or every two months, and then ever more sporadically. Mark told himself he was fine as long as she had space for him in her life *once in a while.* She promised him she would make time for him and that he could also visit her in the hills, that she was building a small, independent house there. It was his money, and he would never begrudge her anything she wanted, in any case.

There was probably no one more ill-suited to Usha. But there couldn't be anyone who loved her more either. Mark would never judge her for leaving. To repay that favour, she dropped in on him every so often and even let him come see her sometimes.

Until, one day, she stopped. And now it's been almost, what, twenty years?

15

Usha, Lost and Found

[January 2024]

'Cross the road to avoid the crazy woman,' Usha says. 'I'm the crazy woman I'm trying to avoid.'

Her thoughts are telegraphed far and wide for those who can hear them, belying her status as spiritually awakened. In the hills, they were mostly unquestioning—not only did she wear the robes of a brahmachari, she was also known to keep her own counsel.

She hadn't spoken much, not for the nine years of recent collective memory. But even in the silence her thoughts consumed her. She had made a strange decision, one she could always justify to herself, but it was in the Monuments of Silence, as she called them, that she felt something had devoured her inside out. And there was no one left to ask for help. The Crank was worse than useless. He had fallen out with her anyway, claiming she had failed him or he had failed her, she couldn't remember which.

The Kind One had moved on a few years ago. He had been at pains to announce her status as an enlightened one first. But then, even then, there had been murmurs. If Usha ever heard the vile gossip, she ignored it. Shorn of all accessories and accoutrements, she was always luminous. Still confused, those days, but still possessed of that enchanting beauty. It was possible then, as the rumours had it, that the Rishi had been taken in—he wouldn't be the first one. After all, to look upon her was to understand the grace of the universe. But then, he was gone and she spoke so little, it was impossible to verify the gossip one way or the other. She had carried on with her practice, impervious.

~

As the years passed, the seasons marked only by the shedding of the deodar's sharp needles—the needles and cones were collected by the younger monks—Usha had stayed on, resolute and unmoved by all the changes around her. The idle comments gradually died down and a not-quite-urban legend grew around her Silence (always spoken of in tones of reverence).

She had attained a remarkable level of balance in her decades outside the city, growing adept in the art of seeing, intuiting the Truth, even healing some parts of her own soul. She finally understood that we were all part of the same web; what pricks you will come back to make me bleed.

It's the thought of blood that gets her head thrumming again.

'Maybe it's like a phantom limb,' a young monk said to her before she returned to the city. 'It's not really there, whatever ghost you're chasing.' He had been distracted by her beauty and wanted to make things right for her—and that had almost soothed her spirit. Like it always had in the past. Almost always, anyway.

Life in this city is not for everyone, though. She had made a terrible choice and it sheared her, she now feels when she lets herself remember. She needs to make amends. It's time. This much she knows. She makes a few trips to Delhi but loses sight of her mission. She's hidden a lot of her trauma from her own self, the decades in between blurring the lines for her, and even today her mind is a shell, even as she stands here at the corner of the street this mid-summer day. She has been staking out a house that seems so familiar that she sees it in her dreams. There's a fog. She has lost something essential, someone, she knows it, but she doesn't quite know when and how it happened.

This person was a piece of her? How to get it back? She scours the news and follows different leads, knowing that at the end of her quest is some sort of rainbow. *Could it be?* She loses track of time but follows the news around her with hyper-alertness.

The story of a little boy who drowns at school breaks her heart. They fished him out much too late. The schoolteachers and staff who found him didn't want to jump in because the water seemed more like industrial sludge. A student—who will go on to win a bravery award—did, but by then it was too late. The newspapers have managed a photo of a ball floating in the water tank. The five-year-old is dead. She starts keening. There is a public mourning, and she turns up there. People presume she is a grief-stricken parent, that she herself must have been recently bereaved, this veiled lady who is in white, head to toe.

There's a sixteen-year-old she read about a year ago, on her last trip. She'd OD'd on her iron pills, her liver giving up on her after she took a friend up on an idiotic dare. Liver failure. Usha had tried to find out when the last rites would be held. She feels for them all, those gone too soon, those who are missing. She'd gone back to the hills and come back today, one last time. The ravages of time had done their bit years ago, the spiritual practice cooling off the tempest in her blood. Haunted by a choice she may or may not have consciously made ... Is it possible in the twenty-first century to trade your soul? And that, too, for something as fleeting as time?

What have I done? she thought, giving herself a new mission, almost desperate for a distraction, but wondering if this might take her further along on her impossible journey to the truth. There was a baby somewhere who had just been abandoned, not far from where he was born on the railway tracks. The news crews heralded him as a miracle baby, to have survived such an ordeal. A teflon baby he must have been, because he hadn't cried when his fourteen-year-old mother finally left him for the second time, wrapped in a shawl at the door of a local kirana shop. He hadn't cried because he'd known she hadn't had any other options, the way she looked at him and wailed, the way she tried to be strong, at least for a few days as she fed him, her under-nourished frame barely able to support him, her hands smaller than his head, almost as delicate.

The girl had been pushed to breaking point. Although the press managed to track her down and get her a few square meals a day, while reuniting her with her baby, that phase didn't last long. The news cycle always moves on. The attention had quickly led to shady, oily men in ill-fitting suits promising sums of money as they patted her on the head (all the while looking down her blouse and thinking, *Well, why not? Especially if we are going to do good*). The girl hadn't had the internal reserve, she couldn't 'dig down any deeper', she wasn't a superhero. She was, quite frankly, starving. Her story didn't make more than a couple of lines past the 'miracle baby' headline before the press moved on. Even the international press, who should have known better.

Worse than that was what the attention got her, worse than the oily politicos, the bastards who had been chasing her from the City of Joy in the first place. Trafficking. The victims of trafficking don't know the terminology; they know their lives are barely worth living. They know they must survive; they know the world doesn't care for them despite the hundreds of hours of footage and award-winning documentaries, despite the outrage and the beating of chests. They are invisible, by and large.

Not this baby, though; he refused.

Usha was obsessed with the story, following it online, on TV, in the newspaper, reading every piece of print, every line of text, even though they were all spouting from the same template, even though the news was awfully limited in the details, even though the story was 'over' for the mainstream media within days. A follow-up one week later, and then it was on to the next big thing. The internet had come to Usha's rescue, keeping the images alive.

She couldn't quite remember how she'd 'lost' what she'd lost, but the pull of this baby had been too much. She'd booked the first ticket she could get to the city mentioned in the news reports, not sure what she'd do when she got there. Years of meditation and solitude, of learning the deeper ways of the universe paid off. She found she was able to go with the flow. She made her way to a kirana shop, followed the shopkeeper's directions to an orphanage, making some sort of plan along the way.

But the baby was gone.

'Arre, you should be happy, sister,' the nurse told the strangely beautiful but haunted-looking woman. 'He has found a good home.'

'Did you know the mother?' the nurse added, curious.

Usha didn't say anything. It's hard to know what she would have done if things had gone another way. She just sat down, the force of what she'd lost hitting home all of a sudden. Everything was connected, like a giant patchwork quilt of loss.

~

She had slowly made her way back to Delhi and started to weave together the strands of her old life like a fraying rope to hold for succour, following it knot by knot to a distant place where she recognised no one.

This city hides so many ghastly secrets, she thinks now. *The roads snake out like dried up veins,* she imagines, a grim picture she's unable to shake, the city having grown exponentially, like a dark beast devouring everything in its path. It's always driven her round the bend.

And it's so loud, with no scope of shelter.

The fissures in her core were spreading, something she had noticed only just recently.

And then, it all comes back to her.

She wails.

There is one space that calls out to her, nothing much to look at, but she lurks about the market for a few days, getting the feel of the place. It's a house that connects them all in such a fundamental fashion; it has its own personality and its own pull for each of them—Maya-then-Mia, Lakshman and Usha, as much as Mark. Especially Mark. Even after all that she'd put him through.

She thinks back to how he'd quietly sat up with her at night, comforting her through the howling, how he'd dropped the work pressures at the door to listen to her acting out, how he'd empathised with her on the grey days when nothing made an impression. He'd been there when she felt that everything was monochrome, when she refused to smile at anyone, the phase when she refused to leave the house, or greet anyone, or interact in any way beyond the virtual. He'd been there through the many phases when she stopped sleeping with him. The phase when she stopped taking a shower and stopped eating.

He'd always been there for her, encouraging, cajoling, calling in the experts when she needed help. When her days became more of the same—grey in and out, through the flashes of energy when she met people (who he had inveigled into coming over, people he remained indebted to), the days she turned into a pallid version of herself, listening and smiling sometimes when she could be bothered to make the effort but tuning into some other frequency he couldn't make head or tail of.

He had done everything he could to remind her that life was worth living, that he was worth loving. She tried to shake it off one day in the middle, tried to get moving, eat proper meals, tried to come out from behind the gossamer-like curtain of unreality. She found her movements slower, as if she was underwater.

It didn't take. She was a changed woman by then, though she and Mark didn't know the half of it. Inside, she was watching, watching the beastie grow, it fed off the darkness and every day it grew bigger and bigger.

I have made a huge mistake, she wanted to scream and shout, stomp her feet and have someone fix it, like in the old days. *I made the wrong deal, promised the wrong kind of payment.* But there was a strict no-returns policy. So she kept feeding the black hole in herself secretly, appalled but fascinated as she watched it eating her alive, inside out.

Today, Usha looks around, sadder, quieter, well-aware that the dark feeds off the light, and vice versa if you're lucky.

Her world's been shattered between two poles, prisms of light sometimes reflecting back to her who she had been, who she almost was, who she couldn't quite bring herself to be. She was a shadow of that old Usha now, her personality subsumed within another's. Or was it the other way around? She had her memories to rifle through, true, but now she knew it was all a cosmic farce. If only she'd known then.

'You're beauteous, glamorous, gorgeous, you goddess,' they used to tell her and she would soak it all up, revel in the attention. The world is so nice to the beautiful and young.

'So stunning and you don't even know it,' they used to coo at her, content to look, and touch if possible, but if not, just to look, to have some of that shine spill over onto them. She'd drunk it all in. She'd known it was a gift from the universe and she had traipsed through life, drunk on that power.

But then she'd started having those moments when she heard melancholy music in her own head, a dirge. She found it difficult to look people in the eye anymore. She yearned to be invisible, to get away from the attention.

'Be careful what you wish for,' her silly sister used to say while listing out all the things that could go wrong.

Her sister, who had insisted on doing a puja to purify the house after Usha gave birth, a puja to ward off the evil eye, a puja to purify Usha after Mark left on a two-month trip, a puja to purify everything when Usha visited after a long time. (*Or was it to curse me, you never know with sisters,* Usha had thought once upon a time, before her stint in the hills where almost everything was removed, including the vestiges of her ego.)

Her sister, who always knew what to say to everyone except Usha, having heard their relatives talking early on about this Manglik business.

And wasn't Chi right, actually? Everything Usha touched turned to dust, her own happiness included. Men, love, laughter, it all died so suddenly, the demons coming to the fore, not even bothering to cloak their intentions—they took Usha down after ripping apart the fabric of her life, pulling out her very lifeblood, entrails and all.

And then Usha started to think, *But wasn't Chi wrong, actually? I managed to give birth, after all.* Damned if her sister hadn't shown her surprise that the babies had survived, before changing her face right back to normal.

'Nothing wrong with being a Manglik,' their father had said. 'There's no such thing, if you think logically.'

But their mother had begged to differ. 'And please don't talk about this in public,' she'd insisted, instantly disregarded, of course, by Chini.

Before Usha had even turned thirteen, there were the family pandits hemming and hawing and there were rings with multi-coloured stones, rumours of a tree ceremony that could fix things. There were the odd looks from relatives, the doting on Chini, the quietened tones when she walked into a room. She had hated it all so much, she inhabited that hate and could never look upon her family the same way, unable to reconcile their attitudes with what she got on the outside, where everyone adored her. *You gorgeous thing, you goddess.*

She had loved it. And what did Chi even know, being fat and plain and forced to be jolly, Usha had wondered, a strong defence mechanism kicking in. She cringes now as she wanders about, more Zen but still hurting. Her sister must be ageing happily with a merry little brood of grandkids or kids.

Is she even happy? Usha wonders. Maybe it won't hurt to visit and find out. There's only one person she'd want to have by her side.

~

Mark isn't even around anymore, it looks like. Usha skulks about the market near their old house. She watches the curtains on the living room door twitch every so often, but if he does come out, it's never while she's around to see it.

She wonders if he's taken a new lover (of course, he must have) but can't bring herself to ask or find out. She wants to go and speak to him, even after all these years. She dreams of collapsing once and for all into his arms (he has always been the one supporting her, after all), but doesn't know if she can go through with it.

Until she spots him at a central market one fine winter day.

'Why would you not come in the first day you got here?' an older Mark, a less patient Mark asks her, when she finally gathers her courage to ask him to coffee.

'I wasn't sure you'd want to see me,' she says and has the good grace to break eye contact, though not before she sees a flicker of rage flare up.

'You weren't sure if … What?' Mark starts.

He brings himself under control, as always. 'My dear, my dear,' he says. 'After all this time.'

He doesn't mind the meeting, he says, 'It's only been two decades in the making.'

But a second later, he asks her almost savagely, without changing his tone, 'Are you happy, my dear? Ah, I hope that at least now you're happy.'

Usha is quite startled by the force of his anger but tries not to show it. *After all this time?*

'It was going to end anyway,' she tries. 'We were going to.'

She falters at this because she can't avoid the truth, much as she'd like to.

'It was bound to end, bound to collapse under the weight of all the bullshit,' she had told Mark when they were young.

'Your bullshit, you mean. Your lies,' he had said, with all the bitterness rising to the fore. 'Your affair.'

'I, my …' she had choked out the words, suddenly sadder than she could ever imagine. 'We're not fundamentally right for each other. You know it. And for the rest, I'm … I'm sorry.'

Structural flaws, she thinks and as is her habit from childhood, a habit she somehow passed on to her daughter, starts to hide inside her own mind.

(In fact, once in a while, even in the hills, she would catch the sound of a little girl laughing, and look and drink it all in. Why, that was Mia when she was little, staring at her with those giant grey eyes.)

'I haven't done right by her,' she tells Mark. 'Or by you. I'm so so sorry.'

She hadn't done right by her, that's for sure, but the understatement of the century.

What about the boy, though? Isn't he around?

'There's probably nothing I can do about any of it right now, but I wanted to try and make amends. Make things right. Somehow.'

Mark laughs. There's a lived-in air about him, but age has made him a little crueller, given him lines on his face, deep scars in his soul, wounds that still bleed vitriol. She knows in that moment he's not been pining away for her as she had half-hoped without realising it.

'What's right! What do you know about that?' he half-laughs again. 'As a wife? As a mother?'

She stays quiet for a while.

'I was never that clear, not like you,' she says, 'I didn't know exactly how I felt about us, or actually, if we're being honest, I knew exactly how I felt, but didn't know how to balance. It was very difficult, Mark.'

'I don't care for your words now, Usha, not in the least. I suppose you have to get something off your chest, is that why you're here?'

'I lost something important, and I'm not sure where to start ...' Her face shows the strain of what she's trying to say.

He cuts in.

'Lost something! Ha!

'I believed in you, you know? Never mind what the others said, what your own sister said. I believed in you. More fool me. When I was there, loving you, thinking maybe it was me, my job, my fault because I didn't have as much time for you as I wanted to, you were out there. Lakshman! The others! You didn't even have the guts to tell me,' he says, bitterly. 'Everyone, everyone close to us knew, by the way. Tried to warn me, too. But nooo, not me. I believed in you. Defended you. Guess what, the joke was on me.'

She cringes.

'Thanks for nothing,' he almost spits out.

The rage is all but spent.

She can't comprehend how the love had turned to hurt, to hate. She wants to make it up to him, to explain, to make him feel better. 'It wasn't …'

He waves at her. 'Don't bother,' he says, but not unkindly this time. 'Try the girl.'

His energy is spent, his hurt can't be assuaged so easily, the lost years gone never to return.

'I always cared for you,' she hears herself saying quietly to no discernible reaction.

It's true, too.

But why do I owe anyone any explanations? She can't help the thought.

A more compassionate side creeps in and she holds her peace. She knows that she has wielded the death blow to the romantic soul sitting in front of her. *Did I do this? Turn him into this horrid shell? Or was it always in him?*

It's another failure, but she will stay the course, she will survive. That's what she's hard-wired to do. She will overcome. And she will find what she's lost, she decides, no ego, only a quest to make amends, banking on her instincts.

And the universe.

16

Love-Hate: Reunion

[February 2024]

'Bad luck just follows you around,' Chini tells her sister, the initial surprise (not to mention politeness) on seeing her giving way to the truth as she sees it.

Usha is too low to even respond, but faintly surprised that her sister doesn't realise that all this is genetic roulette. It could just as easily have been her cross to bear.

'How have you been?' Usha tries.

'Better and better,' Chini laughs. 'What do you think?'

This is certainly not the welcoming atmosphere Chi is known for, but Usha wouldn't know that, never having seen any other side to her sister. *Just cold blows, bad news,* she thinks, the grey curtain blocking her memory of the one time her sister was warm and welcoming, when Usha and Mark came over, a baby in tow (Mark left behind in the car), Usha deciding cruelly back then that Maya-then-Mia would be better off anywhere else. She had revelled in the pain in Chini's eyes.

A silence sets in, fraught with decades worth of emotional warfare.

Usha says nothing, just stares out the window for a while.

Chini softens. 'It's not your fault, maybe. You couldn't help yourself if you tried.'

Stillness and silence. These are Usha's allies now.

Getting no rise out of her sister, Chini continues, 'Not your fault, I guess. Something going back generations, it could be. Ma looked it up with one old pundit once, it's quite possible that it was the curse of the brahmins.'

Usha turns toward her. 'What are you talking about?'

'Yes, a curse,' her sister is saying, gravely. 'There's no way to know unless you do some of those specific mantras. It could go back generations.'

'What brahmins? What curse?' Usha is struggling.

'Well, who knows? That jyotishee Ma knew has died, I think. It was his theory, sister dear,' Chini says, her eyes not warming up one bit to match her tone. 'How else to explain your life? The misery?'

Usha's eyes narrow. 'There's been some miscommunication, surely. I'm only miserable when I'm around here.'

'Oh, really?' Her sister is having none of it. She can't help some of the barbs. 'What, no curiosity to see how your daughter is doing? The baby boy you let go of? No love for the family? It's not natural. All those pujas I did for you didn't even make a dent.'

A bitter laugh from Usha. 'Pujas for me or curses? Don't think I forgot the time the old pundit told you to stop meddling with what you don't understand. What were you trying to do, anyway? Get more attention? I guess it worked!'

Chini looks perturbed for a second but shakes it off. 'He was wrong. I wasn't doing anything.' She's lying though, and clearly remembers how she had tried her hand at black magic at one point; the only guinea pig in sight was her sister. That one didn't go too well.

Usha knows the truth, but also knows that her sister's only felt strong jealousy, never too much malice, and certainly not had that deeper vein, the requisite spiritual firepower to have done much damage. Not any more or any less than she's done with her regular self, that is.

Why did I even come here? she wonders, something driving her to fight through the pain and humiliation and start putting the pieces back together.

She rallies. 'Forget it now, we're too old,' she says. Things have been strange and disconnected for too long for Usha to feel that they might patch up their relationship. It's beyond repair. They wouldn't be the first siblings to devolve into a love-hate-indifference curve of a relationship, after all.

A long period of silence follows, with neither one attempting to break it, until Usha caves. 'But I didn't know this curse theory.'

'Well, Ma thought of asking. She never gave up on you, you know?'

More silence at this.

Usha doesn't believe it, but picks up on something else. She knows that taking care of her mother through a debilitating illness, unto death, has been a huge drain on her sister. She wants to acknowledge that somehow, but, how? *What can we even hope to fix now?*

'She cared, right till the end. She might have forgotten her own name but not you.' Chini is not angry now so much as resigned. It's even more hurtful this way. 'You should have come, at least once.'

'I couldn't. I didn't even know. You never told me when she was taken to the hospital.'

'Hrm.' A snort in reply. There had, after all, been no contact with the family for what seemed like a lifetime. 'Like we even knew how to reach you. Just like when Pi ...'

She gets up abruptly and goes to the kitchen to make them some tea.

The timeout is a good idea.

Softened by her life experience, the intervening passage of time, and most immediately the cup of English Breakfast tea her sister brings out on one of their old family trays, Usha reflects that maybe underlying this entire fractious relationship is a monumental misunderstanding. *Or strike that, a misfitting, of the square peg–round hole variety.*

Maybe her mother didn't know any better than to believe all the vague holy men floating around in their home. Maybe her mother had been trying to protect her or love her in her own way, Usha would never know. But she didn't feel it. Not then, not now.

What do I know anyway? She's feeling old and tired. But thankfully not angry. Those days are long behind her. *What's left to do is fix the future.*

'You can still find out,' Chini is saying. 'There are some mantras that can reveal whether it was a previous generation. We just have to feed some thousand brahmins, I can get in touch with the temple next door.'

'Haha, no re,' Usha says, allowing herself a smile.

Her sister is transfixed, it's been so long since she's seen Usha's features arranged in that fashion. 'Forget it, it's too late for all that. How have you been?'

The next three hours pass in a surprisingly pleasant haze of catching up—the big life events first, Mia coming by to say hello, Gautam in his now-not-so-new job with the Rishi (Usha starts, but says nothing) and calling to chat with Chini every couple of months or so, the people who came by the house in the wake of their mother's passing, the old, ancient folks Chini had gone to visit, to pay her respects. 'It's all ending, you know, we're almost done,' she says, 'I can feel it.'

'It's not,' Usha says, smiling again, 'There's something much bigger. You'll see.'

For once, Chini is impressed by this calm, all-knowing air. But it lifts as they move to trickier territory with Chini describing Mark over the years, stumbling about in his grief, refusing to meet the child he knew wasn't his.

'And Mia?' Usha forces herself to ask for more detail, heart in her mouth.

Chini talks about Mia growing up confused, running away from home, doing drugs, losing herself, making up friends, suffering that mental illness, running away again after her diagnosis: multiple personalities they called it, she tells Usha fiercely.

'Triggered, for all we know, by trauma,' she adds, unnecessarily.

Usha hangs her head further, if it's even possible.

'After Lakshman died and by the time she got here, she had manifested a few personalities, maybe two personas, the shrink told us,' Chi says. 'She went for a few sessions. But then she took one set of meds and vanished.' She's still a bit hurt by her niece's callousness, but tries not to show it.

'The next thing I know it's two or three years later and she's talking completely normally, so ...' she trails off.

Don't ask, don't tell, Usha remembers this side of her sister.

'I had no one,' Chini goes on, more strident in her accusations. 'No one to help. Meena was holding our family together through the tough times. Mishraji kept us posted on Mia.'

Two personalities, poor Mia, Usha's thinking. *Demon babies,* she had said back in her own callow youth. Words resonate.

Her sister continues, oblivious. 'So that's fine. Anyway, you know Mia visited the other day, and she's fine now,' she says. 'Don't spoil it,' she adds, unable to help herself.

Usha says nothing.

Her sister has had the real relationship, it gives her the authority to say what she likes. (Though a few years ago, when she had come down from the hills, ostensibly to give her family life another go, Usha couldn't help but feel that her sister had done her fair share of brainwashing the young child. What else could explain Maya's point-blank refusal to return home with her? Usha had never discussed it with anyone, least of all herself, but the hurt had stayed, her pride wounded for life.)

'She even stayed here for a while last month,' Chini adds, not mentioning that she's getting Maya to house-sit more and more as she plans to travel often. 'Let me show you this lovely stole she bought me,' she trills, knowing that she's turning the knife. *Maya hasn't asked about Usha in years!*

Anyway, Chini moves on, talking about Mark's reemergence on the social scene, his new wife, or is it mistress? She isn't sure, but mentions how he's changed in old age, he's really come into his own, she says. Whether it's meanly meant or not isn't the point—Usha feels it as a blow to the heart.

She hears of his deposits for Mia decreasing along the way but never stopping altogether, not even with Mia about to turn thirty. She's quietly proud of Mark, he always had a heart of gold.

Chini ends with news of Meena and Mishraji's long years of service (refraining from mentioning how they had slowly stopped asking after Usha), their impending retirement, and that they've managed to build a small home for themselves.

'In the city?' Usha asks, so much pain in her voice still, pain her sister doesn't register and cannot help ease, anyway.

'No no, the hills,' Chini says. 'Their daughter is all grown up and working, such a sweet girl she seems to be. Anyway, they want to leave by the end of the year but haven't figured out how to tell Mia yet. Poor baby.'

Poor baby, alright.

Mishraji has actually had enough, but it's his wife who has kept him at it. The two of them have kept an eye on Mia, as they had promised Chini they would, it's the least they can do after all she's done for their family, helping to put their daughter through college and setting aside money for her wedding.

Their fondness for Mia might have dimmed a bit over the years—at least, it has for Mishraji—but Meena keeps reminding him of what a difficult life she's led. And so they are watchful, caring, looking out for her as best they can and keeping her aunt posted on most of her shenanigans, avoiding some of the scandalous news over the years. They don't talk about the frequent breakups and her temper, but sometimes reference her strange friends and her drinking and smoking.

Chini hasn't judged, her heart still a marshmallow as she remembers that little face lighting up every time she sat on her lap. She has a patient ear on those monthly and then increasingly sporadic visits, and tells the couple that Mia is still young, still letting off steam. *Should we find someone for her?* she secretly wonders. *But who? Who would be good enough for the girl?*

And when will she learn to be happy? If she could, she would explain that it's a matter of just dropping all the baggage. *Leave it behind,* she wants to say.

But then, how can she? She glares at Usha sitting in front of her, lost as usual in her own world.

This Usha has been the source of all the trouble, Chini can't help but think.

It's back to square one with these two.

17

Worse, Then Better Again

[February–March 2024]

Dealing with his own aching sense of loss, Karthik is at his wit's end.

Pacing about at home, he tries to steer clear of social media, but can't stop himself from checking out Maya's photos and posts again and again. Not much has changed and these last few months have gone by in a blur. At least he knows she's okay, because she had sent him a message.

'Hey. I'm back on the scene. Just wanted to let you know.' That was it. A long time ago, too.

On social there was that last comment, from Farhan no less, followed by Maya. 'Yaa, wassup?!' was Maya's contribution.

What the heck was he supposed to do with that? He has so much to say but feels too self-conscious.

'What is going on?' he had finally typed out, not mentioning the crushing anxiety he'd felt that something had happened to her. Luckily, he'd deleted some of his older comments so she may not have seen all the poems and tributes. 'Are you okay? You just fell off the planet.'

'Listen, I'm going through a thing. I want to meet you though,' was her last message. 'Give me some time. We'll catch up very soon.'

His moodiness hasn't improved the general atmosphere at home, that's for sure.

'I don't know how Karthik has survived this long without combusting, to be honest,' Om is telling his brother.

'I told you he's got the goods. You should have sent him to me for training.'

'I know, I know,' Om says.

Garima holds on to his arm and adds, 'But it was my fault. I couldn't let him go.'

'No no, no such thing as your fault, or you should have or could have, it wasn't meant to be.'

This sort of reasoning has driven Om P. mad for most of his life, but he finds it comforting now. 'What does he have? Is he going to be in some trouble?'

'Oh ho, no no,' the Rishi laughs. 'You're so dramatic. No. It's just … you know, Death.'

'What?!' Om hears his wife's sharp intake of breath.

'No, no, not his own death, baba, it's Death with a capital D. Interested in him. He's pulling towards himself all those forces of death and destruction. Because of his dreams. He's a bit obsessive and … You know how they say our realities … we manifest our realities?'

Blank faces.

'Life is a waking dream?'

Still nothing.

'Do you chaps listen to any of my talks?'

Garima at least has the grace to look sheepish, but Om is starting to work himself up into a fit. 'That mumbo jumbo.'

'He's got all that intensity, as you call it, it's a psychic strength,' the Rishi says placatingly.

Silence for a bit. 'He always has been intense,' Om says, agreeing for once.

'I think we should get him to reconcile with the girl,' says the Rishi.

'What does that have to do with anything?' Om's voice sounds strangled.

'The same girl? Maya?' his wife asks at the same time.

'Ah yes, yes of course,' the Rishi says, indulging in a hand-rolled cigarette offered to him by some sort of butler he smiles at.

'I think this might end well after all,' he adds. 'Now, where is that Krishn?'

'K? The driver? Is this his fault?' Om asks. 'I don't believe it! The kid's Cab of Death theory is true or what?'

'What? What theory? No. What? I just want to meet him,' the Rishi lies.

'Ah, so,' he says a few moments later when K comes out to see him, his faint smile intact. 'How have you been? Busy of late?'

No reply except a small nod of the head.

'What are we going to do with you?'

Death grins at him. It's been a ride. And he's found his new companion. You can't blame him for having fun along the way.

The Rishi is smiling at him, shaking his head. 'Not yet, buddy,' he says. 'It's much too soon.'

Karthik wakes up suddenly. It's quite possible he dreamt all of this, his shirt is drenched through, he's been out for hours.

How did that even happen? he wonders, not quite realising he had passed out a few hours ago. He has a huge drink of water to calm his nerves and then steps into the living room. Karthik isn't at all surprised to see the man sitting there, holding forth.

'Ah, young Karthik,' the Rishi says. 'We've been waiting for you.'

'Didn't we just meet?' Karthik asks, suddenly unsure of where the dream boundaries end. (The Rishi could have told him that they never do, only merging with what we consider our waking reality, blurry at the edges, but one seamless transition. He will teach him this and more, going forward. And how to leave the dreams in their own world. For the most part.)

'We did indeed,' the Rishi says, smiling. 'I wanted you to meet my young friend Gautam. But he's not here right now.'

'Gautam?' Karthik says the name, questioningly. 'Isn't he …'

'He's known to you, yes,' the Rishi continues, 'or rather, he's known to your friend Maya.'

'Maya! But ...' Karthik's mum Garima tries to say something, but her husband shushes her. He desperately wants someone to get to the bottom of this. None of it makes sense, and he's having the worst time trying to keep track.

Karthik can't help himself. 'Is she okay? Where is she?'

The Rishi laughs at the tell-tale signs of love. 'Well, Gautam, at least, I can tell you about. He and I were at your old friend the Guru's ashram a while ago.'

All three of them must look uncomfortable because the Rishi adds, 'Oh no, no, don't worry, you don't have to go back there.'

Om lets out a sigh of relief.

At which Karthik finally cracks a smile.

'It's okay, Dad, they couldn't force me to rejoin them even if I did go back.'

The Rishi is looking at them all with an unusually shrewd eye. 'Good. There's nothing there for you anymore.' He's more business-like as he continues, 'Now, Karthik, you can join Gautam shortly. He'll text you the address.'

He throws a phone towards Karthik. Om and the Rishi exchange eye contact. It's impossible to get a reading on what's happening, so Karthik gives up.

The phone beeps. It's an address, as promised.

As he gets up, the Rishi's voice booms out, 'And Karthik? Take K and the Audi.'

'But ...'

The Rishi says simply, 'We face our fears and outgrow them, boy. It's the only way.'

Karthik thinks about it, shrugs and walks out.

Om is furious. 'What are you doing? I told you about the dangers.'

This time the Rishi doesn't laugh it off. 'You fight fire with fire, brother, trust me, I know what I'm doing.' He's operating on instinct, sure, but he knows deep down that K is not the threat. He's just keeping his finger on the pulse. 'He'll get it right out of his system, trust me.'

His brother is not convinced, becoming more frightened and angrier by the second. 'That's not good enough, you know. I always knew you were mad, but this is too much. That's my boy out there.'

'He's a wonderful kid. Don't worry about him if you can help it. He's going to be fine.'

Om looks painfully worried.

'Man, trust me. There's nothing wrong with that damn car. You can't possibly believe in this fleet of death, nonsense. Do you?' The Rishi appeals to his brother's logical side and then shakes his head. 'I thought you were the rational one.'

There's no getting rid of the pain but Om mumbles, 'Of course I am rational, but my only son has been telling me obsessively about this car and his theory ...'

'Nonsense. Things are going to be fine. Just trust me.' The Rishi makes one more stab at predicting normalcy. 'He'll be home before you know it, with that girl in tow.'

Karthik's parents look a bit relieved to hear this. They don't know that the Rishi is counting on Maya (and me!) to balance out some of those psychic energies. (Not that he's sure what a baby will add to the mix.)

Halfway across the city, Gautam is on the phone, talking to his sister. 'Dude! I'm going to be there soon. You're at Chini Auntie's only, right? Of course I'll come there. Is she around?'

Maya says that she's not. 'Is the Rishi coming?'

'No, no, actually, Sir gave me the royal ditch again, almost as soon as he got to the city this time,' he says in reply to his sister's question, adding, 'The talk went well, at your old ashram, actually! Sans the old Guru, believe it or not. He's out.'

He can practically hear her smiling over the phone and asks, 'Want me to get you anything from here before I head?'

She may have said no, but he thinks he'll pop into Khan Market and pick up something nice for her. Eating for two and all that, he smiles to himself. He was so relieved that the talk went well, the Rishi just telling him to go enjoy himself and to meet his sister, but then he asked him to text their address. For what, he did not say.

'Sir, but Usha and Karthik?' Gautam had asked.

'It will be fine, young Gautam. What have I taught you? Nothing?'

'But sir, I thought we had to ...'

'We have to do nothing right now. Nothing. Enjoy yourself and say hi to your sister for me.'

Gautam was puzzled as he hung up. Just a few months ago he'd had no idea that the Rishi knew the boy Maya was interested in, let alone that he was the boy's uncle, nor that he'd arranged any number of meetings by himself, whilst keeping his disciple in the dark.

But he had to trust that things were going to be okay. *What else can I do? Just go with the motherfuckin' flow.* (He had some rap on his iPhone these days.)

~

The siblings are just catching up, quite an unsuspecting audience, when the curtain goes up—the perfect little storm lands on the doorstep of the flat with its intangible pull on our particular group of inter-connected friends and relatives.

Usha barges in first.

Ahhhh. She really is stunning, superlatively beautiful, even now, even at this age, Gautam thinks when he sees her.

She's panting, like she ran up the stairs.

'Hey, what ...' Maya starts. 'Oh, it's you!'

She's equally startled a few minutes later when Karthik follows Usha.

'Hey!' she says in a different tone.

Gautam instantly recognises the young man from his dreams and half-looks around for the fleet of death trailing flames. He peeps out the window—there's a fancy car parked below, but nothing weird about it, so he says nothing.

He sends off a quick text: 'She's here. So is your nephew.'

The Rishi writes back, typing slowly. 'Good. Be there, stay by the phone. Be rational.'

And then he sends another message: 'I'm right here and will get there when I'm needed.'

Gautam can't argue with him but would much rather have had him in the room. Just in case.

Maya, meanwhile, has walked towards Karthik, her hand out as if to shake his hand. She's smiling sheepishly and he melts. He envelops her in a bear hug and looks like he's bursting to say something.

It's Usha who speaks first, though. 'Ohhh. Lovely,' she says.

'What?' That's Maya.

'You both.

'And congratulations.'

'Ummm … for what?' Maya says. 'And excuse me, but what are you doing here?'

'I came here to say sorry,' Usha starts, trailing off into silence. 'I really feel like I need to say sorry to you all.'

Silence for a tick. Maya can only hear heartbeats. *Can everyone hear them?*

'Umm,' Maya makes a face—a plea of some sort—to Gautam, but neither knows what to do or say.

'I could have the baby if you like.' Usha's tone is so rational, the contrast with what she's saying couldn't be starker. 'I could make it up to you.'

'What now?' asks Karthik, who is a bit out of sorts. 'What is she talking about, a baby?'

He was actually just preparing to castigate Maya (lightly, mind!) for scaring the bejesus out of him, but she's let go of the hug, half-turned away to this older lady. In the stunned silence that follows, it's just as startling to hear Gautam laugh at the inevitable absurdity of the universe.

'What are you laughing for?' Usha eyeballs him, not knowing that he's just channeling his inner Rishi.

'Just the timing.'

'What?' Maya asks.

'The universe.'

'Ahh,' Usha says.

'What baby?' Karthik asks. He feels something plummet to the pit of his stomach and doesn't know what to make of any of this. *Whose baby? Can't be ours, right?* he wonders, turning from side to side as he follows the conversation. *After that one time? Or even the second?*

Is that why she's been avoiding …?

'Excuse me though, how do you figure?' Maya's hand is hovering protectively over her belly.

'You don't even want it, do you, darling?' Usha says. 'Or do you?'

She sounds sad suddenly. 'I lost mine.'

'What? Not want it?' Maya's starting to get worked up.

'And excuse me. Lost yours? You didn't lose yours. You walked out on her. On me, I mean.

'How dare you … what do you even mean? After being gaayab all this time?' Maya's here but Akira is starting to surface, anger fizzing through the cracks.

Usha smiles, a gentle smile.

'You know, Mia, I really am sorry. So sorry. I don't know if you remember this, but I came by the house to see you when you were little, just to see you,' she says. 'And then, that last time, when I came by to ask if you'd mind moving with me to the hills, do you remember?'

Silence.

Gautam tries to remember whether Maya had ever mentioned this, but draws a blank.

'I don't, actually,' says Maya.

'It's okay,' Usha says, a slightly wan look on her face. 'I told you a terrible story, I was quite hurt that you chose Chini.'

Gautam remembers being told about this, and looks over at Maya. Her face is white.

'But that's okay, that's okay,' Usha hastens to add, seeing the impact her story is having.

They're all a little taken aback by the affection in her voice.

This isn't what I expected. It's a bit anti-climactic now that she's shown up, Gautam can't help but think.

'You were always more like me than anyone else,' Usha is saying to Maya. 'You've grown up so much better, though, so much better than I could have hoped …' She trails off.

What the hell? No one saw that coming. No one's even sure what's what, right now.

Is it true? Is she more like the Pahaari than the others? Maya's brain is spinning. *Is that the missing piece?*

Usha's face changes and she sits down. 'It's just that I didn't know what to do. It didn't come naturally to me, being a mother.'

It's not possible, right? She didn't say those words out loud? Maya looks at Gautam for backup, but he's also looking puzzled, brow furrowed and everything.

Everyone goes quiet.

Karthik goes to the window where a beady-eyed little crow is staring at him, head cocked to one side. He doesn't know what on earth is going on; it feels like he has cotton wool cradling his brain. He certainly can't hear clearly. It doesn't seem polite to speak right now with all of this happening, but he can't help himself. 'What baby, Maya?'

Maya moves towards him but then stands frozen as Usha starts speaking again.

'She'll have the trademark eyes,' Usha continues. 'Oh, I can't wait to see her,' she says, sort of to herself.

'But, but ...' Maya tries to sound more coherent. 'You never liked children.' She ends on this strange note, sitting down with a thump.

Usha smiles at her, a sad smile. 'I know, I made a huge mistake. It's been a huge loss. Mine more than anyone else's.'

'But ...'

'I used to send you those long letters, you know. Even though I knew you wouldn't write back.' Usha stops, trying to take the words back. 'I ... guess I stopped some years ago.'

Maya looks like she's about to start crying.

Gautam interjects, 'Hey, hey, hang on.'

'There were no letters.' Maya's crying now. 'Why would you lie? I even came to find you and ...'

'Hang on,' Gautam repeats. He puts a hand on Maya's shoulder. He's seen her through her strange childhood, he knows this is a huge moment but ... she needs some time.

'She needs some time,' he starts to tell Usha, who nods sadly.

'I'm not lying,' Usha says, and then realisation dawns. 'Oh. Oh, of course Chini would have kept them and not shared.'

'Hey, leave her out of this,' Gautam says. 'At least she was around.'

'I'm sure she thought she was doing the right thing,' Usha says. 'I just wish I'd known then what I know now.

This taking a village business,' she trails off. *If only someone had told her she might be better with older kids, but there's no room in life for the what ifs, is there?* That's something she's learned the hard way.

Karthik moves to stand next to Maya—he has so many questions.

Gautam intercepts him. 'Wait, hold on buddy, hold on. You and I, we need to talk.' Gautam really is at his protective best.

'Do I know you from somewhere?' Karthik asks. 'You look awfully familiar.'

'Well, I don't know about that. But we need to talk about these dreams of yours. You know, fireballs, destruction …'

Karthik looks embarrassed and a bit subdued.

Maya makes a huge effort to speak. 'Wait, is this about that Cab of Death thing again?' she asks Karthik. 'I would have thought you were over that.'

On the stairs, a landing below, a smile in the shadows.

Karthik somehow manages to look even more crestfallen than usual. 'These strange dreams. They're getting pretty bad. I don't know how to stop them.'

'Oh my God, Karthik, like I've been having these weird bloody dreams too. In the daytime, even.'

He seems surprised to hear this.

'Death, fire, that accident we saw …' Maya stops.

He makes some sort of strangled noise in his throat. 'Really?'

Gautam is a bit perturbed by all this. And Karthik has so many questions, you can see it, but their private conversation is cut short by the larger drama unfolding.

It's Akira's turn now. And she comes out all guns blazing.

She turns towards Usha, face contorted, barbs flying. She chokes on a word and then it comes out.

'You ... bitch.'

She's not done. 'You've been such a bad-mother-horrible-person. How dare you come back?'

'Listen to me, listen to me, Mia,' Usha's trying, her hands raised as if to ward off the onslaught.

'It's not Mia, you asshole.'

'Maya.'

'You wish,' Akira snarls. 'It's all your fault—every single one of our problems. I hate you.'

Karthik looks ashen-faced but to his credit says nothing. Maybe this is what was bubbling up, maybe Maya's just been trying to deal with all of this, an extra ... voice? *Is that what it is?*

Gautam puts his hand on his shoulder and shakes his head. 'Don't say anything right now.'

'What kind of woman would you even have to be to think that you have a place here, in our lives?' Akira isn't done.

There's no reply to that at first.

'I just,' Usha starts, but is unable to finish her sentence.

'Yeah, exactly that, you didn't think,' Akira goes on. 'As self-centred, selfish and evil a Manglik as you've always been.'

Usha starts at that, not knowing but not entirely surprised that her sister's been drip-feeding her niece all that superstition for donkey's years.

'It's disgusting,' Akira says, with eyes for no one but Usha. 'You're disgusting. You never even for one second think about any consequences of anything. Not for Mark, not for Chini Auntie, not for Maya.'

She's working herself into one of those fits. Gautam starts to panic. *Who can I call now?* The Rishi had said to get hold of his old friend, Dr G, if required. But that might be too much, given Maya's terrible experience as a teen.

(It's okay, Maya will tell him in a bit. She's already texted her therapist an SOS. 'Hiiii, I'm so sorry to trouble you, but something dramatic is going down, like full-fledged family drama. Any tips on how I can stay calm? I don't want to take anything, I don't know if I got a chance to tell you, I'm expecting. SORRY I didn't connect earlier and hope I can come see you soon.')

'I just wish ... you were dead like you've been all along,' Akira's voice is harsh, cruel in the silence.

There's something going on here that I can't quite understand, Karthik thinks. *I can help her though, I know I can.* He gets up and tries to put a hand around Maya, but Akira shakes it off, her rage falling off her in cascades.

'Fuck off, just go on and fuck off out of our lives.'

'Hold on hold on, hold on,' Gautam tries to interject, dialling the Rishi, who surely is the right person to come here and sort this out. *The adults, we need the adults!* He starts to panic.

'Fuck you too, you fucking loser,' Akira lays into him now. 'What the hell is wrong with you?'

Ouch. 'Hold on, just a second, please just sit down,' Gautam says. 'Akku ... please.'

Everyone is quiet for a second.

'Akku?' asks Karthik.

'Not now,' Gautam says. Too many things are happening.

Usha's look, her entire demeanour softens. 'Ohhh.'

'Come on, Akku, come on,' Gautam tries again. 'There's no need for names. There's nothing wrong. Just hang on.'

'Nothing wrong?' Akira's cold.

'One sec ...' Gautam has reached the Rishi for an intervention. 'Sir, I really think it would be good for us if you were ...' He pauses. 'You are?'

The Rishi manages to calm Gautam down and tells him to hold fast. 'Things will be okay.'

'Nothing wrong ... Well, there's nothing wrong with me,' Akira is still lashing out. 'But what the hell happened to you? Joined a cult in the end, or what?'

Akira's voice is razor sharp. 'Sir isn't really a doctor anymore, Gautam, you know that, right? Just your wannabe father figure.'

Gautam's face turns ashen. This is a new development. *All this chaos can't be healthy for the baby*, he thinks.

'And you,' Akira has turned back to face Usha, 'you absolute bitch.'

Goodness, he's never heard her talk like this. And with that, a strange thing is happening to Karthik, who till a moment ago felt the usual panic bubbling up, and rage. He screws up his face, actively trying to deep breathe his way out of this, actively trying to avoid this vision or waking dream which is blazing across his eyeballs like some sort of chariot with flames billowing.

(Hi Dad! It's me, I want to say.*)*

He can all but see it. *What the hell is going on,* he wonders, *how do I stop it?* It seemed under control this morning, briefly, when his new-found uncle was around. *Maybe I can just close my eyes* … He opens his eyes shortly and catches sight of Maya again, a twisted version of Maya.

She needs me to be the rational one, the calm one. This can't be good for her.

The fight continues, oblivious to anyone else's feelings.

~

Usha starts to raise her voice. 'Darling, you need to calm down.'

'I'm not going to calm down until you fuck off back to the fucking hills,' Akira says, her breath ragged. Her words have never had a crueller edge. 'And don't "darling" me.'

'Guys, GUYS!' Karthik yells, red-faced, a vein in his forehead popping. 'Everyone calm down.' He rarely loses his cool in public or even asserts himself, so it's quite a moment to behold. He takes the entire tension of the room, absorbing it.

Gautam exhales loudly.

He didn't even know he had been holding his breath through this entire heated exchange.

~

Pin-drop silence interrupted by …

(Ping: 'Maya, goodness, of course you can text me. Listen. Well, congratulations first. Remember the deep breathing and grounding exercises? Please start doing them. Try to remove yourself from there if you can.' A message from Reena Gupta)

Well, on the upside, it's good to air out the family laundry sometimes, Usha thinks. She starts laughing.

They all look at her like she's gone bonkers. Maybe she has at that. 'This is brilliant,' she says, laughing. 'Brilliant.'

'I'm sorry?' Gautam is back to his polite self, but you can almost hear his pulse thundering in his veins.

'You guys are … ah … still so young.'

'What?'

'You poor babies. I thought I had missed out on everything, but I guess I haven't.'

Akira, or is it Maya, is looking deflated, her energy spent for the moment.

'We need to get you to a doctor,' Usha says, matter-of-factly now, looking at Maya and Gautam. 'In case you're taking it again, you'll have to check your medication against the pregnancy, right? Trust me, I know a little something about this.'

'How the …'

'Taking what …' Gautam starts to say at the same time.

'What baby? Whose baby is this?' Karthik asks plaintively. 'Maya?'

'She's making sense actually,' Maya says. 'My therapist has pinged me back to say you all need to take a step back and give me some space. I need some space, please.'

There's a lull—no one is sure how to do that. They're not even sure how to concede, or what to do. There are so many questions, not enough time, and for the moment, the surfeit of love—though present—isn't all that evident.

A mini timeout is a thing of grace.

'How do you even know what you're talking about?' Maya's question takes precedence.

Usha's not sure how much to share. 'I went through some of this myself,' she starts to say but her voice catches and she just looks down. The thing is, no one can deny she's radiating something positive, feel-good, almost like she's trying to hug them all. Even Karthik can feel it, and it's sensational.

Gautam is moved as well. *I can feel the love,* he marvels to himself. He has to admit that there's something touching about the way she's opened up to her daughter. Something human, more human than they had thought she would be.

But it's not enough.

Not yet.

'Un-fucking-believable.' Akira is having none of this normalising. 'You absolute BITCH. Talk to me. Speak to me.'

She gets all their attention. 'What right do you have to even be here?' she's asking Usha.

'None, you're right,' Usha says, unusually contrite. 'But …'

'But, nothing! Doesn't it matter to you that the payment is in peace of mind? Mark's … now Maya's. Do you even care about anyone?' Akira won't stop, her words firing relentlessly, and no one has the heart to stop her.

Certainly not Usha, but not Gautam either, who remembers how much his sister had longed and yearned to see her mother, all those years ago.

'If you go up to the hills again,' she had told a young Gautam, 'don't love her, just tell me what she's wearing and if she has a new family.'

He remembers that suddenly and feels like he might start crying any moment. It's too much. *The Rishi should be here to handle this, isn't HE the real adult.* But he knows it's up to him to reconcile them somehow, if he can. 'Maya, Akku … listen to me. None of us know … Listen, none of us …'

Usha starts speaking at the same time. 'I know I messed up, I know …'

'Messed up? Messed up? You have no idea what you're talking about. You didn't mess up. You didn't mess me up. You gave me the best gift in the world. A family that actually cared for me.' Akira's eyes are blazing; she dares someone to contradict her.

They don't.

'I didn't need you. I never did. Why are you back here? Don't think you can just come back here and ruin everything again …'

'So that worked out well then,' Usha tries again, softly. 'You're obviously a lovely, happy girl with …'

'Don't you come here and tell me what I am and what I'm not,' Akira snaps. 'What are you doing here? What do you want?'

The tension is unbearable now and Maya is starting to feel very sick, *very* dizzy and very nauseous.

(I am too, but this may not be the moment.)

'My family. I want my family back,' Usha says simply.

There's a gob-smacked silence.

~

'Whaaaa?' Gautam is glad to see Maya sitting down again. He exchanges a glance with her, eyebrows raised.

'I want you to think about coming and staying with me,' Usha is saying. 'I came here to put all my cards on the table and ask you to let me make it up to you.'

Does anyone else think it's weird the way she's talking to me, Maya wonders. *Like she really sees me?*

'Ummm ... that doesn't ... This isn't something we were expecting,' Maya says, her tone remarkably balanced.

'Darling, me neither. But we're part of this shit storm together.'

Maya can't help but think there's logic in that. *The crazy old lady is right. She's always been part of the fabric of our lives. Whether or not we admitted it, and mostly, we didn't.*

'But never mind that for now ...' Usha says. 'Take your time. I'm not going anywhere this time, not again. We can figure ...'

'Well, first, we need to figure out a space that's safe for the baby,' Gautam butts in. 'Away from all this,' he gesticulates. 'Too much commotion.'

Maybe this is the new normal, Maya marvels, subconsciously realising she's never going to be alone again. *Isn't that something?* They all love her too; she can feel it. *That's the second epiphany, Papa, the real one,* Maya wants to tell

Lakshman. *The world does owe you that much,* she thinks but … her brain is getting loopy.

She's really feeling dizzy now and more than a little sick.

'We'll find a space that's safe,' Gautam asserts. 'I don't think you should worry about …'

Karthik looks pleadingly at her.

'Hey, don't worry, we'll talk properly. Let these guys just …' she starts.

Oh God, she's not looking too good.

'RRRhmm.' A grown-up cough in the air goes unnoticed, except by Gautam.

'Krishn?'

Karthik makes a move towards the driver.

'Sir ne message kiya tha.'

The driver has brought some ORS liquid mini-tetra packs and hands them to Karthik gingerly, gesturing at Maya. He's super-stressed by all the yelling, triggered right back to his own unhappy home. *They'll sort it out though,* he figures. He'd thought they were such an interesting family, and the young miss had brought so much sunshine, with all her chatter. It's made him smile despite himself.

'Oh.' Karthik's features change completely. 'Shukriya.'

Maya doesn't have the energy, but wants to laugh, knowing what she knows about his inane fears. She closes her eyes, a bit wiped out.

'Maya, Maya, just take a swig.'

She forces herself to sit upright, taking the ORS gratefully.

Gautam and Karthik are both trying to make eye contact, one is holding her hand even. And that's when she starts laughing, startling everyone. It's the loudest Gautam has ever heard her.

'Just look at this! The only thing that's not crazy here is me.'

They can't argue with that.

She wants to shout it out loud. *Finally!* She knows where she fits.

Usha smiles at her daughter, HER daughter. She wants to laugh out loud too. She looks at how worried the brother is and smiles in Gautam's direction.

'Hey, it's going to be fine.'

Gautam doesn't look convinced.

Usha's quiet.

'You've been such a trooper, I always heard.'

'Wait, what?' Maya comes back to the present moment from another perspective, surprised that Usha is talking so much to Gautam all of a sudden.

'What did I miss?' No one hears Maya this time.

Usha smiles at him kindly, but Gautam can't be sure. He's very confused right now.

'I don't know, how much do *you* know?' she's asking him, with a strange smile. She doesn't mean it the way he takes it, but he's already feeling the upheaval. *What? This isn't making any sense.*

Gautam had an equally strange childhood, Maya thinks, *never quite knowing where he stood with their father, for some reason.* A hidden part of her is whispering what has been buried at the back of her mind. *Surely, the old man would have told him, right? Given all the family dynamics? Surely, he would have mentioned this possibility.* It never really came together for her till this moment.

Gautam, meanwhile, tunes out everything that's non-essential. Unusually for him, he's unable to get a handle on his thoughts, which are a mishmash, but this may not be the time.

'Let's just take a minute,' he says. 'Let Maya feel better, and then we'll figure out what to do next.'

He offers everyone some water, cold drinks or coffee/chai, whatever they want, taking the opportunity to collect his thoughts.

There is some faintly soothing conversation that follows, more to do with breathing and taking it all in, as Maya reads from her therapist's texts.

'No wonder you needed a timeout,' Karthik says. 'This is intense. But Maya ... the baby.' Karthik's voice is a bit strained. 'The baby?' His look is so plaintive. He's not sure if it's his or her ex's. *And why didn't she tell me in the first place? Is that why she disappeared?*

She had almost forgotten how he made her feel. 'Yes, I'm pregnant. I'm pregnant,' she laughs. 'Can you beat that?' Maya knows what else he's asking.

'Is this why you ghosted me?'

'Noooo ...'

'I need to know,' he's saying, but again, it sounds like he's speaking underwater. Or is that just how he feels? He can't be sure. *Is this another part of my weird dream?* 'Is it mine?'

Maya smiles at him, their own private smile.

Why does Usha look at me so familiarly? Gautam isn't done puzzling it out, but he smiles back at her.

Hearing some murmurs of a conversation, he turns over to glance at Karthik. *Something's going on with that kid,* he realises. 'Hey, come here for a sec,' Karthik says, pulling Gautam to a corner.

Five minutes of conversation later, he's got Karthik doing some deep breathing. 'There's a lot we don't know, right,' Gautam is saying, 'but for now, just try and find some Zen.'

He asks Karthik a few simple questions and tells him it sounds like all the visions and agitation are linked to his patchy sleep cycle. *(He's half-right … but the agitation? Well, that's his, mine and the Tribe's, but he doesn't know that yet.)*

'The Rishi will sort this out,' Gautam says, confidently. 'Your uncle will. Don't worry.'

Karthik's life is going to get a lot more complicated before it stabilises, but there's something to be said for hope. Not to mention love. He goes back to Maya. 'Listen, about the baby? What do you need from me? Anything.'

'Karthik, you know I haven't even …' Maya starts, then realises everyone is listening. 'Can we talk about this in private? Later?'

Karthik nods, but his face feels—and looks—funny. Pained, almost. She reaches for his hand.

He really is a good sort, Gautam finds himself thinking. *Maybe he will be good for Maya*.

They're quiet for a little longer, the silence like a cocoon for each one.

That's them, there, in the moment. Maya is still sitting, one hand on her stomach, Gautam looks strangely forlorn, Karthik is just blinking in silence. Usha is rocking herself on the chair, unaware of what she's doing, but soothed by the movement.

And Akira … well, Akira's still in a rage, unfortunately. She's not done yet.

She's ready to burst that last bubble of childhood sunshine. *This Gautam, he's clearly a clod, not on our side. He's turned completely. Look at them together.*

'Wait a second,' she starts. 'Wait a goddamn second.'

They're starting to recognise her by her voice, which is much harsher than Maya's, and commanding somehow. 'We're not done here.'

'Akira …' Gautam tries, his tone placating.

'Don't,' she warns. 'Actually, wait, so did you know she was here?' This last bit she spits out at Gautam, gesturing at Usha.

'Huh?' he asks, pleading with his eyes for her to calm down. 'I had no idea,' he says.

'Of course not,' she sneers.

Akira is crystal clear that she has to protect Maya—everyone else is collateral damage. Every single thing else is collateral damage. *All those years of trying to not find her and this woman is still a gargoyle who will harm her.*

'You don't ever know anything,' Akira says. 'Lost in your own world of make-believe with your pretend father. I mean, yes, all these years later, let's talk about that, shall we? Your parents.

'Your father with his affairs, and with you lost in your own fantasy land, your mother just had to grin and bear it …'

That snaps the last shred of his patience.

'Keep my mother out of it!' Gautam's voice is clear and cold. 'What are you trying to say—my father what? What does he have to do with anything?'

'Your father...' Akira starts, but Usha butts in, trying to be gentle with the big reveal.

'Your father ... was a wonderful human being,' Usha says. 'A gem.'

There's a pause that is turbo-charged.

'Of course he was,' Gautam says. *Wait, why would she say that?* He looks at Akira, or is it Maya?

'I have no idea what you're talking about,' he says out loud. He can hear his heart beating into his skull. *But wait, what the hell does ...*

'What do you know about it?' he asks Usha.

She is silent, not sure how to keep her word to Lakshman; a promise made in another era.

'Well, since you ask ... Mark let something slip years ago,' Akira says, coldly, not mentioning the full context, that Mark had let something slip while sharing that her bloodline and parentage didn't matter to him at all, that he'd keep supporting her as long as she went to the shrink Usha had refused to see.

'No, no, no,' Usha says, feeling Mark's pain belatedly.

'Your father destroyed this family,' Akira tells Gautam.

Gautam is still trying to catch up. 'What?'

'Our family,' she says.

'It was one affair,' Gautam tries to sound firm.

'Let's be honest now. Man up, Gautam, remember?' She's almost mocking him now, but he's still not getting the whole picture.

'What is she talking about?' He's just gawping at Usha at this point.

'You don't know the half of it,' Akira says, jeering. 'Man of the family, I believe ... but which family, Gautam? Poor little Gautam.'

~

'Two babies,' Usha whispers. 'Twins.' *'Demon babies,' the universe reminds her of the anger that rent the family and her soul.*

'What?'

Luckily for Gautam, who needs this time to process, there is a staggered silence.

Usha seems to be near tears again.

(That makes two of us—so much emotion and heartbreak here.)

'So wait, somehow, Mark is my father? What?'

'No, Gautam,' Maya emerges, wanting to protect her brother. 'Same … Papa. Lakshman,' she says softly, tears streaming down her face. She's known, but also not; it's been blocked out somewhere in her brain.

Gautam thinks frantically. *I can't have been adopted too, I would have known, surely, my mother would have said something.* There's no one to tell him about the agonising decision his parents had come to, unable to have kids themselves. His mother was fine with one adoption, at least of the boy, but Neeti had thrown a shit fit when Usha dumped the girl on them too, years later.

Usha tries to tell him. 'We all loved you,' she starts, but doesn't know how to tell him the rest.

Neeti will, in time. Her lousy luck, her husband always had such a glad eye. But the boy, she had always loved the boy.

Gautam doesn't know what to say or how to say it. The confusion and denial are making way for anger.

Wait … Akira knew this whole time? 'You knew, Maya, and didn't tell me?'

'I don't think so, Gautam, I didn't know.'

Usha is just looking at him, desperate to spare him any hurt.

'Uh.' Her choices and their repercussions are spiralling out even now. Surely by now things should have been a bit calmer, the karmic debt had to have been repaid.

'There's nothing I can say,' she says. 'I know I hurt you. I'm so sorry. I'm so proud of you. I'm so so sorry.' Her voice trails off, she wants to give up, this is too hard.

But this time she has to do it; power through, or she won't forgive herself. *Look at them, my babies.*

'And you,' she turns to Maya/Akira. 'Maya, Akira, is it? Just listen to me, listen to me. I messed up. I did. But you're Mark's and mine. And Lakshman's, yes, but also Chini's and Pi's. It takes a village sometimes, don't they say?'

'What?' Maya is slightly taken aback, reminded of what she used to hear from Chini Auntie as a child. *It does fit, now that I think of it. We fit together.*

'It's what the Rishi calls the Tribe,' Usha tries to add.

'Wait, what?' Gautam is still looking shell-shocked. *Why is she quoting the Rishi now?*

'The universe—cradling you all,' Usha says, 'I didn't see it at first.'

She's saying without saying it, 'We all love you.'

That they can feel. Weirdly, given all the build up from her absence over the years.

'I was lost myself, I made such terrible choices, such terrible choices. I won't be able to undo … I can't even ask you to forgive me. But I'm here now, I promise you.'

Everything is out of focus for Gautam. He always thought he was the one in charge, taking care of everyone, no one to take care of him, to protect his feelings. Not his father, not … his sister. *So, not adoptive but real—*

'More real than real, we used to say,' she's cry-laughing.

'I can't believe you didn't tell me. How could you?' His tone is accusing, his eyes flat. She's never seen him like this before, not since their father died.

Gautam's feeling too foggy. He's silent for a heartbeat, his pulse hammering in his head like there's no tomorrow.

He sits down abruptly. Maya tries to hold his hand, flinching as he pulls away.

He's looking so naked, vulnerable. She knows he needs her now. It's her turn. She knows how it feels, exactly how it feels. *I love you so much, Gautam.* She will be his anchor through this, she decides. It doesn't matter how long it takes. All the love, the hurt, her black days, she's got a fount of strength to work from and she'll use it for him, just like he's always been there for her.

But one thing has to change.

Her anger takes root, in strength. In love. In knowing in her bones what's what.

There's no space for this other persona who's been flitting from periphery to centre stage and back.

She walks to a little corner of the room, grabbing the phone to call, her voice croaky and small. 'Hi … yes, please.'

'How are you holding up?' asks Reena Gupta from her clinic half an hour away.

'I'm okay, thank you.

'So, I need that referral. The sooner the better. Does he do emergency house calls by any chance?''

'Yes, we'll get that done. You can do this,' Gupta says. 'We're going to get through this.' She shares some instructions on creating her own space on her own terms.

Bolstered by that, Maya takes charge.

'This … this is over.'

Maya speaks out loud to the group in the room, just to set the tone. It's a new tone at that. If only it were that easy. 'I'm going to need you to give me room. Give me, give us some space to breathe now.'

Something does shift with that.

The silence is only punctuated by the *'kaabaaaaaaaadi'* wail from downstairs. The man on the cycle has no idea of the drama unfolding or his role in its denouement—his voice piercing the air, breaking up some of the tension.

…

Of course it fits; no wonder we always stay connected, reading each other's thoughts with ease, Maya and Gautam think together. Twins.

But he's firm on one thing. *Biology be damned, Neeti is my mom, she always has been.*

Maya can't understand it, but nods.

'Listen,' he starts to say to Usha, but she's just smiling at him. 'I know,' she says.

Akira is stone-cold silent. No one notices when she leaves the building.

It's at this moment everyone's grateful for Karthik.

He calls a final timeout. There's a lot to process. And they're going to need a lot of time, not to mention professional help.

Maya writes in her journal much later, not sharing anything on social this time:

Akira, Akira … Apparently could have been my coping strategy.

This may be what's been happening when I skip time.

Those memory patches are trauma-induced, they say.

Just when the reality was too much to bear, I guess.

I don't know.

But I know I'm not embarrassed anymore.

This is me—vulnerable, weird, messed up, it's all okay.

We're getting through this. Together. There's a full circle of trust now.

'Excuse me?' Akira can't believe this 'bullshit' when she surfaces again, months later in therapy. 'Listen. She doesn't know how to fight back. She's such a pushover,' she'll share in a session. 'She crumbles, she needs my protection. I've been making things better for her, her whole life. That no-good gargoyle, she's just going to hurt her again.'

Maya, on the other hand, is finally realising that she's gotten through the worst. And she's more than ready for the 'better' that comes next.

Epilogue: Orion's Belt

Orion's Belt is the constant—she looks up every night, just as her father had taught her to, some thirty-four years ago. Every night she goes through the same ritual, even when she is almost too sad to remember.

'You're seeing the light from the past,' he had told her, and it sounded magical.

It still does. Even if a lot of other truths were hidden from her, even if he'd lied, by omission, about some fundamental things, this one thing still holds. She can lean her full weight on it.

She's shared the same constellations with me, tracing them out for me in the night sky. That's right—it's been a few years now and I'm fully in the mix. (We've met before, but it's official now!)

She sits with me every night, sharing her stories, somehow managing to share the yearning, the courage … and the legacy of being almost the bravest girl in the world.

'Sometimes we have to walk an awful long way to find our way back home,' Mum tells me, kissing me on my head after one story session. (I'll say!)

'How do we manage? If we get lost?' I ask her.

'You won't, I'm here,' Maya laughs. 'But anyway, your little feet will lead you back home.'

'My feet?' I look surprised. 'You mean my heart!'

(It's the one thing we can trust, after all.)

She laughs again, her glorious, unfettered laugh.

'Isn't that what happened for you and Dad?'

'You know it is,' she says.

She smiles again, a proper hundred-watt smile. I snuggle up to her, asking her to stay in bed until after I fall asleep. And so she does. Her warmth seeps through my winter clothes and she vows, as always, that I will never know the feelings she grew up with, not if she can help it.

Maya thinks about Karthik, about their partnership, how his uncle talked him through all his fanciful theories—maybe his eyes were open in utero, he said, maybe that childhood brush with blindness clicked on his third eye, as he imagines. Or maybe his family dynamics made him an emotional sponge, triggering deep dysregulation of his emotions, who knows.

'What we do know is how to control the ebb and flow of the energies around us,' the Rishi teaches, 'creative and destructive both.

'You don't get to pick one over the other, that's the thing,' the Rishi teaches us all. 'Usha learned it the hard way. You can learn it your way—how to be in sync with the universe.'

So now Karthik—with his parents urging him on, having seen how much he's changed since Maya and the baby and his uncle came into his life—goes every so often to do his 'short-term' spiritual training course with Gautam and the Rishi. Gautam can use the distraction; it's taken him a lot of time and love to get over his sense of betrayal. He's still a bit shaken, a bit upset from time to time that he was lied to his whole childhood, but he must admit that it weirdly all does make sense now.

Om heaves a sigh of relief that things are fine with their family again, and the business is looking up.

Maybe the boy will take over? Or maybe not, he sighs, pragmatic as always, *but at least he's okay.*

'The girl, now she is a revelation. She may just have a head for business,' he tells Garima gleefully.

~

Maya is comforted, knowing that they're all looking out for each other, and especially for me, 'little one' as she keeps calling me. I stir a bit but go back to sleep; I know how she feels now, heart full.

Usha wasn't lying about that part and even though she has more of a guest role in all our lives now (all minus Chini Auntie, who needs her own 'timeout')—the rest have got over the surprise about all that she brings to the table. From profound insights to babysitting me, her cherished granddaughter, she's around these days. And authentically so. Not for her any faking it to make it—Usha's never known how to do that in the first place.

~

And finally, far away, across the city, a surprisingly tender story plays out.

Someone's coming up the stairs, Mark notices, peering out from his study.

The first thing he notices is the aura.

Then her smile.

He knew she'd be back. He'd always known.

Now that everything is different, now that she looks like a crinkly old overcoat, all folds and stains, she smiles more fully.

'You do realise how beautiful you are,' he says, as she stands there in silence. 'You know that, right?' he persists.

'Well, that depends,' she says, still smiling.

'On what?' he asks.

'The time of day.'

He laughs, knowing that she has returned to him, after all. Just about intact.

Acknowledgements & Author's Note

[October 2024]

My gratitude first and foremost to you, dear (gentle) reader. If you've reached this page, I'm pretty humbled and impressed (though I'm not going to lie, if you're like me, you started here!)

Thank you to my friends and fam, and friends-like-fam … including my now-not-so-secret weapon, Abhishek. What a year and adventure of a lifetime! The original dedication is in *The Sibius Knot* and with that, I, like the dude, abide.

Suren, the original ray of sunshine and game changer (wiser than your years and wiser than me, that's for sure!), thanks for so many things, not to mention the comics collection (woohoo!) and all the stories and adventures and conversations.

Mum, you're the one who kept asking when I was coming back to this, so it's entirely your fault this is out. Though I should add that this one also has a massive, huge parental advisory warning! Do not read beyond this page. I can't believe your book is coming out around the same time! #Prouddottie

Sometimes I wake up thinking I just need to call my Dad and ... well, there's that jolt of realisation. I first sent out a draft of this story when I was grief-stricken and somehow, some of the story kept me going. (It really wasn't ready, though. I suppose I was trying to produce something, anything! To gain some modicum of control in a year when I had none. Some of you might know what I mean ... take a gentle hug if you do.)

Big love to Shoili (I borrowed your nickname and I hope you like the character and this book!) and Pallo the Pea, for all our profound conversations; I should have assigned the proofreading to you, but wanted the story to be a surprise. Love and light also to Bedi, Van, Gerry, Bea, part of an amazing global sisterhood.

Huge thanks and shout-out to the one and only Karthika V.K., my editor. She *is* as good, smart, patient and amazing as you've heard. Thank you for 'getting' it even in the before times! And here's to more coffee catch-ups and pizza lunches.

Major thanks due to Ratna, for being an early reader (so long ago you may have forgotten it), for re-reading it, giving me your honest take (as always) and some hugely helpful insight and notes. And thanks for the use of 'Nan'! (Let's make that plan to meet, minus a concussion this time!)

Thanks so much, Dr Amit Sen, for answering my rambling questions about dissociative identity disorder and whether some of these plot points could hold (namely, could Akira exist?), and how different ego states can present and why. Thank you for all that you do!

Any mistakes are my own and I'd like to emphasise that this is entirely a work of fiction, not a mental health guide. Decisions have been taken along with the characters themselves, often to move the story forward.

Having said that, what I do know is that our rational selves and evidence-based treatment systems co-exist in this land with other faith-based belief systems, superstitions even. That's the nature of the beast. Nowhere in this book do I want you to conflate treatment for mental health conditions with spiritual journeys—I don't mistake delusions of grandeur and waves or bursts of 'psychic energy' (those dreams of destruction) with the cold, hard corners of reality or the need for professional help.

I know that, above all, none of us can 'win' alone. And that too many of us feel alone and truly forsaken, when it comes to darkness or despair.

You know, sometimes storytelling can feel like a luxury, a privilege, especially when you juxtapose it with things like medical science and people who save lives, doing tangible good in a world that's gone to complete shit. And of course, it is a luxury and a privilege to be able to share stories, to be a storyteller. But it's also essential.

I've come to realise that it is the stories—whether we stab at fragmented truths in our fiction or try to re-ravel strands of truth in our non-fiction—it's the stories that keep us going. The stories give us hope, and hope is something tangible, something real, even when the times seem dark. (As they inevitably do, these days.) Stories show us our humanity, enable us to learn empathy, compassion, even. Sometimes they show us a way out and through. *(There's better after the worse …)*

My work at The Health Collective and the conversations that have kept that mental health initiative going (with more than 500 stories at last count) have taught me so much … and nothing more profoundly important than the fact that we are all the gatekeepers of our own mental health, and that people with lived experience are the real experts of their own journeys.

It is not a sign of weakness to ask for help, far from it.

There are evidence-based treatment options for mental health disorders and conditions, and professionals out there equipped to deal with many of those conditions. We share some resources on The Health Collective for folks in India, including helplines, psychologists and psychiatrists, and that invaluable iCall crowd-sourced list of experts pan-India. (http://healthcollective.in/contact/)

If you take one thing away from this book—know that whatever you're going through? You're not alone.

~

Okay, that's it! You can always share your comments and feedback with me on social.

I am still on X: @amritat.

The Health Collective is @healthcollectif.

Insta: @healthcollectiveindia.